A trio of treasures . . .

Faced with her strange destiny, the elf Glissa and her companions must travel through the metal world of Mirrodin, seeing the mysterious being at the heart of the world.

What does he want with Glissa? What role do the sinister vedalken play in the drama that is unfolding beneath the moons? And what are the three treasures that Glissa must now find to fulfill her quest and avenge her parents' death?

Jess Lebow continues the story of a search that leads to the very center of Mirrodin.

EXPERIENCE THE MAGIC™

MAGIC
The Gathering™

MIRRODIN CYCLE · BOOK II

THE DARKSTEEL EYE

Jess Lebow

Wizards
OF THE COAST™

THE DARKSTEEL EYE

Distributed in the United States by Holtzbrinck Publishing. Distributed in Canada by Fenn Ltd.

Distributed to the hobby, toy, and comic trade in the United States and Canada by regional distributors.

Distributed worldwide by Wizards of the Coast, Inc. and regional distributors.

Cover art by Brom
First Printing: January 2004
Library of Congress Catalog Card Number: 2003111900

9 8 7 6 5 4 3 2 1

US ISBN:0-7869-3140-X
UK ISBN: 0-7869-3141-8
620-96473-001-EN

U.S., CANADA,
ASIA, PACIFIC, & LATIN AMERICA
Wizards of the Coast, Inc.
P.O. Box 707
Renton, WA 98057-0707
+1-800-324-6496

EUROPEAN HEADQUARTERS
Wizards of the Coast, Belgium
T Hofveld 6d
1702 Groot-Bijgaarden
Belgium
+322 467 3360

Visit our web site at **www.wizards.com**

Dedication

To R.D.L. This one is for you.

Acknowledgements

Thanks go first to Peter Archer for his insightful
editing and selfless mentoring.
Thanks also to:
Will McDermott and Cory Herdon for helping me
create such a fantastic story.
Jeff Grubb and J. Robert King for creating the backbone
of the Magic story world.
Philip Athans and Mark Sehestedt for simply being brilliant.
Steve Whitman and Philip Tasca for also being brilliant.
And the baristas at my local coffee house for not
throwing me out after I finished my cup.

CHAPTER 1

Alone in his laboratory, Memnarch closed the latch on the arm cuff and finished strapping himself in. A giant humming construct covered by tubes and funnels crouched high over his bulbous frame.

"Yes, yes," he said. "Everything is working properly."

Memnarch eyed the straps and glittering lights covering the artifact.

"So much effort for something so simple," he said. "Would it have taken so much if you had built it?"

He listened.

"I thought not."

He cleared his throat and fingered a tiny lever. Gargantuan articulated arms on the back of the device unfolded then unfolded again. They moved with a practiced precision, a simple grace that belied their size and the bulky tubes attached. The metallic limbs enveloped Memnarch in his cushioned restraints. They buzzed with magical power.

"You see that," he said, admiring the leather straps that held his body. "These bonds, Memnarch, endure in your name. The self-imprisonment of worship. If ever you doubted, now you know. Memnarch is a true disciple."

Memnarch's right appendage moved. Three red beams issued

from each of the mechanical arms, crisscrossing his flesh. Tiny pinpricks of light moved over his skin, illuminating the tissues and vessels underneath with an eerie orange glow. A soft click echoed through the laboratory, and the arms shook a bit as they locked into place.

"But you never doubted. Memnarch knows."

Memnarch closed his eyes and leaned his head back into a padded cradle. The soft curve held him firmly, and for a brief moment, the being strapped inside his device relaxed, breathing a gentle sigh. This would be the most peaceful instant of his day, and he wanted to enjoy it. In that brief moment, there would be a balance of pleasure and pain, darkness and light, good and evil.

After that, there would be work to do.

With a deep breath, Memnarch focused on the mana that would start the infusion. He felt the warm glow of power flow up his spine and out his finger tips, and he braced himself against the restraints. The hum of magic filled his ears then the sound of bubbles coursing through thick liquid filled his laboratory.

The serum transference began.

The magical process did not hurt, but the infusion was not without pain. The liquid was thick, thicker than his blood, and it took a while to enter his blood stream. As it crossed from the storage vessels into his body, he could feel the strain on his body. It felt almost as if he were drowning but from the inside out.

Slowly the serum made its way through his body. When it hit his heart it burst into flame, and he felt as if he were being burned alive, an excruciating pleasure that both exhilarated and tormented him. This was the moment he had built the artifact for—the reason he strapped himself in before each dose. After several pumps of his heart, his whole body was flooded with the serum. It hadn't been like this before. It hadn't taken so much effort, but he hadn't needed so much of the serum then.

Every muscle tightened as he tried to hold back the unbearable pleasure. He screamed, or at least he thought he screamed, lost in the overwhelming sensation that he couldn't honestly say what the rest of his body did while he suffered. After a moment more, the fire entered his brain, and he opened his eyes.

Every morning he followed the same ritual. Rarely did he see anything—nothing definitive. Tears filled his eyes and ran down his cheeks. The dark gray tiles lining the floor of his laboratory swirled together with the blue of the walls. Light coming through an enormous window mixed in reds and yellows. The artifacts, weapons, and scrying instruments inside his laboratory were invisible through the pleasure. What Memnarch saw resembled a puddle of liquid silver, reflecting and distorting the colors of Mirrodin.

"Master, you've come."

Memnarch held his eyes open, fearing that if he blinked the distorted image before him would disappear.

Then the burning would peak, climbing to the point where it could get no better—or no worse.

Lingering at the height of pleasure and pain, he held his breath. The serum's effects receded slowly, leaving him soaked with the memory of its presence.

As the burning slipped away, turning back into a knife blade and drifting again into the dull sting of an insect, it revealed to Memnarch a new power. His mind became clearer, his thoughts more brilliant, his understanding of all things more perfect. His overlarge, bulbous felt more nimble, less burdensome, more alive. His four hydraulically enhanced limbs felt stronger, and his six magically perfected eyes now revealed the true secrets of the world.

The tears ran away, clearing his sight—his vision of the creator, his master, slipping away. The floor and walls took shape. His scrying pedestal rose up from the ground, cradling in its basin a pool of silvery liquid, and the massive window that formed one whole wall of his laboratory came back into view. Beyond it, the glowing blue-white ball of pure mana at the center of Mirrodin pulsed, and its rays warmed his face.

Memnarch gazed out the window. Crystal-shaped chrome spires rose up from the curved ground, reaching for the mana core like plants to a sun.

"Odd how organic life copies artifice," he said. "Is it the same on all the other planes?"

He listened.

"Yes, that is what Memnarch thought."

The door slid open, and a figure entered the room. It was a metallic bipedal creature, similar in shape to the elves or humans of the outer world—noticeably lacking the enhancements and improvements Memnarch had given himself.

Memnarch recognized the creature immediately. "Malil," he said. "Come in. Come in."

"Is everything all right, Master? I heard screaming."

Memnarch maneuvered controls, and the articulated arms withdrew. The straps holding his body inert during the ritual released, and the device let out a long slow hiss.

"Yes, yes, everything is fine, just fine. Is it not?" Memnarch scuttled across the floor toward his servant, the tips of his metallic crablike legs clicking as they tapped the stone tiles, the base of his gigantic abdomen dragging along behind him. "Thank you for asking us." He could feel the muscles in his back relax and a sensation of simple calm wash away the last remnants of exhilaration from the infusion.

Malil stepped to one side, looking past Memnarch at the huge device.

Memnarch watched Malil examine the device. He smiled at the metal man's obvious wonderment. Pride swelled within him, and he looked down on Malil's face—a face nearly identical to his own.

"He is curious," said Memnarch, looking away from Malil. "Shall we tell him what we have created?"

Malil turned to Memnarch and blinked. "Yes, Master." He turned back to the device. "What does it do?"

Memnarch smiled. "Many things, Malil. Many things."

"What kinds of things?"

Memnarch crossed his laboratory again. Looking into a glass funnel full of milky white liquid, he stroked it gently as if it were a favored pet. "To begin," he said, not turning away from the device as he spoke, "it harvests and stores blinkmoth serum. Is not that right?"

Malil stood completely still, not making a sound.

Memnarch laughed, slowly at first. The problems he had faced only the day before seemed trivial now. Why had he been so concerned over such insignificant thoughts? His laughter became hysterical, and his body convulsed.

"Is not . . . is not . . . is not that . . . wonderful?" he asked between breaths.

"Yes, Master," replied Malil.

Memnarch abruptly stopped laughing.

"Why must we be surrounded by such puny minds?" he said, slamming his fist against the edge of the device. "On one side Memnarch is in the presence of greatness, on the other, the presence of nothing." Lifting himself to his full height, he moved around to the control unit, touching one of the arms. "Yes, yes, Memnarch knows. You are right."

He turned back to his servant, continuing his tour of the device.

"Here is the delivery system," he explained, rubbing a smear mark from the brightly polished chrome.

"Delivery system?"

Memnarch spun on Malil, his legs clicking against the tile. "Yes, the delivery system." He crossed his arms over his chest. "You see what Memnarch must deal with? How he lacks the intellect to understand?"

Malil lowered his eyes to the floor. "I see."

Memnarch scrutinized his servant. Malil was tall by elf standards with an ordinary pair of legs and matching arms. He had a wide, strong chin, that mimicked that of a human and narrow, gently sloping shoulders. Except for the fact that he was made *entirely* of metal, Malil could pass for one of the humans on the surface.

Memnarch turned away, toward the window. At one time, he had looked just like Malil. At one time, he too had been made entirely of metal. The thought made him sad. He looked down at his hands. A line of red liquid seeped from the edge of his fist where he had slammed it against the device.

Memnarch touched the spot with his finger. He actually bled! Memnarch, the Guardian of Mirrodin, was bleeding! His sadness turned to anger.

"Is this what you intended for me?" He held up his bleeding fist. "When Memnarch was made, was this what you envisioned?"

Malil shuffled forward a step. "Master?"

Memnarch looked up at his servant. "Silence! If Memnarch wanted you to speak, Memnarch would have addressed you."

Malil stepped back, remaining silent.

Memnarch looked back down at his arm. "This is not what the creator intended. Is it?" Memnarch shook his head. "You who *made* Mirrodin then placed it in Memnarch's custody did not want this."

He listened but heard nothing.

"Has Memnarch not been faithful?"

He listened again.

"Of course. Of course. So why have you forsaken Memnarch?"

Memnarch paced the lab. He ran from the room, then he paced back the way he had come, his feet making a high-pitched grinding noise on the tile as he spun.

"You have not?" he continued. "Memnarch's perfect body, the body you gave Memnarch, created for Memnarch, is slowly turning to flesh. If this is not your wish, then whose? If you had not wanted this, why is it happening? Has Memnarch failed?"

Memnarch shook his head. "No. No, Memnarch could not. Memnarch would not. Memnarch has been given the task of protecting Mirrodin, of caring for it until the creator himself returns. Memnarch has done that. Memnarch has done everything you have asked of him—and more!"

"Master?"

Memnarch looked up.

Malil blinked, watching him. "Master? Are you all right?"

"Yes," he said then smiled. "Why would not Memnarch be all right?"

The scrying pedestal in the middle of the laboratory began to change colors, wavering in a dark blue. Memnarch scuttled over to it, lifting his considerable girth off the floor so as not to drag it along behind him. Settling down before the metal pool, he looked into the silvery liquid. Ripples formed at the center of its perfect circle, spreading out in rings toward the edge of the basin.

Images began to form, images of a gigantic metal tunnel.

"The blue lacuna." Memnarch brought his head closer to the basin. "Someone is coming down the blue lacuna, coming to see us."

Malil crossed the room and stood beside his master, gazing down into the pool.

More images began to form—fuzzy pictures, and they were moving fast. Memnarch squinted, focusing his attention on the scrying pedestal. The images grew clearer. They were bipedal and moved upright. There were several figures, perhaps two dozen, maybe more.

"Vedalken," he said.

Malil shifted his weight. "Why would vedalken be coming now?"

"A good question." Memnarch waved his hand over the pool. "Memnarch has not granted them an audience. . . ." His voice trailed off. "They seem to be chasing something. We do love a good chase." He stared into the scrying pool. "This is most unusual."

The wavering silvery liquid suddenly grew crystal clear. A tall, slender female elf appeared. Her arms and lower legs were, like most creatures of this world, covered in thick metal that seemed to grow from her skin as if it were a part of her body. Her medium-length hair was held back by a strip of tanned hide, and she wore a leather jerkin that covered most of the rest of her body.

"She is here," gasped Memnarch.

"Who, Master?"

Memnarch looked up from the pedestal. His skin tingled with delight. His bones ached with excitement, and his mind raced over all the work he still had unfinished.

"She is here," he repeated. "The one." He turned to Malil. "The elf girl."

Malil straightened to attention. "What are your desires, my master?"

Memnarch rubbed his hands together, and he ran his tongue over his dry, parched lips. "Bring her to us."

Malil bowed his head, turned on his heels, and exited the same way he had come in.

Memnarch leaned down over the silvery pool once again. "Memnarch had not expected you so soon."

* * * * *

Malil marched at double speed along the long, curved corridor. His path led him in a gentle downward spiral—a long way to go to get from Memnarch's laboratory to the next level.

As he descended, he ran over the scene with Memnarch in his head. He'd spoken of the elf girl before. Malil didn't claim to understand everything. He knew only those things Memnarch told him and the things he'd witnessed for himself, but both of those were considerable.

Memnarch's regular scolding repeated itself in his ears, "You do not need to know everything. You need only follow Memnarch's directions."

The metal man redoubled his speed. Stepping off the causeway, Malil entered the observation platform. This room, by design, was completely empty, and the outer walls were made of one contiguous piece of magically curved glass. From here, he could see the entire interior of Mirrodin.

Out the window, at the center of the plane, a huge ball of blue-white mana floated above everything. Below that, the ground curved up in every direction, encircling the glowing sphere and eventually meeting itself on the other side, forming both the floor and the ceiling of the interior. Pointy chrome towers, called mycosynth, rose from the ground, reaching up like gnarled, sharpened fingers grasping for the ball of power above them.

Malil crossed the open chamber to a spot at its very center.

There a red circle marked the floor, and the metal man stepped onto it.

"Ground level," he said.

The room filled with the hum of magic, and the floor descended, slowly at first then picking up speed. It slowed and finally stopped. Malil walked down a short ramp, stopped at a waist-high railing, and looked over the edge at a legion of metal warriors.

Each was identical. They had curved heads, each with a singular glowing yellow eye in the center. Their arms came from their sides, growing wider and thicker as they extended, ending in gigantic, razor-sharp blades. The warriors' torsos were armored with metal plates, interlocking over the other so that they could move independently without exposing their delicate insides to harm. Where a human or elf would have legs, these warriors had two wheels tipped with heavy spikes sharp enough to puncture even the strongest metal. On their backs, every one had a short, trifold sail, which they used to steer themselves across the vast open expanses of Mirrodin.

The metallic killers crouched, quietly ready and loyal, prepared to stay where they were for an eternity or cut down an army at a moment's notice.

Malil smiled. "Open the gates," he shouted. "The Guardian wishes us to bring back an elf."

CHAPTER 2

Glissa ran. She ran with all of her might, all of her being it seemed. The earth before her sank down and down. If she didn't know better, she would have thought this great hole in the ground through which she descended led right through the middle of Mirrodin and out the other side. Of course, that couldn't be the case.

Slobad ran beside her. His wrinkled little goblin body moved surprisingly fast, considering how short his legs were. His tool pouch bounced against his body as he ran. It always did whenever they were running away from something. It seemed as if they had been doing that since the day they met.

Glissa spared a glance over her shoulder. Bosh, the artifact golem, tromped along right behind her. His rusting iron frame seemed to lumber along, but what he lacked in agility, he made up for in size and strength. Each one of his footsteps measured more than three of Glissa's. It was a good thing too. On more than one occasion it had been Bosh's long legs that had saved their necks.

The clanking sound of his heavy metal feet colliding with the ground was dampened by the glowing mossy substance covering every inch of the tunnel and lighting their way. The funny thing about Bosh was that no matter what he did, his face always held the same stoically serious expression. Right now, that look of utter concentration and contemplation seemed appropriate.

In the giant construct's outstretched arms, the newest member of the group rode, her face curled up tight in a grimace of pain, her hands gripping her leg. She had been hit by a harpoon while standing beside the Knowledge Pool. They had already removed the metal shaft, but the leg was still broken. Bruenna was a human wizard of considerable power, though none of those powers could heal her broken leg.

Glissa turned her attention back to the mossy ground before her. It gripped her feet, making each step more tiring.

The lacuna tunnel through which they ran was round and regular and traveled downward in a curved line. The slight bend in the passage blocked Glissa's view of the warriors pursuing her. That, at least, was comforting.

Though she couldn't see the vedalken, she knew they were there. She could hear their marching feet squish the mossy ground as they gave chase. Of course they were going to chase her. She and her friends had broken into their most sacred place. Even though it was for a good reason, Glissa didn't think the blue-skinned, four-armed creatures saw it that way. In fact, she felt certain they wanted her dead.

Rounding a bend, the lacuna split in two.

Glissa coasted to a stop, breathing hard. Were this the Tangle, she would know which path to take, but she was a long way from her home now—in a place that until a few minutes ago, she never knew existed.

"Bruenna. . . . Which way?"

The wizard looked down through pained and teary eyes. "I ... I don't—"

"Left." Bosh's voice boomed over Bruenna's.

Glissa looked up at her metal companion. "Left?"

"Left," he repeated.

"How you know?" Slobad asked, now gasping beside the elf. "Your memory back now, huh?"

The golem's voice rumbled through the tunnel again. "Yes. I remember this place."

The sound of the marching vedalken army grew louder in the curved tunnel. Glissa looked to Bruenna. The human shrugged.

"We go left," announced the elf. She continued her sprint down the tube. The goblin loped along beside her, as the clank of Bosh's massive feet resumed.

The tunnel continued on, and the mossy covering grew thicker, more dense. After another long turn the passage straightened, and a bright blue-white light beamed in. Glissa shielded her face, her eyes painfully adjusting from the dull glow of the moss that lit the tunnel to the blinding light now cascading down on her.

Slowing down, she asked, "Where is that light coming from?"

"I don't know," replied the mage.

"The mana core," answered Bosh. He nudged Glissa forward with his great bulk. "It is a long way off. We can travel on safely."

The elf shook her head. "I hope you're right."

"Hope it not levelers," added Slobad. "Slobad not dismantle whole army."

"No," said Bruenna, "but the vedalken army will dismantle us if we don't keep going."

Not the most ideal set of options.

Glissa took off without another word. Bruenna was right. It didn't matter what the light ahead of them was. They couldn't stop. Better to head for the possibility of escape than cower from it and be killed by the vedalken.

The light grew as the comrades ran. Glissa could make out the end of the great tunnel. Back-lit shapes began to form between the light and the thick carpet of moss.

At last elf, goblin, golem, and human burst from the lacuna.

Glissa fell to her knees at the sight before her. Her stomach churned, and her eyes seemed unable to focus. The world she had known, that had been changing daily for days now, was once again turned upside down.

"It's true," she whispered. "Mirrodin is hollow."

The interior of Mirrodin was more beautiful and terrifying than anything Glissa had ever seen in her life. It was as if all the world had been turned inside out and stuffed down the lacuna. Since Chunth's final words to her, she had tried to imagine it, but imagination fell short of the reality.

A whole world rolled out before them. Spires of crystalline chrome rose from the ground, reaching toward the sky like the trees and brambles of the Tangle, but unlike the great metal forest, these structures were not so close together. At their tops, where branches and leaves should have been, these spires came to a jagged point. The towering growths rose from the ground toward a blinding blue-white ball in the sky.

A low, electrical buzz issued from the hissing core—made up of mana, Glissa guessed—filling the interior of the plane, settling over all creatures and structures as if it were a blanket. It didn't drown out all other sounds, but it created a barrier that other sounds couldn't escape. If Slobad or Bruenna were too far away, Glissa felt certain they wouldn't hear her call their names. The sensation from this all-encompassing noise was odd but somehow comforting to the elf, as if in this wide-open space a little piece of it had been reserved just for her use.

Above the interior "sun," hanging from the ceiling, more of the pointed chrome monoliths jabbed downward. From where

Glissa stood, the interior of Mirrodin looked like a rotting, toothy mouth, poised to bite down on the mana core at its center.

The mossy carpeting continued from the lacuna, covering the ground and everything in its path. Here and there, straight patches had been seemingly stripped away, making lines on the ground like the veins of a leaf. In these openings, polished metal shone through, reflecting the light of the mana core overhead.

In the far distance, a tall blue tower distinguished itself from the rest of its surroundings. It stood above the other pointed towers and ended in a rounded bulb at the top. Though all the other spires were covered at the base by the mossy ground covering, this one was not, and it shone brightly, reflecting the blue-white glow that touched everything.

Looking out over this mythical world, Glissa became dizzy. She felt as if her brain were growing, as if it might burst from her puny skull. There was so much to take in, and none of it seemed to make any sense. The monsters her parents had spoken of in bedtime stories were now all suddenly real. A whole world existed inside her world—but that was impossible.

"What is all of this?" she asked, not really expecting an answer.

"These tall chrome structures are called mycosynth," replied Bosh. The metal golem lifted Bruenna, pointing with an outstretched finger at the shining structure in the distance. "That is called Panopticon."

"How do you know all this?" asked the human wizard suspended in his arms.

"I used to live here—"

Bosh's explanation was cut short by a high-pitched wail. Slobad jumped up and down, pointing toward Panopticon, squealing.

"Levelers! Levelers! Levelers!"

Coming down one of the pathways, a mob of artifact creatures sped toward them. The levelers were sleek and curved, like giant metal prawns with killing blades for tentacles and spiked wheels instead of tail fins, which seemed to push them effortlessly through the sticky moss.

At the front of the group, atop a modified leveler, rode a silvery manlike creature. From this distance, Glissa couldn't make out much detail. Except for its reflective skin, the creature could have been an elf or a human from the outer world.

"Run," shouted Bruenna.

"No wait," replied Glissa. "If this place exists, it means Memnarch exists."

"And?" asked the impatient wizard.

"And," snapped the elf, "he's responsible for the death of my parents." She looked at each of her companions in turn. "This is my destiny. Eventually I'm going to have to face him, for good or ill."

Bruenna looked down from where she was being cradled in Bosh's arms. Her face was pale. Sweat ran down her brow, and her eyes seemed sunken. Grimly she smiled. "You're right." She shook her head. "But if you try to confront him now, it'll just get the rest of us killed."

"But—" started Glissa.

"We don't have time to argue about it," said Bruenna, cutting her off as the levelers closed in. "We can avenge your parents and save the world another time. Right now, we have to go."

"Where?" Glissa turned. The vedalken hadn't appeared in the lacuna yet, but she knew they were coming, and heading back up the tunnel would mean suicide.

"This way," said Bosh. "I remember another tunnel to the surface."

The metal golem took off at a run, charging away from the

opening to the blue lacuna, the approaching horde of levelers, and the strange structure he had called Panopticon. Glissa grabbed Slobad by the arm and followed.

They were running again. Glissa was tiring of running. Not even on the hunts in the Tangle did she remember running so much. An elf had her limits. She shrugged. She supposed she was about to find her own.

Slobad struggled against Glissa's grip, straining around to look behind him as they ran. "They're gaining."

"Run faster!" shouted the elf.

"He's right." Bruenna looked back over Bosh's shoulder as he carried her. "Bosh, how far is it to this other exit?"

"A long way."

The human wizard lifted her arms out to her sides and spoke a single word. Her hands flashed with a blue light. The open space between her upraised arms congealed into a silvery membrane, and Bruenna vaulted into the air.

Hovering above Bosh, she said, "I guess we have no choice." She looked at Glissa. "We stand and face your destiny after all."

*   *   *   *   *

Malil rode atop a specially designed leveler. This beast had been outfitted with a set of steps and two curved handles. The metal man crouched over the killing device as if he were riding a dolphin. Gripping it with his knees, Malil didn't so much steer the creature as tell it where to go. Through one of the handles, a magical conduit, the leveler could "hear" his thoughts, and it obeyed his whims. Absent this connection, the leveler would respond to his verbal commands, but that was less satisfying. Malil liked to simply think about where he wanted to go and let the beast take him there.

The metal man had ridden from Panopticon at the head of a battalion. The leveler he rode was slower than the others since it carried his weight in addition to its own, and ultimately, he knew, it was he who held back the entire pack. Once they had the elf and her companions in sight, Malil gave the order.

"Catch them," he shouted to the levelers rolling along beside him. "Bring me the elf. Kill the others."

The killers took off ahead of their general. Malil nodded his approval. Soon he would have the elf in his possession, and he would fulfill his orders from Memnarch.

The metal man leaned forward and watched his quarry grow nearer.

*   *   *   *   *

Glissa turned. The levelers were much closer than she had imagined them. She had seen these creations before, even fought them, but never had she been witness to so many collected together into one space. The sight was terrifying, and a shiver flushed down her spine, making all the skin along her back tingle.

The metal beasts were close enough now that Glissa could clearly see the humanlike figure at their head. He was tall and thin, not clearly elf or human, and he wore a long blue robe that billowed out behind him as he rode his leveler forward. His shiny silver skin made the expression on his face hard to read, but Glissa thought he might be handsome were it not for the fact that he was charging toward her atop a killing device—the same sort of device that had taken her parents, her sister, and her best friend from her.

The tingling sensation faded, giving way to a palpable anger that heated her blood and steeled her spine. She could feel her lip curl up and her eyes narrow. She didn't even know who this silvery man was, but already she hated him. He had much to answer for, and if this were the fabled Memnarch, he had an enormous debt to repay.

"Time to settle," she said, lifting her hands high over her head and drawing green mana from the far-away Tangle. She was surprised how easily it flowed to her. The arcane energies flooded her body, and she felt strong.

Bosh stepped in front of Glissa and Slobad, his hammering footfalls shaking both elf and goblin to the bone. Their big friend came to a stop, and the rumbling of the levelers replaced the pounding of the metal golem's feet.

For a moment, all four companions were silent, watching the approaching throng. Glissa took a deep breath, channeling the mana she held. Looking out at the charging artifacts, she singled out the closest. As she released her spell, the mana gushed down her arms, ripping across the open air in a green zigzag.

The magic smashed headfirst into the oncoming leveler. The creature exploded. Interlocking metal plates shot out at all angles. The animated device's wheels spun off wildly, smashing into other levelers who simply ran over the dismembered parts of their one-time comrade without slowing down. The creature's scythe blades flopped uselessly to the metal ground, tumbling end over end, then coming to rest.

The levelers continued on, the silvery man unflinching.

Over her head, Glissa watched a glowing blue orb race toward the horde. Bruenna, she thought. The spell struck a charging artifact, and its spiked wheels suddenly stopped spinning. The metallic beast shuttered, skidding sideways before coming to a halt. Another leveler plowed into the back of the stalled beast, knocking it over and getting tangled in its bladed arms and steering sail. The two creatures lay on the mossy ground in a heap, forcing the constructs behind to smash into them or drive around.

Bruenna's spell had caused a break in the advancing enemy line, and the once orderly artifact creatures now looked like a rioting mob.

The first leveler closed in on Bosh, and the golem smashed it to smithereens. With one swing of his heavy fist, he bashed it flat. He swung his other fist. The shriek of metal bending and glass shattering followed a loud crash, and another of the artifacts went down.

As the front line of levelers reached the companions, Slobad jumped atop the first one he encountered. Raising its scythelike blades, the leveler turned toward Glissa. Its spiked wheels tore up the ground, greedily eating up the space between itself and the elf.

Holding onto its steering sail, the goblin pulled a narrow crowbar from his pouch. Jamming it between interlocking plates, he pried the device's outer shell free, opening a hole large enough for him to stick his fist inside. Reaching in, the goblin tinkered with the leveler's innards.

Glissa watched it come, the goblin on its back. Seeing him dig into that artifact creature brought a smile to Glissa's face. When it counted, Slobad was the bravest goblin on Mirrodin.

A whistling sound brought Glissa from her reverie. Diving forward, she managed to duck and tumble away from a second leveler's blades as they came down where her head used to be. Coming to her feet, Glissa pulled her sword. It seemed silly to try to dismantle a device with a sword. She wished she could turn that pointy blade into a pounding hammer.

But this was no ordinary sword. She didn't know where it had come from, only that she had found it inside the Tree of Tales in Chunth's chamber. It was more powerful than any weapon she'd ever wielded, and for that, at this moment, she was grateful.

The blade rang as she bashed back the new leveler's attacks. Sparing a glance to her left, she saw the leveler with Slobad on its back was almost on her. Looking back and leaning in, she lunged for the artifact's glowing yellow eye. Her blade struck the seam, lodging between the housing and the lens. Twisting her sword, Glissa popped the creature's eye from its socket, and the device swung side to side, grasping with its arm blades like a blind man trying to catch a thief.

Glissa turned to the leveler with Slobad on its back. The construct brought its arms together, scissoring down on the elf with its razor-sharp grasp. The artifact was close, closer than Glissa had thought. She rolled backward, falling onto her behind and ducking away from the blades. The creature missed her but just barely, and it opened its arms, ready for a second deadly embrace.

Glissa scooted back with little room to move. The leveler behind her still flailed blindly. The one before her leaned down, ready to take her head from her body. The killing device brought its blades together, right down on her. Pushed back against a flailing, blinded leveler, she had no room to move. Glissa cringed, bracing for the impact—but it never came.

The artifact creature veered to its right, turning away from Glissa and lunging at the flailing leveler behind her.

"Kill it," shouted Slobad from the creature's back. "Cut it up." The device followed his orders.

Glissa rolled away and got to her feet. The two levelers cut into each other. Sparks flew as Slobad's fighter slashed through the blinded monster's torso. The goblin leaped onto the back of another device, his crowbar gripped in his three-fingered hand.

Bosh smashed devices with both fists. Bruenna froze the

oncoming monsters in their tracks or blasted them away with gusts of wind. Slobad turned them against each other or dismantled them as fast as his little fingers could pry them apart. Glissa battled them back with her sword and her magic.

Still, the mass of sharpened creatures came on, endless and unrelenting. The flood of levelers swarmed over Bosh. Their spiked wheels pushed them up his body. Their scythe blades struck him, and his body rang out like a tolling bell. In a matter of seconds, the giant metal man disappeared under a pile of killing devices.

A high-pitched squeal filled Glissa's ears. Slobad had jumped from one device, and he now rode on the back of another. His arm was buried to his elbow inside the creature's metal frame, and his face was held tight in a pinched, pained expression. With the fist of his other hand he beat on the leveler's hide, pushing, pulling, and squirming to get his hand free. Something had gone wrong. Slobad was caught.

The leveler he rode reached its arms back and swiped at the goblin. Slobad ducked, but the tip of the creature's scythe blade caught the side of the goblin's head. A chunk of Slobad's scalp sliced away, and blood spurted down his neck.

Glissa's heart sank. Her stomach felt as if she'd swallowed a bottomless pit, and the hairs along her back and neck stood at attention. She watched as the beast took another swipe at Slobad. The goblin disappeared from sight.

The creatures swarmed in, climbing on each other's back to reach into the sky and pluck Bruenna from where she flew. Glissa heard the human wizard scream as she was brought back down to earth. The horde of metallic monsters closed in on the elf, blocking out the reflected blue-white light from the mana core.

Thrashing about with her blade held high, the elf fought

off one leveler after another. Scythe blades fell to the ground. Eye sockets went flying. Spiked wheels were cut in two. Still, the circle closed down, and there were too many to fight on her own.

Slipping her blade into the crease between two metal plates, Glissa lunged to kill another leveler. As she stretched out, a sharpened claw tore into her side, then a spiked wheel collided with her leg, and the elf fell backward onto the ground.

In seconds she could feel her arms pinned and her legs immobilized. Someone pulled the sword from her grip, and the tip of another blade touched her exposed belly. Spreadeagled, limbs held firm, a deadly weapon pressed against her gut, Glissa thought about her family—and Kane. She was going to die, and with any luck, she'd see them again in whatever place elves went to after they left the horrors of this world.

Even the thought of seeing her parents again couldn't quell the fear inside her. Life on Mirrodin had been no picnic, but she didn't want to die—especially not at the hands of a leveler. Over the past few rotations she had come to believe, really *believe*, that she had a destiny, a greater purpose, but her quest had become a monumental failure. She had traveled to bring her parents' killer to justice, only to be slaughtered in the same fashion. It seemed tragic.

She wasn't the only one here. She had friends now, friends who had followed her to this place. Though she couldn't see them, their faces flashed in her mind: Slobad, Bosh, even Bruenna whom she'd only recently met. They were all going to die.

Glissa's fear once again gave way to anger, and she screamed. Not a shriek of terror or the startled scream of a little girl, but a feral, predatory screech that dripped of power. She took in a deep breath. The pounding of her heart filled her head, and the grinding wheels of the levelers filled her ears. She looked up at the metal beasts holding her down, and she hated them. She wanted to smash each and every one into greasy bits of scrap metal.

Then something inside snapped. Glissa felt as if a door had been opened deep within. Power flowed out over her body, and all her muscles tensed. A wave of green energy exploded over the battlefield, filling the interior of Mirrodin with a bright flash of light—followed by silence. Nothing could be heard, not the grinding of levelers, not the buzzing hum of the mana core.

All was quiet.

The light subsided. Levelers were flung back. As if a switch had been flipped reversing gravity for a brief moment, the killing devices were launched into the air. Their blades flailed. Their steering sails flapped side to side without result. Just as suddenly, the switch was re-engaged, and the constructs fell back to earth, smashing into other levelers and crashing into a tangled heap.

Glissa was free.

Beside her, Bruenna hovered. The artifact monsters that had pulled her from the sky were thrown away, and the wizard launched herself back into the air—no longer a captive.

The pile of killing devices completely covering Bosh were torn off, tossed to the metal ground like discarded children's toys. Their heavy carapaces had cracked on impact, sending metallic sinews and glass lenses flying in all directions. Metal torsos collapsed in on themselves, smashing the mechanisms inside. The glowing yellow lights in their eyes went out.

All the climbing devices were flung away, and the great metal golem was revealed. Bosh wasted no time. Stepping over a wall of bent and ruined metal, he reached down and picked up the leveler with Slobad on its back. Squeezing his fingers together, he pinched the beast's lower back. Its head popped off, and the mechanism's insides squirted out.

Slobad's arm slipped free of the creature's carapace, escaping from whatever had held it, and he climbed up Bosh's chest, crouching on the golem's shoulder.

"Thank you," cried the goblin, holding Bosh's neck. "Now, run, huh?"

Bosh turned, and his feet resumed their heavy drumming on the metal ground.

From the distance more levelers advanced. Before Glissa, a crescent-shaped portion of the ground was clear of levelers and rubble alike. It was as if the elf's anger had created a giant gust of wind that had blown everything back, but it had been more than that. Where her spell had touched a leveler, it had been destroyed.

Bosh reached down and scooped up the young elf where she stood. He continued on, Bruenna flying beside him.

Slobad looked at the elf with wide eyes. "How you do that, crazy elf?"

Glissa looked down at her hands. "I don't know. I just . . . did."

"Think you can teach Slobad that trick? Make taking apart levelers easier, huh?"

"Yes, it would," replied the elf, "but I still haven't figured out how to do it myself. It just sort of happens."

Bruenna swooped down closer to Bosh. "Where to?"

Bosh lifted his face, pointing with his chin. "Just over that rise. There's another entrance to the blue lacuna."

Glissa wrinkled her forehead. "The blue lacuna?"

"The tunnel we came down," explained the golem. "It is called a lacuna."

"I know that, but you said the 'blue lacuna.' Are there different colors?"

"There is a red one and a blue one but no green."

"How you remember all this stuff, huh?" asked the goblin. "Dross finally leak from your rusty head?"

"The Pool of Knowledge," interjected Bruenna, nursing her injured leg as she flew. "The pond we jumped into that led us down here." She grimaced. "I told you, my father was right. The vedalken have a way of putting all of what they know—everything every single one of them knows—into the serum inside. Our swim through must have revived Bosh's memories."

"Yes," replied the golem.

"Wait." Over Bosh's shoulder, Glissa watched the surviving majority of the leveler battalion start to regain their composure and line up behind the strange metallic man. "We can't go back into the tunnel . . . the blue lacuna. The vedalken are inside."

"This entrance should bring us back to where the tube spilt into two paths. If we are lucky, we will avoid them."

Bosh headed up a slight incline, and Glissa turned. Just ahead, barely visible in the near distance was the opening to the tunnel the golem spoke of. She looked back to the levelers.

"Better hurry," she said. "They're gaining again."

CHAPTER 3

Malil sat atop his leveler, stunned. How had the elf done that?

Memnarch would not be happy.

"Form up," he shouted.

The broken line of levelers obeyed his command. Despite the spell the elf had cast, most of Malil's army was still intact, if scattered. In a few moments, the killing devices were in formation and ready to roll.

Someone else emerged from the blue lacuna.

"Pontifex," said Malil. Spinning his leveler, he once again ordered the pursuit. "After them."

The mob of metallic creatures rolled on. Malil, atop his killing device, stayed put. Instead of the sound of wheels tearing at the metal soil he heard the voice of Memnarch inside his head.

"Bring the vedalken to us. We want an audience with Pontifex."

Here, inside the interior of Mirrodin, the Guardian could speak to Malil, no matter where he was. From what the metal man could tell, Memnarch could see through his eyes as well. No doubt the Guardian had been watching the whole encounter with the elf. There was no way for Malil to be sure of this, no indication inside that told him when this was happening. For all he knew, Memnarch could be watching constantly. Malil behaved at all times as if this were the case, just to be safe.

Malil urged his leveler forward—toward the opening of the blue lacuna.

* * * * *

Pontifex stepped from the tunnel. With the head of a broad-tipped spear, the tall, slender vedalken shielded his eyes from the mana core's glow. Bright purple spots clouded his vision.

A team of warriors filed out behind him.

"Marek, where is that elf?" he shouted.

The four-armed bodyguard shrugged. "I don't know, my lord."

Pontifex had to catch that elf. He *needed* that elf.

The spots began to fade, and for the first time he saw the leveler horde. The killing devices rolled up and over a curved pile of wreckage, speeding off into the distance.

"Follow them," he ordered.

The army of skinny, blue-skinned, four-armed beings behind him took off double time without a word, the heads of their spears gleaming in the preternatural light.

To Pontifex, the interior of Mirrodin was a wondrous place. He had been here many times before on official visits to Memnarch, but this time was different. This time he came as the newest leader of the Synod. This time, he hadn't been invited.

The thought of being chided by Memnarch tugged at the back of his thoughts. The freedom he took in coming here with his warriors was exhilarating.

As if his thoughts had been broadcast across the interior of the plane, Malil, Memnarch's personal servant, appeared, riding his leveler toward the vedalken.

Malil was new. Memnarch had created him some time between the last two blue moon cycles and the current convergence, and Pontifex had only encountered him once before. Still, there was no mistaking whom he served. Atop his lithe metal body, Malil had the face of his creator. From the shoulders up, every curve, nuance, and gesture was replicated exactly.

Talking to Malil produced mixed emotions for Pontifex. Malil was a servant, but he looked so much like Memnarch that it was hard to look him right in the eye. Though he was unsure if it were true, Pontifex assumed Memnarch could hear everything Malil could. Certainly, the guardian of Mirrodin could see everything on the plane from inside Panopticon. Why wouldn't he be able to hear what his servant heard?

This annoyed Pontifex. He was the most respected researcher on Mirrodin, and now he was the leader of the vedalken Synod. Why should he have to speak to an intermediary? He hadn't before. Now, instead of talking directly to his lord, he had to get past a mere servant. The whole process was humiliating.

Malil pulled up and stopped his leveler. "Greetings, Lord Pontifex."

"I have no time for pleasantries, Malil," replied the vedalken lord. "Where is the elf?"

"She is headed for the second entrance to the blue lacuna." The metal man who looked so much like the Guardian of Mirrodin pointed toward the receding column of levelers.

Pontifex spun toward his army. "Halt," he shouted.

The order worked its way up the line of marching warriors, the words echoing in different voices all the way to the front. The line stretched out and finally stopped. Marek returned to Pontifex's side at a sprint.

"Your orders, my lord?"

"They're headed back up the lacuna, through the other

entrance," Pontifex snarled. "Go back up this way and cut them off at the break."

"Yes, my lord." Marek spun and ran back to the other soldiers, shouting orders as he did.

Pontifex turned to the metal man. "Thank you, Malil, you've been very helpful. Now, if you'll excuse me I—"

"The Guardian has requested your presence," interjected the metal servant.

"The Guardian has frequently requested my presence."

"The Guardian has requested your presence *now*."

Pontifex narrowed his eyes at Malil. "Surely my lord has seen that I am in pursuit of the elf."

"Yes," replied Malil, "but now he requires to speak to you. He has sent me and the levelers to capture the elf. Your help is no longer needed."

"My help is—" Pontifex cut himself off. Gripping his four hands into fists, he took a deep breath then continued. "Of course, I'll report to his lordship at once."

"I shall escort you to Panopticon."

Through gritted teeth, Pontifex said, "As you wish."

* * * * *

Malil led Pontifex up the lift. The two rode in silence. When they reached the observatory, Malil spared a glance out the window. In the distance, he could see his levelers, a column of rust rising into the air marking their progress.

The metal man and the blue-skinned vedalken climbed the curved entranceway to Memnarch's laboratory at the top of Panopticon. Beside the door stood a rectangular pedestal, which rose from the floor to the height of Malil's waist. Embedded in the top, a triangular red stone pulsed with a soft internal light.

This was the portal to the laboratory, and only Memnarch and Malil could open it.

Malil placed his hand on the stone, and the door to the chamber slid open.

Turning to the vedalken, he indicated the door with a wave of his hand. "You are free to enter."

Pontifex glared at him as he brushed past into the laboratory.

Inside, Memnarch gazed out over the interior of the plane. From behind, the Guardian of Mirrodin looked like a four-legged metal crab. His rounded abdomen rested on the floor. His long, pointy legs were bent, the joints poised above him ready to lift his bulk with a thought.

"Pontifex," said the Guardian without turning around. "So good of you to come to see us."

The vedalken researcher fell to his knees, lowering his face to the ground and spreading his arms in an elaborate bow.

"Of course, my lord." He lifted himself then bowed again. "Forgive me for the intrusion. I know I was not invit—"

"Enough babbling, Pontifex," interrupted the Guardian. "Memnarch will forgive your incompetence." The crablike creature turned away from the window, scuttling around without lifting his midriff from the floor. "We forgive your intrusion."

"Thank you, great lord." Pontifex stayed prostrate on the ground, though he raised his head enough to glare at Malil again.

The swollen joints in Memnarch's legs whirred into action, and the Guardian lifted his girth from the floor. Once his weight was up and balanced on his legs, he moved with a smooth grace that belied his size. He headed across the laboratory to his scrying pool. Pontifex shifted himself on the floor as Memnarch moved so that his head pointed toward the Guardian.

"We see that you brought your warriors," said Memnarch.

"Yes, my lord. We were chasing the elf."

"Yes," replied the Guardian. "She is a hard one to catch. We have yearned for her, yet both you and Malil have failed to bring her to us."

"I am sorry, my lord," replied Pontifex.

Malil stood stock still beside the open laboratory door but did not say a word. He wished it was him lying prone on the floor, being berated. It was worse to be chastised for his failure indirectly.

"Once again, Memnarch will forgive your incompetence," said Memnarch, "but that is only because the Creator wishes it so." He waved his hand over his scrying pool and looked into its depths. "We have more time."

From where he stood, Malil couldn't see what Memnarch saw, but it apparently did not please the guardian.

"The next great convergence is coming," the Guardian said. "The mana core is overripe. It will erupt soon. When that happens, we must be ready. We must. We must." Memnarch ran his finger through the pool. "Memnarch is almost ready. Is not that right? Only a few more preparations to take care of, and all will be as we have planned. . . ." Memnarch went silent, his voice trailing off, staring intently into the pedestal.

Malil stood quietly for several minutes. Pontifex did not move from the floor, his face pressed hard against the tile.

After a long while, Memnarch spoke. "We must have her by then. Do you understand us?" He waved his hand over the pool once again.

"Yes, my lord," replied both men in unison.

Memnarch raised his fist into the air and brought it down inside the pool. Blinkmoth serum slopped from the pedestal in a huge splash.

"Damn, damn, *damn!*" he shouted. Spinning away from the scrying pool, he turned to Malil. The guardian pointed at Pontifex, still prostrate on the floor. "See him out," he said. "Memnarch must speak with the Creator again." The Guardian raised himself to his full height. "In private."

Malil nodded and crossed the floor to the worshipping Pontifex. "Time to go."

Pontifex looked up at Malil, hatred in his eyes, but he got up off his knees and followed Malil from the laboratory. "I will bring you the elf, my lord," he said over his shoulder on the way out. "This you can count on."

The metal man led the vedalken lord down the curved corridor and waited until he was aboard the lift.

"You know the way out," he said.

The lift descended.

Pontifex slipped silently through the floor, disappearing from sight.

* * * * *

Memnarch paced in circles around his laboratory. The clicking of his sharpened limbs mingled with his words as he spoke.

"Things were easier when Memnarch and the creator were the only creatures on the plane." Memnarch laughed. "Yes. Yes, they were. There were occasional visitors, and sometimes the Creator left for long stretches at a time." Memnarch pointed his finger in the air. "Still, he always returned.

"Now things are different. Memnarch has explored the entire plane. There is no more sense of wonder." He shrugged. "There was not much to it really, at least, not before Memnarch brought in the test subjects. Back then, the only unique things on the plane were the blinkmoths."

He listened.

"Sure the towers and chambers you created for us were

interesting, but how much can an observer really learn from a tower? The blinkmoths, though, they could be studied, dissected, and experimented upon. Memnarch found the most amazing things. Yes he did." He giggled, rubbing his hands together. "Memnarch discovered their separation anxiety. Yes. And found their threshold for distance."

He cocked his head, listening again.

"Yes, Memnarch remembers the first experiments. The solitary moth taken more than a few meters from the other moths became frantic, smashing around inside its containment cube." He laughed again. "As if it could build up enough momentum to break the glass walls." Memnarch lifted an empty containment cube from the desk. He looked at it with all six of his enhanced eyes, admiring his own handiwork. "It could not, of course, Memnarch had seen to that. Eventually the moth expired. Separated for too long and at such a distance proved to be fatal.

"At first, Memnarch was saddened by the deaths of these delicate creatures. They had died of loneliness." He shrugged. Putting the cube back on the desk, he headed across the lab. "That is what led us to populate Mirrodin with test subjects. Yes. To eliminate loneliness and to have more creatures to experiment upon.

"But that was a long time ago. A long time ago."

Memnarch strapped himself into his apparatus once again. Before he had the device, he had created a portable tank that would deliver the serum to him in measured doses throughout the day. It was uncomfortable and limited his movements around his laboratory, so he preferred to simply dose himself while he worked within Panopticon. If he needed to leave his fortress to tend the soul traps or take specimens off the mycosynth growths, he wore the tanks. Today, though, he was working hard and would have no time to leave.

The straps came down around him, and he guided the articulated arms into place.

The door to the laboratory slid open, and Malil entered.

Memnarch looked away from what he was doing, examining his servant as he came into the lab. "Damn him," said the Guardian. "He's so perfect, so metal. Oh, to be made only of metal again." He sighed. "If only to be able to remember what it was like to be blissfully ignorant again."

Memnarch tilted his head, nodded.

"True, the serum has expanded Memnarch's intellect, but who would have known that consciousness could be such a burden? You never spoke of such things."

"Master, is everything all right?" asked Malil as he stepped closer.

Memnarch channeled mana into the device. "Yes. Yes." He turned away. "Perhaps achieving the state of planeswalker relieves some of the strain. Memnarch hopes so. It is a lot of work to struggle with the responsibilities of running an entire plane."

He pushed his head back into the soft cradle, and the red lights raced over his skin.

Memnarch looked across the room at Malil.

The metal man stood stock still, watching.

"Do you understand what we are doing?" asked Memnarch.

"Yes."

"Perhaps soon we will let you taste the serum."

CHAPTER 4

Glissa's eyes adjusted to the dark inside of the lacuna. The mossy ground glowed as it had before, but its light was far dimmer than that of the mana core.

"Can you see where you're going?" she asked Bosh as he bounded up the tunnel, carrying her and Slobad.

"Yes," came the metal man's reply.

Bruenna hovered along behind, just off Bosh's shoulder. She looked up the lacuna, and when Glissa looked over the golem's shoulder they were almost face to face.

"How's your leg?" asked the elf.

"It hurts."

"How long will that spell keep you in the air?"

"Long enough to get us back to Lumengrid—if we don't run into any vedalken or levelers."

"Don't look now." Slobad stuck his scrawny arm out in front of him, pointing down the tunnel. "Well, maybe should look, huh?"

Glissa turned to see the point where the two paths in the lacuna joined, heading up the surface as one tunnel. Coming around the corner, spears held high, was the front of the vedalken army.

"Hurry," shouted Bruenna. "If we can get past these few

before the rest of them make the corner, we might be able to get by."

Glissa could feel Bosh's whole body rumble as he spoke. "Good plan." The golem took off at double speed.

"Hope crazy elf can do that trick again," said the goblin as they closed on the slowly growing group of blue-skinned soldiers. "Better figure out how to make it happen, huh?"

"Yeah, right," replied the elf.

* * * * *

Marek turned the corner and looked down the other passage of the blue lacuna.

"There she is."

"Sir, we've cut them off," said a soldier beside him.

"Lord Pontifex will be pleased."

"What should we do?"

"We should . . ." Marek looked back over his shoulder.

More vedalken soldiers filled the tunnel. It would be some time before his entire squad could march up the passage and join the fight, but more than a dozen soldiers already stood by his side, and more were arriving every minute.

"Sir?" asked the soldier.

"We should delay them, give the rest of the squad enough time to catch up with us. Don't let them get past, and don't let them go back down the lacuna. When more of our soldiers arrive, we'll capture the elf girl and kill the others."

"Sir, there are more than enough of us here to capture an elf, a goblin, a human, and a rusty old metal golem."

"Perhaps." Marek looked into the warrior's eyes. "But we will do things my way, and you're going to follow my orders. Right?"

"Yes sir," replied the soldier. "We will delay them until the rest of the army arrives."

Marek smiled. "Good. Make sure the others have their orders."

* * * * *

"Are you sure we can get through?" asked Glissa as they scrambled up the lacuna.

"No," replied Bruenna, "but what choice do we have?"

"We could go back."

"The levelers have surely followed us into the lacuna. We'll be trapped between two armies."

Glissa looked ahead. The vedalken had lined up shoulder to shoulder, ten wide, across the tunnel, waiting. A second line had formed, and a third was beginning behind them as more soldiers came around the corner.

"What are they doing?" asked the elf.

"Clogging the tunnel," said Slobad. "They hold us here for levelers. Cut us to little bits. Dead goblin. Dead crazy elf, huh?"

Bruenna nodded. "He's right."

"What do we do? We can't fight all of them."

"No," said Bosh, "but we can bowl them over."

"What—?" Glissa's question was cut short.

Bosh lifted both she and Slobad off of his shoulders. A huge section of rusted iron opened on his chest, and the metal golem stuffed the elf and the goblin inside.

"You might get dizzy." Bosh replaced the metal piece.

Glissa sat, knees jammed against her chest, in complete darkness. The heavy thumping of Bosh's footfalls echoed loud inside the chamber.

"Is this going to work?" she asked.

"Don't ask Slobad," grunted Slobad. "Slobad don't know what crazy golem doing."

* * * * *

Bruenna flew behind the stomping golem. "What's your plan, Bosh?"

"Stay behind me," he said, "and stay close."

With that, Bosh pulled his arms in to his sides. To Bruenna, it looked as if they were retracting. His head did the same thing, dropping down inside his body and disappearing from view.

The metal giant took three more bounding steps and leaped into the air. When he came down, he'd retracted his legs, and his whole body had turned into a perfect ball. The metal sphere rolled at the waiting lines of vedalken.

"Good plan," muttered Bruenna, and she followed the rolling golem as he crashed into the soldiers.

Spears, helmets, and other accoutrements went flying, making a terrific noise as they smashed into one another and came down in a heap. Those soldiers who didn't immediately jump from the way were squashed flat under the weight of the rolling metal ball.

Bruenna slipped in behind, following Bosh as he bowled the vedalken down like a patch of razor grass.

* * * * *

Marek couldn't believe his eyes. One minute, there was a golem charging down the lacuna at him and his men. The next, a giant ball careened into his soldiers. Blue-skinned, four-armed vedalken were knocked every which way, many of them maimed or killed as the ball rolled over them and through the ranks. Marek dived out of the way to avoid being smashed.

Getting up from the ground, the vedalken lieutenant dusted himself off. He watched the still rolling ball and the flying human wizard as they passed swiftly through his shattered ranks, and continued up the lacuna toward Lumengrid.

"What was that?"

Moans were all he got in response.

* * * * *

Glissa braced herself against the inside of the golem's empty chest. The steady beat of Bosh's feet on the metal ground was interrupted by several loud slamming noises and one long grinding sound, then the world began to tumble. She wasn't able to see anything in the lightless chest cavity, so she had no way of knowing which side was up. Whenever her head hit something hard, she figured she was upside down. Her legs, hands, and hair had become tangled with Slobad. Eventually, the two companions clung together for dear life.

"Slobad scared," the goblin shouted.

"Me—"

Glissa's response was cut short when her back smashed into something hard, knocking the wind from her lungs.

"—too," she finished when she had regained enough composure to scream.

There were several loud thumps that sounded like something hitting the outside of the chest cavity. Abruptly, the tumbling stopped.

"Thank the maker," said Glissa.

She had landed on her head. She was sure of this only because her neck hurt, and her feet seemed to be touching nothing but thin air. Flipping over, she untangled her body from Slobad's and lifted herself up off the dark ground.

"Goblins not made for rolling, huh?" said the goblin. "Slobad sick."

His words were followed by a gurgling sound, and the splash of liquid on the chamber floor. Glissa felt the wave of fluid flood over her feet.

"Nice, Slobad."

The door opened and light poured in.

In the dark, Glissa hadn't noticed how dizzy she had become. When she saw the wall of the lacuna, her head spun one way, and her eyes the other. She vomited.

Bosh's stubby digits reached in and pulled the two nauseous riders out into the light.

"You must stop that," said the golem. "It tickles."

Glissa looked up at Bosh then leaned over his hand and threw up once again.

"Thanks for the warning," she said. "What did you do?"

"We can cover that ground later," interjected Bruenna. The wizard hitched her thumb over her shoulder. "Right now we've got a bunch of angry vedalken to outrun."

Bosh lifted Glissa and Slobad onto his shoulders and took off along the tunnel.

Glissa clung tightly to the seam in Bosh's neck. The fresher air and the light were helping her to regain some equilibrium, but she was still a little queasy. Slobad looked even worse off. Every few steps, his limp little goblin body threatened to fall from the golem's shoulder. He hung on with all his might, his knuckles turning pale against his rumpled flesh. Every time one of Bosh's feet landed on the ground, Slobad let out a little moan.

Bruenna hovered behind them. "You two going to make it?"

Glissa looked up, shrugged, then nodded.

"Good, because once we get up the Pool of Knowledge, we've still got to get out of Lumengrid."

Glissa grabbed her head. "I'd forgotten about that. I'm not sure if I *can* make it."

Slobad gagged. "Me neither."

The company continued up the lacuna. The mossy stuff on the ground began to give way to simple metal, and the tunnel grew darker. The vedalken warriors were nowhere in sight, though Glissa knew they couldn't be too far behind.

"We're nearing the top," exclaimed Bosh.

The giant metal golem came to a halt. On the floor, the edge of the tunnel rippled. An opalescent oval broke the regular metallic sheen before them—the bottom of the Pool of Knowledge.

Glissa looked at it. "I didn't like this on the way out."

"It's easier on the way in," said Bosh.

The golem lifted his two passengers off his shoulders then knelt down. He poked his finger at the floor, and the silvery substance gave way, letting the golem's whole hand pass through. Waves rippled off in every direction, as if a drop of water had hit a puddle.

"That all serum, huh?" said Slobad.

Bruenna nodded.

"But how does it stay there? Why doesn't it just drain into the lacuna?" asked the elf.

The human wizard shrugged. "If I had to guess, I'd say magic."

The sound of booted feet coming up the lacuna echoed up the tunnel.

Slobad dashed for the silvery wall. "Good enough for Slobad," he said. The goblin dived upward into the serum.

The wall wavered but none of it came into the tunnel.

Bruenna levitated into it as well, disappearing from view after a *bloop*, *bloop*.

Glissa looked after her friend. "I don't know, Bosh—"

"Time to go," interrupted the golem and shoved the elf into the serum.

Glissa slipped through the wall, her mouth still open from her last word. The world around her was thick and slow. She felt the weight of the pool on top of her, and her chest seemed empty. Her ears felt as if someone had his hands cupped over them, and everything had gone silent.

Opening her eyes, Glissa looked up. The world was blurry. The top of the pool looked like the wall she had just passed through, only it was a long way away and wasn't in focus. Ahead she could see a small, frantic green thing that looked like a child's drawing. That must be Slobad, she thought. Behind him, a fluidly moving blue streak raced toward the surface. Though nothing was recognizable, Glissa knew this must be Bruenna.

Turning around, she watched Bosh transform from a disjointed reflection beyond the wall to a ghostly blob as he slipped into the serum. The golem moved toward her in a rush. Grabbing Glissa by the arm, he forced her up to the surface.

Kicking her legs, and with Bosh's help, Glissa rose through the thick liquid. Her lungs burned, and her mouth was full of serum. She wanted to spit it out and take in a big breath. Looking up again, she tried to focus on getting to the surface.It seemed such a long way away. The pool hadn't seemed so deep on the way down.

Glissa kicked harder, pulling free of Bosh's grasp. Still, the surface came no closer. Reflexively, she tried to take in a breath, but there was no air, and all she managed to do was collapse her cheeks. She felt trapped, panicked. She might drown in this pool. Her heart pounded in her ears, and her limbs ached with fatigue.

She felt Bosh's hand again, and the top of the pool dropped toward her. She could see the surface clearly now. There were lights, and where they hit the serum, a star formed. There was something else—dark figures moving around the edge of the pool. She couldn't make out what they were. She squinted, but it was no use. Whatever they were, they slipped from view as her head breached the surface.

Glissa spat out serum and sucked in a huge breath. Blowing it out, she took another gasp.

"I didn't think I'd make it out alive," she shouted, wiping the serum from her eyes.

"You won't," said someone in a gurgling voice. The words sounded as if they had come from underwater—far away and muffled.

Dragging her hand over her face once again, Glissa looked out over the edge of the pool.

A dozen vedalken guards filled the room. Two of them held Slobad by the arms, while another pair pointed their glowing halberds at the wounded Bruenna.

"Get out of the pool," said the same far-away voice.

Glissa couldn't tell which one was talking because all of them wore heavy helmets filled with what looked like water or blinkmoth serum.

"I said 'out,' " commanded the voice.

"All right, all right." Glissa began pushing herself toward the edge. From underneath, she felt a large pulse, as if a huge bubble rising from below had hit her legs.

Then she was airborne.

Serum trailed from her limbs as she rocketed toward the ceiling. Waving her arms in a circle, Glissa managed to keep herself upright. As she reached the apex of her upward arc, she drew her sword from her belt and glanced down at where she had been. Below her, the pool writhed and bubbled, as if a hundred deadly fish were fighting over the carcass of a zombie. Bosh's head had burst through the surface, and he rose like a piston—climbing to a height with tremendous speed then falling back under the serum.

Waves lapped over the golem's shoulders as he slipped back into the pool. The elf came down atop a vedalken guard. Her boot heel smashed through the creature's face mask, spilling the liquid underneath. The guard dropped his halberd and clutched at his face.

Glissa turned on the next vedalken guard. This one was ready with his halberd. Angling in, the four-armed warrior brought the head of his weapon down on the elf.

Glissa just managed to get her blade around in time, blocking the vedalken's strike. Had she missed, she would now be missing an ear. Twisting away from the blow, the elf stepped in, pulling her sword free.

The guard was defenseless, unable to bring his long weapon in so close, and he backpedaled, but it was too late. Glissa cut a long gash across his belly, opening his robe and abdomen in the same stroke. Pink and purple blobs of flesh poured from the warrior's open stomach. Glissa assumed they were vedalken entrails, though she'd never seen the inside of one before.

The guard went to his knees, scooping up his guts in both arms and trying to stuff them back in. Glissa turned away, sure that he'd cause her no more trouble, at least for the foreseeable future.

Four halberd blades descended on her at once, blocking each of the cardinal directions.

"Drop your weapon," came another gurgling voice.

Glissa bashed away one of the great spears, dodging through the hole as she did so and coming around behind the circle of guards. As she spun, something caught her foot, and the world spun with her. For the dozenth time in as many minutes, the elf landed on her head and saw stars.

"Not again."

Glissa tried to sit up, but her path was blocked by a trio of spearheads.

"That's far enough."

Glissa looked up into the eyes of a vedalken guard. His head swam inside a helmet full of serum, making his lips and eyes appear stretched and rubbery. He looked like a cross between a fish and a human—no elf could ever be so grotesque.

Glissa lay on the ground, panting. "What do you want?"

"I want you to drop your sword."

Up this close, Glissa could see the creature's lips move as he spoke. Somehow the words seemed to be coming from his neck or the top of his chest.

The vedalken jabbed his spear into her belly.

"All right." Glissa released her blade, and one of the other guards kicked it across the floor, away from her open hand.

A great splashing sound echoed through the room, and a wave of serum spilled over the sides of the Pool of Knowledge. Bosh's head and chest rose into the air. The golem lifted himself from the pool, his feet coming down with a thud as he landed on solid ground.

"Stop right there," sputtered one of the guards.

Glissa felt two pairs of hands reach under her arms, and she was yanked to her feet by a vedalken. To her left, Slobad and Bruenna were being held in the same fashion, their arms pinned back by a pair of guards, blades to their necks.

"On your knees, golem, or your friends are dead."

Bosh looked to Slobad and Bruenna then to Glissa.

She shook her head. "No."

A guard grabbed her by both cheeks, immobilizing her head and jaw. The elf struggled, but it was no use. The vedalken had a good grip, and all she could do was move her eyes in their sockets.

"On your knees," repeated the vedalken.

Slowly, Bosh lowered his head and dropped himself to the ground.

A pair of four-armed warriors rushed over and pried open a metal plate on his back. Flakes of rust fell to the floor. Bosh flinched at the sound.

"No," shouted Slobad. "Don't turn him off. I just turn him back on, huh?"

A guard shoved the goblin to the floor and knelt on him.

Glissa felt a cold chill run down her spine. She'd gone too far. All of this had started because she had vowed revenge for her parents' death. Along the way Bosh and Slobad had joined her, and this personal quest had turned into something bigger. Now Glissa had dug too deeply, and they were all going to die. She closed her eyes. She couldn't bear to watch.

A clank rattled around inside the room, echoing over the pool and the walls. Glissa cringed, remembering how she and Slobad had found the golem, sunk and forgotten, lying in pieces in the Dross, and a tear ran down her cheek.

There was another clank, and another, followed by the sound of footsteps and shouting.

Glissa opened her eyes.

Humans, wizards and soldiers alike were flooding into the room. They all wore blue robes, and most carried wicked hooked staves, ending in jagged points, covered with glowing jewels.

Half of the vedalken guards holding Glissa broke off, heading to intercept the humans. The elf's head and jaw were again free.

"Bosh, get up," she shouted.

The iron golem anticipated her command. Standing in a single fluid movement, Bosh brought his hands together—behind him. The clap crushed a vedalken to pulp and shut the golem's open access door at the same time. Spinning to face the remaining guard, the golem let the vedalken's limp body fall to the ground.

Glissa didn't see any more. With her arms still held firm by two guards, she kicked her legs into the air, flipping over backward and coming down behind the vedalken. Twisting, she got one arm lose. That was all she needed.

Funneling mana into a spell, the elf willed her body strong as a bear, her skin tough as bark. Her arms grew thick and muscular, and her once-lithe elf frame doubled then tripled. Reveling in her new found power, Glissa scooped up the guard who still had hold of her arm and lifted him over her head. With a feral grunt, she heaved him against the wall of the chamber. His face mask cracked from the impact, leaving a wet streak down the wall as he slid to the ground.

Turning, Glissa reached for the other guard, but he was gone. A human soldier had the crook of his staff wrapped around the vedalken's neck, the tip dripping blood as it poked from his throat. The rest of the vedalken guards had suffered similar fates, and as quickly as it had started, the fight was over.

Bruenna, her arms draped over the shoulders of two soldiers, hobbled up to the elf.

"They got here just in time," she said.

Glissa looked around. "These are *your* soldiers?"

Bruenna chuckled. "You saw the marketplace. Many people from my village work inside Lumengrid."

"But they seemed so scared before. Everyone scattered when Pontifex came through." She scratched her chin. "What makes them so brave now?"

"There is no love for the vedalken in my village," replied Bruenna. "When the time comes, we take care of our own."

Bosh stepped up beside the women, Slobad on his shoulder. "No time to waste," he said. "The other vedalken warriors will be coming from the pool any minute." He ran his huge, glowing eyes over the floor. "I do not think they will be happy to see us."

CHAPTER 5

Glissa leaned back onto a comfortable bed and pulled her boots from her feet. Quicksilver rushed onto the floor. As Bruenna had said, it had been an easy thing to catch a vedalken transport from Lumengrid. The humans far outnumbered the blue-skinned, four-armed creatures. Once the group had hit the lower levels, they disappeared in the crowd of human workers.

Now she was safely inside the human settlement of Medev. Bruenna had been immediately carted off to a healer. Glissa, Slobad, and Bosh had been shown to a large metal building, not unlike Bruenna's own home. Three well-made beds with soft cloth coverings greeted them inside. Slobad lounged on one of them now. Bosh sat beside another, his body much too large to fit on the frame.

"I've never seen a bed like this before," said Glissa, as she dried the remainder of her body. "In the Tangle, there isn't much cloth. The leaves and thorns tear it to shreds pretty quick. My mother had a shawl, but . . ." Glissa felt something stick in her throat, and tears welled up in her eyes.

Slobad sat up on the bed, leaning toward the elf. Glissa smiled at him then looked away. She closed her eyes to keep the tears from running down her cheeks and took a deep breath. Behind her, the bed sagged under the goblin's feet.

Slobad put his arm around Glissa's shoulder.

"I miss them," she said.

Slobad sat down. "Yes."

"I think about them every day." Glissa tried to hold back her emotions, but they were too overpowering, and she let out a sob.

"I know."

The elf looked up at the goblin, puzzled. "How could you know that?"

The goblin shrugged. "What? Think goblins got no feelings too? Slobad hear you talk 'bout parents, sister, friend Kane. Slobad lose friends too."

"I didn't mean that. I know you have feelings."

Slobad smiled.

Glissa wiped away a tear. "Will you tell me about some of the friends you lost?"

Slobad nodded. "When Slobad little goblin, go with other goblins to hunt squirrels." His head drooped as he spoke. "Little goblins surprised by two clockwork dragons."

"Clockwork dragons? I thought they were just a myth."

"Think Slobad make something up, huh?" snorted the goblin. "They real, you bet. Kill all the goblins." He nodded. "Except Slobad."

"What happened?"

"One minute Slobad deep in crevasse, poking for squirrels. Then screaming. Slobad hit head." The goblin rubbed his scalp, as if he was remembering the pain.

"Someone was holding you?" Glissa scratched her head. "You mean like with a rope?"

"No. Crazy elf. By ankles. Never catch squirrels before, huh?"

"What?" Glissa shifted to face the goblin. "By the ankles? I've hunted a lot of things but never that way."

"'Course," said Slobad, he held up both arms. "How you think goblin get really good squirrels, huh?"

Glissa laughed. "That's a good question." She settled back into her place on the bed. "I guess I hadn't thought of that. Anyway, what happened next?"

" Slobad climb back up, nothing of other goblins but bloody bones and bits." Slobad cringed.

"That's terrible."

The elf and the goblin sat silently for a while, looking at the floor. Glissa massaged her forehead and eye lids, feeling the wetness from her tears cover her fingertips.

"Do you still think about your friends?"

The goblin nodded.

"Every day?"

The goblin nodded again.

"Does it ever get any better? I mean, does thinking about them hurt less?"

At this, Slobad lowered his eyes. "Depends. Sometimes, not so bad, huh? Other times . . . not so good."

Glissa nodded. She wiped the rest of the tears off of her face and looked at Bosh still sitting at the foot of his bed.

"How about you?" she asked. "Now that you have your memory back is there anything you miss?"

"Yes," replied the golem, his voice rumbling in his chest. "I miss being all metal." Bosh lifted his arm up to reveal a large tear near his elbow. A thick red and black liquid dripped from the opening.

Glissa jumped up from the bed. "You're bleeding." Crouching down beside the golem, she examined the wound.

A large patch right above his elbow had changed from a dark gray to a lighter peach color that resembled the complexion of human skin. Up close, it looked as if part of Bosh's forearm had simply transformed from metal into flesh.

Glissa poked at the wound with her finger. The flesh was primarily just on the surface. She could feel the metal underneath. Only near his elbow did it feel more like the deep, meaty flesh of an elf or a goblin.

"Does it hurt?" she asked.

"Hurt?"

"Can you feel my finger touching you?"

"Yes."

"Does it feel bad?"

"Yes."

She and Slobad spoke at the same time. "It hurts."

Glissa examined the golem more extensively. In several other places, the dark metal seemed paler. She turned and looked at Slobad.

"How could this be happening? I mean every flesh creature has some metal in her body—" she held up her own arm as proof— "but I've never seen a metal creature become flesh."

This was true. Every organic creature on Mirrodin had some metal attached or growing from its body. The only completely flesh creature she'd met had been the troll Chunth, but he was very old. Everyone else, Slobad, her parents, even the other trolls, had bits of metal on their bodies. Glissa's own forearms and shins were covered in metallic scales and claws.

Slobad jumped down off the bed and padded over to his two friends. He leaned in close, looking at the fleshy patches on Bosh's arm and abdomen. The goblin climbed up the golem's shoulder, made a fist, and knocked on Bosh's head.

Bong . . . Bong . . . Bong.

"Feel that?" asked the goblin.

"No, but I can hear it."

The goblin grabbed a piece of peach-colored flesh between

two fingers. "How 'bout this, huh?" He pinched Bosh.

The golem flinched, tossing Slobad from his shoulder. "Yes."

The goblin landed hard on the bed behind the golem. The frame creaked, the mattress sagged then rebounded, and Slobad was tossed back into the air, bouncing twice on the soft bed before finally coming to rest.

"Please," said Bosh, "stop touching me. It feels very strange."

"I'm sorry, Bosh," Glissa said. "We're only trying to help."

"I know," replied the golem, hanging his head.

"It makes me sad to see you this way, Bosh." Glissa touched his arm lightly. "I wish I knew what was happening."

Bosh nodded.

"Until we figure it out, you're going to have to be more careful about what you smash into."

"Crazy elf is right," agreed the goblin. "Slobad can fix broken golem, not broken person, huh?"

Bosh poked at the wound on his arm. "I am still a golem."

"Yes, you're still a golem, but now you are…" Glissa fished around for the right word.

"Fleshy," finished the goblin.

Glissa glared at rumpled green creature. "You're not helping, Slobad." She turned back to Bosh, watching the metal man poke and prod at the blotch of skin that was now part of his frame. She took a deep breath and threw her arms in the air. "Now you're just more like me."

Bosh stopped his examination and turned his attention on the elf. "Like you?"

"I guess so. I mean, I'm mostly flesh, but look." She held up her leg, tracing the line between where her shin stopped and the metal plate that grew from her skin began. "We live in a metal world. The ground, the trees, even the grass is made of the stuff."

"So are golems," interjected Bosh.

"Yes, and so are golems. Even so, with everything else made of metal, maybe it's not so bad to be a little 'fleshy.'"

* * * * *

"Damn this flesh body." Memnarch lifted himself from his serum infusion device. "Why is Memnarch cursed with such imperfection?"

Malil stood by the door, waiting out another of his master's tirades.

"But with the elf, yes, with the elf, Memnarch will be metal again." He crossed to the scrying pool. "No. Memnarch will not be metal. Memnarch will be better than metal." The guardian shuffled across the floor of his laboratory, shaking his head. "No. No. That is foolish. There is no such thing. Is not that right, Malil?"

"What's right, Master?"

Memnarch lifted himself away from the scrying pool, turning his whole body toward his servant. "Have you not been following what we have been telling you? How do you expect to learn if you do not listen to us?"

"I have been listening, Master, but I must confess, I do not completely understand."

"Memnarch understands enough for the both of us."

"Yes, Master."

"The Creator understands enough for all three of us and worlds beyond."

"The Creator, Master?"

Memnarch scowled. "Yes, the Creator."

"I apologize, Master, but you were my creator. I know no other."

Memnarch nodded. "Yes, yes. His mind is too weak to

understand us. No. No. Memnarch will educate him." The Guardian gazed into his pedestal.

"Educate who, Master?"

"Do not be obtuse, Malil. You know full well who we are talking about."

Malil didn't but went along anyway. "Yes, Master."

"That is better. Now, let us start with what you *do* know." Memnarch looked at Malil. "What do you know?"

"I know many things, Master."

"Yes, yes, but what do you know about the elf?"

"I know that she came from the Tangle and she has something you want." Malil stopped there. He knew other things, but they seemed inconsequential at the moment.

"What does she have that we want?"

Malil shifted in place. "I'm sorry, Master, but I'm afraid I do not understand what it is that she has."

Memnarch shook his finger. "It is enough that you know what we want, not why. For our sake, and the sake of Memnarch's boredom, we shall explain." The guardian ambled over to the long window and looked down on the interior of Mirrodin. "Come, Malil. Look out the window."

Malil did as he was told.

"Tell Memnarch what you see."

Malil looked out over the verdigris ground, the chrome spires, and the blue-white mana core. "I see Mirrodin."

"Yes, yes, but what is Mirrodin?"

Malil focused on the ground then on the sky. He followed the path of a leveler as it made its way toward Panopticon, then he shook his head. "I don't understand, master."

Memnarch put his hand on the metal man's shoulder. "We will tell you what Mirrodin is. Mirrodin is perfection. Mirrodin is the creation of divinity. It is the work of a god."

Malil didn't fully understand, but he felt it was in his best interest to keep that information to himself.

"What is our job here on Mirrodin?"

"To do the Master's will," replied Malil.

"Precisely." The Guardian turned away from the window. "Memnarch is the protector of divinity. We are the keeper of all that you see below and all that is above." Memnarch hung his head. "Despite that great responsibility, the honor we have been given, Memnarch is still not satisfied."

"Why, Master?"

Memnarch looked own at his arms. "Memnarch is imperfect. Yes, it is true. We do not understand it. It was not always this way. No. No. Something happened. Something that changed Mirrodin made perfection imperfect." Memnarch shook his head. "Mirrodin was Memnarch's responsibility. To guard and care for the creator's plane. Despite our best efforts, a plague has stolen past Memnarch and taken root inside of Mirrodin."

"The elf girl, master? Is she responsible?"

"No, Malil. The elf girl is not responsible, but she can help us cure the plague." Memnarch stroked the hard scared skin on his fleshy arms. "She provides the key to making us perfect again." He looked up at Malil, and his eyes narrowed. "She can make Memnarch just like Malil—all metal and perfect—but so much more."

Malil was confused. "Why would Master wish to be like Malil?"

Memnarch scuttled across the floor over to his servant. His four spindly limbs lifted him high above the ground, and he had to bend down to see eye to eye with Malil. Memnarch touched the metal man's face, ran his finger over his metallic arm, then stepped back.

"We will show you." Memnarch lifted a vial of opalescent

liquid from a pouch on his belt. He handed it to the metal man.
"Drink this."

"Drink the serum, Master?"

Memnarch nodded. "Yes."

Malil lifted the stopper from the vial. Swirling it around, he
watched the thick substance adhere to the sides of the vessel,
clinging as if it were trying to climb to the top and escape over
the edge. Instead it sank back down into the vial, sticking to the
edges where it had clung, slowly slipping back down to collect
in a pool at the bottom.

"Go on," urged the Guardian.

Malil thought back on all the times he'd seen his master
infuse himself with the serum. He thought of the massive containment tanks Memnarch wore and the pressured containers
attached to the infusion device on the opposite end of the lab.
What he held before him was an insignificant amount in relation
to what Memnarch ingested several times a day—a tiny raindrop
in comparison to his master's Quicksilver Sea.

The metal man placed the vial to his lips then lifted the end
into the air. The thick liquid rolled across his tongue and down
the back of his throat. The sensation was odd. He was unused to
eating or drinking as the organic creatures did. He had no need.
What was more, he had no idea where the liquid would go or
what it would do.

It hit him. A sudden rush of power flooded through his body,
and he felt stronger. He looked at Memnarch. His master was
gazing at him with great interest, intently watching for something. Then the light in the room seemed to grow brighter. It was
as if someone were turning up the lights, over and over again.
The light did not diminish, but it never became unbearably
bright. Still, Malil could have sworn that the room was constantly getting brighter.

The edges of the tables and beakers became sharper, more clear. The experiments lining the desks and table made more sense to him, their purpose more evident and desired results more useful. The whole world made more sense to the metal man, and he smiled. So this was why his master ingested blinkmoth serum.

In the next second, the world expanded. Nothing inside was as Malil remembered. It was as if he'd left Mirrodin altogether. Where once there was a scrying pool, now there was a towering geyser. Where Memnarch's infusion device had been now stood a grotesque, metallic juggernaut with long curved tusks and gaping, wide eyes. The creature watched Malil, curious but unconcerned about the metal man's well-being. Where the windows of the observatory looked out over the interior of the plane were now only swirling colors and lights. It had all become one connected, living breathing creature that refused to take shape or be defined by those who viewed it.

The spike of power and enhanced mental capacity had pushed Malil into a new arena, one that he had never before seen. It was a place so out of control and ominously large that Malil feared for his own life. He hadn't chosen to come here. In this place everything made sense. It was all connected, everything working in concert to become so much more than the sum of each of its parts. In that moment, Malil realized how terrifyingly little he actually knew.

He had traveled all over Mirrodin, but he hadn't even scratched the surface.

Dropping to his knees, the metal man curled up, holding his legs to his chest.

"Please," he said. "Help me understand."

The gargantuan Memnarch crossed the room, no longer walking but stretching his body so that he encompassed the space between where he had been and where he was now.

"Now that you have tasted Memnarch's burden," said the Guardian, placing his hand upon Malil's shoulder, "you can never go back. We are sad for you. With true understanding comes the lose of innocence. Funny thing perfection. Only the imperfect can see it for what it truly is, and those who possess it are too blind to appreciate it."

Malil reached out to Memnarch. "Master, please help me."

Memnarch chuckled. "You will understand, Malil. Trust us. You will be fine."

* * * * *

Pontifex rose through the Pool of Knowledge aided by a simple magic enchantment that propelled him effortlessly toward the surface. He did not have to hold his breath. Vedalken had developed gills that could not only remove oxygen and nitrogen from not only water but nearly any liquid—even liquids as thick as blinkmoth serum.

His head breached the surface as he reached the inner sanctum inside Lumengrid.

"What in the name of the Creator happened here?"

Lieutenant Marek stepped to the edge of the pool and extended his hand. "The human warriors from Medev, Lord Pontifex."

Pontifex reached up and took hold of Marek's hand, lifting himself from the pool in a practiced motion. "The humans happened?"

"No," replied the lieutenant. "A fight happened. The humans caused it."

Pontifex looked straight into Marek's helmet. "What happened to you?"

Marek put his hand to his face shield, partially covering a crack in the glass. "It's . . . It's nothing."

"I didn't ask you what it was, I asked you what happened. I'm not playing word games here, Marek, I'm trying to ascertain what went on in my absence."

"Of course, my lord." Marek stood to his full height, straightening his back. "We encountered the elf and her companions in the lacuna, but they managed to pass us." He pointed to the crack in his helmet. "This is a result of that encounter."

The halberd in Pontifex's hand glowed a deep blue, and the vedalken lord blew out a breath, forming bubbles inside his face mask. After a moment, he began pacing, tapping the end of his weapon on the floor as he walked.

"You can give me the details later, but tell me this: How long ago did they get away, and have you sent someone after them already?"

"When I arrived, they were already gone. That was nearly an hour ago." Marek lifted his chin. "I formed a sky glider team, and they will be leaving in pursuit shortly."

Pontifex tapped his fingers on the glass of his face mask. "Call back the gliders."

"My lord?"

"Call them back," snapped Pontifex. "We will go after her in due time."

Marek nodded. "As you command."

Pontifex smiled. "Good, Marek." He placed a finger on the crack in the lieutenant's mask. "I'm glad you're all right. Give the orders then go get this fixed up and meet me in my chambers. I have something I would care to discuss with you."

* * * * *

Pontifex paced in his chambers. The damn elf had gotten away from him, but it was no matter. He would get her. He would find her, and he would deliver her to Memnarch. For now, there were other matters to take care of, matters a little closer to home.

A knock came at the door.

"Enter."

The door to Pontifex's private chamber slid open, and Marek entered. The commander of the vedalken elite guardsmen had removed his helmet and was now dressed in simple, functional robes. A sterile-looking bandage covered his forehead—an almost imperceptible dot of blue blood staining its surface—but otherwise the warrior appeared unfazed by his earlier ordeal.

Marek went down to one knee, bowing his head.

"Lord Pontifex."

The vedalken leader admired the supine warrior's neck.

"Rise, Marek. Do you have word of the Synod? Have they managed to enact a 'Special Assembly'?"

"I do not mean to be presumptuous, Lord Pontifex, but wouldn't you rather hear about the elf girl?"

Pontifex smiled. "All in good time, Marek, all in good time. Right now, I'm more concerned with the other council members. They will not be pleased that a human, the elf, and her companions marched into our fortress—into our holiest shrine, and entered the Pool of Knowledge." Pontifex crossed the room, his woven metallic robes grinding against the polished floor. "They will try to hold me responsible."

"My lord, you are the head of the Synod. Surely you can convince them that you—that we did our best to capture the elf and—"

Pontifex cut him off with a wave of his hand. "What you say makes sense, Marek, but I'm afraid there is much you have to learn about the politics of rulership." He touched the warrior on the arm. "Despite our best efforts, there are those who will point to this event as evidence that I am not fit to rule the Synod. They will try to use it to their advantage. This 'Special Assembly' the other councilors are calling is nothing more than a grab for power. Anything they perceive as a weapon, including the escape of the elf girl, will be used." He looked into Marek's eyes, nodding his head. "Power has just shifted hands. At no time after this will my grip on the Synod be less secure. The other councilors are smart enough to recognize this, and they will not hesitate to make a move with whatever means are at their disposal. Do you understand?"

"Yes, my lord." Marek bowed his head.

Pontifex ran his hand over Marek's scalp, tracing the edge of his fresh bandage with his index finger.

"Good, Marek."

CHAPTER 6

Glissa stood alone outside a large building on the edge of a rushing river. The sky was black. None of Mirrodin's four moons shone overhead, a rarity. Glissa had seen times when more than one of the moons seemed to occupy the same place in the sky. One would cover the other, bathing the Tangle in an inescapable blinding light. Strange things occurred at these times, and it was always one of these convergences that marked the time before a festival or ritual.

Now times of darkness were fewer and far between. If one side of the plane was in darkness, it meant all the moons were on the other side—at the same time. Glissa knew what it meant when two of the moons were in alignment. It was time for the rebuking ceremony, time for all elves to give up their memories. It had been this ceremony that had caused her the most trouble while she had been in the Tangle. Giving up on all the things she'd experienced in this lifetime seemed like such a waste. It had been her decision to forego the Rebuking that had touched off the strange series of events that led her to her present situation.

This darkness was deeper than others she'd seen. This was no simple Convergence. Numerous Rebuking ceremonies had come and gone since she was a child. This time, however, *all* the moons were lining up—something that had never happened in her lifetime. If the runes on the Tree of Tales could be trusted, it was something that had only happened four times in the history of the world.

That was why she'd come to see Bruenna.

Glissa knocked on the door of the wizard's tin home, but there was no answer. Pushing aside the chromelike curtain, the elf slipped inside the square building. The entryway was dark, but she could see a faint blue glow coming from a room deeper in the house. Following the light, she made her way to the place where she had first seen Bruenna looking over a series of maps spread out over a large table.

The room was still quite dark, lit by a magically glowing stone that hovered in the air. It cast a perfect circle of light on the floor, throwing the rest of the room into long, deep shadows. Below the glowing stone, Bruenna sat cross-legged, her hands pressed together as if in prayer, and her eyes closed.

Glissa stepped quietly inside the room.

"Hello, Glissa," said Bruenna, not opening her eyes. "Please, come join me."

Glissa crossed to the female wizard, circling around the long table still covered in rolled maps. She sat down facing Bruenna.

"I didn't mean to disturb you."

Bruenna smiled but still didn't open her eyes. "You're not disturbing me. I'm doing a meditative exercise my people call *mulla bunda*. It's a practice to still the mind and heal the body."

Glissa was a little uncomfortable. She'd never seen anybody sit that still. It seemed like a luxury—and boring.

"I'll try to be quiet," she said.

Bruenna's smile widened. "There is no need. Part of the exercise is to focus while confronted with distraction. Please, talk to me. Tell me what you need."

Glissa shrugged. "Okay." She paused. "Bruenna, the moons are aligning."

"Yes, I noticed. It's very dark, darker than I've seen in my lifetime. This Convergence is different."

"In the Tangle, when the moons align, it marks the coming of a new phase, a time of cleansing and renewal."

"I've heard of the elf rituals."

"Well, I've never been much of a believer in these things," admitted the elf, "but until I'd seen it with my own eyes, I didn't believe that Mirrodin was hollow."

"And now you're beginning to question yourself."

Glissa took a deep breath. "Well, wouldn't you?"

"Yes, I would," Bruenna opened her eyes, her smile gone. "I am."

Glissa felt a sudden rush of relief. "I'm frightened, Bruenna."

"As am I." Bruenna lowered her hands to her lap and nodded. "But that fear is comforting."

"I don't understand."

"I would be more concerned—about myself as a human—if I felt nothing during a troubling time. It is natural for elves as well to fear things they don't understand. The question we must ask ourselves is not whether or not that fear is something we should be feeling but how are we going to react to it?"

"You mean, we should be trying to figure out how to stop the moons from aligning?"

Bruenna smiled. "No. There is nothing we can do about the forces of nature."

Glissa wrinkled her brow. "I don't understand."

"We have surprisingly little control over our destinies, yet we still manage to accomplish many things in a lifetime. Changing the course of the moons isn't within our power to control, but how we react to such an event—personally, emotionally, spiritually—we do have some ability to steer. The question we must ask ourselves now is not what we must do, but are we afraid of our own shadows?" Bruenna leaned forward. "Are you going to let the convergence of the moons stop you in your task? Or will you face your challenges—fearful but unstoppable?"

Glissa did not hesitate. "I must go find the trolls again. They're the ones who started me down this path. They'll be able to answer my questions, maybe even tell me more about my role in all of this."

Bruenna nodded. "I have heard that the trolls are very old. They may know a great many things."

"Will you come with me? I could use the help."

The wizard shook her head. "I cannot. My leg needs more healing, and my people need my guidance. There will be much to deal with when the vedalken come."

It was Glissa's turn to nod.

"I will promise you this, though—when the time comes, we will fight with you. We will help you free this world and fulfill your destiny."

"Thank you."

"No, Glissa, it is I who should thank you."

* * * * *

After several long rotations of travel, the trees of the Tangle rose up tall before Glissa, Bosh, and Slobad.

"It's good to be home," said Glissa. "It's been a long time."

Bosh lifted the pair off his shoulders and set them gently on the ground. "Where will we find the trolls?"

"In the Tree of Tales," explained Glissa, "deeper inside the Tangle."

Elf, goblin, and golem made their way through the metallic

forest. As they went, Glissa ran her eyes over familiar ground, bringing back a flood of memories.

She saw clearly her mother, father, and sister, their faces calm and comforting. They drifted away, replaced in her memory by the horror of the leveler attack that had killed them all. She would never forget the terrible sound their scythe blades made. And the blood. Everything was slick with blood.

*   *   *   *   *

Her memories faded, replaced by visions of trees—trees with leaves—and of a world with soft things and a sky of deep blue. A wind slipped lazily through the trees, and Glissa looked to the ground. Patches of green wavered in the breeze. She reached down, and her fingers ran over the edges. She pulled her hand away, expecting to see blood where the leaves had cut her flesh to ribbons—but there was nothing, just smooth, soft skin. No cuts. No blood.

She examined her hand more closely. There was no metal. The blades that extended from her knuckles were gone. She checked her shins. They too had no metal. Her whole body had transformed. Everything was flesh: soft, warm, and forgiving.

She was filled with panic. She reached for her sword, but it too was gone. She was defenseless, with no weapons and no claws. A crash made her look up. Two huge trees cracked in half, each falling away from the other, tumbling into the other trees, smashing away limbs and scattering branches as they hurled toward the ground. Between them towered a gigantic construct. Its gleaming metal chest stood out in stark contrast to the forest and soft plants all around. Its head, arms, and legs were a glowing blue, as if they were formed completely from magic.

The creature stared down at Glissa. She felt very small and

tried to turn away. She wanted to run, but her legs wouldn't move. The creature took a step toward her, and the ground trembled.

Glissa tried to scream, but no sound came from her mouth. She drew a breath and tried again—still, nothing. The construct took another step then bent down, reaching out. Its huge, glowing fingers wrapped around Glissa's body, and she was lifted from the ground.

* * * * *

Glissa came to on the ground, Slobad's face right above hers. "You okay, huh?"

Glissa nodded. She had these visions from time to time. They were called flares, and she dreaded them. They were flashes really, pictures that ran in her head. All elves had them, but Glissa's were stronger, more vibrant, than most. No one knew for certain what they were. Glissa thought of them as waking dreams—the possibilities of her mind showing themselves in brilliant colors.

The elders in her tribe had claimed the flares were visions of the future. Most elves did not believe that. Who could really see into the future?

Sometimes the visions blinked in and out, as if she were opening and closing her eyes while she spun in a circle. Each time her eyes focused again, a different scene filled her vision. It was only for a split second, then it was as if her eyes closed again, and she moved on, looking moments later upon something entirely different.

"No golem," Glissa said.

"No golems?" Bosh seemed concerned. "Are there no golems allowed in the Tree of Tales?"

The elf shook her head, dazed. "Uh . . . no. That's not what I was talking about. I'm sure they'll allow you in." She stood up. "They'd had better let you in."

"What you talking about then, crazy elf?" asked Slobad.

"I had another flare."

Slobad stood upright and looked at her with wide eyes.

"No, it's okay. I'm fine."

"What did you see?" asked the big golem.

"I saw a different world again. A world without metal."

"A world without golems?"

"No. There was a golem, or at least what I thought was a golem." Glissa shook her head, trying to clear it.

"It mean something, huh?"

"I don't know, but it seemed like a nice place." She looked at Bosh. "All except the part about the golem. I'm not sure it was a nice golem—" she touched Bosh's arm—"like you." She shrugged. "There were soft things there, like the blankets and beds we stayed in at Bruenna's village. Even the grasses and bushes were soft."

The goblin gasped. "Soft razor grass?"

"It wasn't really razor grass. It just looked like it." She straightened and headed deeper into the Tangle. "It was nothing. Get going."

The trio walked on in silence for some time. The closer they got to the Tree of Tales, the more memories crept into Glissa's mind. She thought of Kane, wearing the armor of the Tel-Jilad Chosen. A deep sadness filled her chest. It felt heavy, as if a vorac were standing on her chest. A knot in the bottom of her stomach moved and fluttered as if she'd swallowed a live bird.

A voice brought her from her reverie. "Glissa."

Glissa looked up from the ground. The figure before her

wore the red ceremonial armor of the Tel-Jilad. For a moment, Glissa saw a different face.

"Kane?"

The elf looked at her sideways. "No."

Glissa looked around. While she had been thinking of her best friend, she had walked right up to the front of the Tree of Tales.

The guard stepped to one side, indicating the side of the tree with a sweep of his hand.

Glissa stared at him, confused. "What's this? You're just going to let me inside the Tree."

The Tel-Jilad nodded.

Slobad sidled up to her. "You sure 'bout this, crazy elf? Last time we here, they think you kill old troll, huh?"

Glissa nodded. "They haven't attacked us yet," she said. "Besides—" she looked up at Bosh—"we've got a golem."

Slobad threw up his hands and the three of them headed toward the tree.

Glissa stepped between the roots, pushing through the rounded vines that hung down, obscuring the entrance to the Tree of Tales.

Inside the tree, the trio were greeted by a large, imposing troll. His face was round and covered in warts, and his shoulders were slouched forward, as if his head were too heavy to be held up by his thick neck.

"Young Glissa," said the troll in a deep rumble, "we were expecting you."

"Do I know you?"

"No," said the troll, "but Master Drooge knows *you*. He is awaiting you upstairs."

The elf eyed the troll. His manner was controlled and introspective, the exact opposite of threatening, and he appeared harmless—harmless for a troll. He carried no visible weapons and moved with a swiftness that belied his great size.

"Who is Master Drooge?"

"He is the eldest," said the troll. "The newest leader of the trolls." With that, he bowed his head and stepped aside, indicating with a flourish of his hand the stairway leading deeper into the tree.

Glissa looked at the other two. Slobad sighed but nodded, and they headed up.

The steps were cut from from the tree itself. Circular scoring, covering every inch of the tarnished steps, formed a pleasing pattern. It almost seemed as if someone had polished the shape of the stairs into the metal, leaving a series of tiny circles. None of the circles was complete, each having a vague beginning and ending that seemed to flow into the one beside it. At the top of each step, the linked swirls bent at the edge and continued up, wrapping from the side of one step onto the top of the next. The interconnected circles formed a collection of chains that led up and around the spiral staircase.

The surface of each step was rough, not magically honed like the scythe blades of the levelers or the wings of the hover guard. These had been made by hand. It made Glissa's back hurt just thinking of the amount of work it would take to scratch out such a feature in a solid metal tree. Judging by the obvious wear and tear and large patches of heavy tarnishing, this had been done a long, long time ago.

The group moved on in silence, finally reaching the top where the stairs opened into a large room. A set of rising bleachers edged the chamber, and sitting on them, three rows deep, were perhaps a hundred or more trolls. All of them resembled other trolls Glissa had seen. Their skin was green and loose, their hands and shoulders covered in warts and scars, and each was dressed in tattered woven-metal fabrics. Even to the elf, who had grown up in the Tangle living near such creatures, she couldn't tell them apart. Now, seated here, they looked like the fungus or verdigris that grew on the base of fallen trees.

Opposite the stairs, in the center of the curved bleacher seats, a single troll perched on a stool. All the others had their bodies turned toward him and their eyes focused on his large frame. This one, unlike the others, wore newer clothing. He held himself more erect and seemed to have more energy than the others. His eyes darted around the room. This was not a contemplative examination or the sluggish struggle by a slow mind to understand. This was the intelligent look of a decisive creature.

The troll at the head of the room held a bone staff in one hand. With the other he waved the trio forward.

"Come in. Come in."

Glissa and Slobad did as they were told, stopping amid the throng of trolls just before the bone-wielding chief. Bosh, though, had a difficult time getting inside the room. At his full height, his head was much taller than the ceiling. The golem tried to bend at the waist, but ducking didn't provide enough room for him to bring his massive frame into the carved-out chamber.

After several attempts to fold himself in various different ways, each of which proved more ridiculous and less useful than the last, Bosh finally collapsed his legs and head half-way, telescoping them inside his body. The truncated golem waddled as he walked, but he managed to fit, if tightly, inside the room.

The troll looked them over. "We have been awaiting your arrival."

"So we've been told," said Glissa. "That disturbs me."

"Why would that disturb you, young Glissa?"

"Well, to begin with, the last time I was here, Elder Chunth died in my arms."

Drooge nodded, his eyes to the ground. "A tragic blow for

us." He took a deep breath. "You should know that we do not blame you."

"You don't?"

The troll chief shook his head. "No. The elder council has found you innocent, and the traitors among us have been purged."

Glissa looked around at the trolls on the bleachers. They all hung their heads. "Traitors? You mean there was more than one?"

Drooge nodded. "I am afraid so."

Glissa stood in silence. She was relieved that the trolls didn't think she had killed their chief, but she was saddened as well. All of this treachery and infighting was due to her. If she had been at home that night, if she had been killed along with the rest of her family, none of this would have happened to the trolls.

The troll chief tapped his staff on the floor. "You have other reasons for being disturbed by our welcoming you back?"

Glissa swallowed then nodded. "Well, yes. Everyone seems to know where I'm going and what I'll do before I even do it."

"Yes," replied the troll. "I see your point."

"And since they know where I am at all times, I seem to be everyone's favorite target for ambush."

"A role none wish to play," said the troll, "but one that falls upon the shoulders of a hero."

"A hero?" Glissa stopped to think about that word. "Why would you call me that?"

The troll cocked his head, looking at the young elf. "Because your efforts are not just focused on yourself."

"Wait a minute." Glissa shook her head. "How do you know what it is I want or even that I was coming here?"

"A simple deduction," replied the troll. "The last time you were here, you wanted to know about the Guardian. You did not believe us then. You have returned. Thus, I suspect that you have seen proof, that now you are beginning to believe that which Chunth believed, and you wish for answers."

"What did Chunth believe?"

"That you have a destiny beyond the borders of the Tangle. That your path is far longer than you know." The troll smiled, his stained, ground-flat teeth poking from his wart-covered lips, looking menacing yet warm at the same time.

Slobad pulled on Glissa's arm. "Who this guy, huh?"

"That's a good question," said Glissa. She looked up from the goblin. "Who are you?"

The troll bowed. "Forgive my lack of hospitality. I am Drooge, chief teller of tales. These—" he waved his arm to indicated the collected trolls— "these are all that's left of my kind."

Glissa scanned the room. There were a lot of trolls here, more than she'd ever seen in one place at one time. Still, the thought saddened her. This was *all* of them. Every last one.

The group no longer seemed so large.

She laid her gaze again upon Drooge. "So you figured out that I would come back, but that still doesn't answer my question about why you called me a 'hero.' What makes you think I'm not just looking out for myself?"

The troll placed his hand on his jaw, rubbing his bumpy chin. "Sometimes, a hero is not a hero by choice. Sometimes, a hero is just a hero because her actions make her one. Whether you know it or not, your quest is one that will benefit many people. Perhaps everyone on Mirrodin." Drooge lowered his head. "Although the trolls have known about Memnarch, have known not only that he existed but also that he controlled the levelers and devices that plague the land, we . . ." His voice trailed off. The rumpled troll stared at the floor for a long while.

Glissa looked at him, bending her knees and trying to get

down close enough to the floor to get his attention. "Yes?" she said, trying to coax it from him.

"We . . . We have been . . . afraid," he said finally.

"But when last I was here, Chunth was very reluctant to talk with me. He told me very little and seemed quite…guarded, almost as if he would be punished for telling me what I wanted to know." Glissa paused, watching Drooge stare at the floor. "Now you rush me inside and greet me as if I were one of you. Why such a drastic change?"

Drooge raised his eyes. "Chunth was the oldest among us and the wisest. Now he is gone, and a new fear has entered the troll tribe: the fear that we will all be gone, taken from this place as Chunth was. As you can see, there are only a very few of us left. We cannot face Memnarch and his armies of devices alone. We are too few." Drooge paused, taking a deep breath. "We are too afraid."

"What does that have to do with me?"

"Your destiny has been set in motion. There is no longer time to debate 'if' or 'when.' It has come. The time is now, and events will continue forward whether you are ready or not."

"I still don't understand."

Drooge raised his bone staff. "We all have kin who have fallen to the Guardian's armies. We want to see you succeed."

"Are you saying you're going to help me confront the Guardian?"

Drooge once again scratched his chin. "When the time is right. Yes."

Slobad pulled on Glissa's arm. "When that be, huh? We come back then."

The troll laughed in the back of his throat. "I'm afraid I cannot tell you the future, only that the trolls will participate when all has been prepared."

"Prepared?" Glissa shook her head. "What are you talking about. You make it sound as if there is some sort of predetermined course that we're all destined to follow—that I'm the one leading. Am I missing something here?"

Drooge rose from his chair and ambled forward. The quickness of his words and the sharp intelligence in his eyes had distracted Glissa from noticing one important detail about the troll chieftain.

He had only one leg.

The bone staff he had been holding was a crutch, and he leaned on it as he moved forward. His steps were awkward and metered, very much as Glissa expected from a troll.

When he came close enough to touch the trio, he stopped and smiled. "I am sorry, I do not mean to confuse you. I forget that all this information is new to you. For the trolls, it has been a way of life, a belief." He leaned down, lowering his face so that he looked into Glissa's eyes. "We do not belong on Mirrodin. The trolls—" he waved his hand around, indicating all the creatures seated in the bleacher seats— "we are not from this world. We do not wish to stay here any longer than we must."

"Wait." Glissa sank down on the metal floor. "You're from some other world?"

"Yes."

"How is it that I can help you? It's not as if I can lift you to some other plane."

"You can help us escape from the tyranny of the Guardian," explained the troll. "That is the path you will travel. That is the destiny that has been chosen for you."

"You speak as if I don't have any choice in the matter."

"You do not."

The elf snorted.

"If all of you—" Glissa ran her gaze around the room, taking in the entire troll tribe— "with your big muscles and strong fists, can't stand up to Memnarch and his devices, what makes you think I can?"

"Because you are not afraid."

"*Of course I'm afraid!*" Glissa shouted. "In fact, I can't remember more than a brief instant of my entire life when I *wasn't* afraid of something."

The troll nodded, apparently unperturbed by her outburst. "Yes, it is something that transcends the racial boundaries. Fear binds us together and makes us all the same." Drooge placed his huge hand on the petite elf's shoulder. "What makes us different, you and I, is that despite that fear you go on."

Slowly Glissa nodded. Now she understood.

Drooge turned and limped past his seat. "As I said, when the time is right, the trolls will come to your aid." When he reached the far wall of the chamber, he placed his crutch aside. Flattening his palms against the metal, he spoke a single word, and a cabinet appeared.

It was a square box, about the size of a small goblin, the same color and texture as the surrounding wall. If Glissa hadn't been watching, she might have thought it had been there the whole time. It blended with the rest of the chamber as if it had been carved from the tree, just like the steps. Drooge reached into this cabinet and pulled out a small casket.

"Do not think that I would send you away empty handed."

The troll waved the trio forward.

They approached, and Glissa put her finger out to touch the casket. It was of exquisite workmanship, carved in patterns she did not recognize. She didn't want to stop touching it.

"You like that?" asked the troll.

"Yes," said Glissa. "What is it?"

"It is from the wood of a tree not of this world. Many thousands of years ago, it is said that my people, the trolls, lived in these trees."

Glissa's eye's nearly bulged from her head. She couldn't even imagine another world. Just running her fingers over the wood calmed her nerves and made her feel . . . feel . . . happy.

"You're giving this to me?"

The troll laughed. "No, " he said. "I am giving you what is inside."

Glissa was disappointed. "Oh."

"It is nice," said Drooge, his eyes lit up with amusement, "but I doubt this casket will help you along your path. No, I am giving you this." The troll lifted the lid and drew forth a helm. Inset along its rim in a brilliant circle were five gemstones, each one a different color. At the top, carved deep into the metal surface, was a sigil or rune. It was a circle, broken into five wedge-shaped pieces by five different lines—like a wheel with five spokes.

Drooge handed the helm to Glissa.

"It's beautiful." The elf ran her finger over the stones—a diamond, an emerald, a ruby, an onyx, and a sapphire. Each of them sparkled.

Bosh waddled over, and Slobad lifted himself up on his tip toes to get a better look.

"What does it do?"

* * * * *

Pontifex paced outside the door leading to the Grand Assembly Chamber. Inside, the other members of the Synod waited. The lord of the vedalken knew what to expect when he entered. He knew what they had planned. The whole scheme had unfolded in less than a cycle.

Despite the very real power he now wielded over the vedalken people, and for that matter the Synod itself, he had been powerless to stop this. Sometimes the game of politics is simply more powerful than the politicians who play.

Pontifex steeled himself and stepped forward. The doors before him slipped silently aside, and he entered the chamber. No one spoke, but the room was filled with the shuffling sound of bodies trying to get comfortable. The assembled vedalken went still upon seeing him, and the room fell completely silent.

The Grand Hall, as it was often referred to, was nothing more than a giant spiraling pit dug deep into the ground. Wider at the top than it was at the bottom, the room itself had been designed by a vedalken architect who had taken his inspiration from the swirling storms and whirlpools of the Quicksilver Sea. A narrow platform, just wide enough to fit two vedalken guardsmen in full uniform side by side, wound down the edge of the pit, running in a spiral from the very ceiling to an open floor far below. To Pontifex, it looked like a corkscrew, winding its way down into the bowls of Mirrodin. That image amused him, and he smirked.

A railing skirted the edge of the spiraling platform. The original designer had wanted the room to feel—and be—dangerous. One false step and a vedalken could find himself on the floor in a big hurry. Down lower, that wasn't much of a problem, but from this height, a body falling that far would be smashed into jelly.

This room is dangerous, thought Pontifex as he looked down at the collected vedalken, even with the safety precautions.

Gathered on the spiral, the assembled citizens of the vedalken empire stood against the outer wall or leaned up on the railing. Where Pontifex stood at the top of the winding platform he could see down on everyone, including the other two members of the synod who awaited him at the bottom. Beside them stood a third figure. Pontifex did not know this man, but he knew what his presence here represented.

"Lord Pontifex," said a voice from far below, "so nice of you to join us."

The round, lifting design of the chamber allowed every word spoken to be heard by all. It mattered not if the speaker were on the floor or along the railing near the ceiling, all had a voice here. However, any citizen who spoke out of turn or without being recognized was removed by force and thrown into hard labor for two full moon cycles. Many who had been punished in such a fashion didn't live long enough to be released back into society. Consequently, while inside the assembly chamber, very few spoke at all.

Pontifex recognized the voice. "Hello, Tyrell," he said, looking down to the floor at the vedalken. "It's always a pleasure to be in the esteemed company of my fellow Synod councilors—" he circled his finger in the air, indicating the collected vedalken in the assembly hall— "and the elected citizen representatives." He descended the long spiral platform toward the floor. "Welcome."

Quiet clapping filled the room, and the vedalken representatives bowed their heads as their lord moved past.

Pontifex loved this. He loved that these people loved him. He had experienced nothing quite like it, and he relished every moment.

"Now that you have arrived—"

The vedalken's clapping stopped.

"—may we proceed with the inauguration ceremony?"

These were the impatient words of Sodador. The younger, more hot-headed of the other two councilors, Sodador walked with the aid of a cane.

Yes, thought Pontifex, looking at him with narrowed eyes. You are anxious to lead the Synod.

But the councilor's overzealous demeanor hadn't won him the political power to challenge the previous leader, Janus. The latter had had too many allies.

Ascending to the head of the Synod was a nasty business. Assassinating one's predecessor didn't cast one in the most politically flattering light. It would be some time before Pontifex could overcome the negative image his rise to power on the body of Janus had gained him.

Pontifex smiled to himself. They might win this battle, but he'd make them pay.

"Oh, my, this is embarrassing, Councilor Sodador," said the vedalken lord. "Don't you think you're forgetting something?"

Pontifex was nearly half way to the floor at this point. Sodador's features cleared.

"I am most certainly not. We have followed every parliamentary procedure in calling this special assembly of the elected representatives."

Pontifex stopped his descent, stepping to the railing between two representatives. He raised his finger. "Forgive me, Councilor Sodador, but isn't a vote of the council required before we can bring a fourth member into the Synod? Certainly before we have an inauguration, we must have a vote. I don't know about you, but I don't remember voting on the inclusion of this person into our council." Pontifex pointed down at the third figure on the floor. "In fact, I've never even been introduced to this man."

There was a slight gasp from several of the collected representatives, and both Sodador and Tyrell seemed to squirm. Pontifex smiled. Their scheme hadn't been covert, but now their motives for arranging the special assembly were called into question.

"Well," he said, resuming his downward spiral, "am I wrong?"

"As you will recall, Lord Pontifex," replied Tyrell, "this meeting was called in accordance with the law, which very specifically states there must be four members seated on the Synod at the start of each new moon cycle." Tyrell ran his hand over his bald scalp. "It is dark outside, my friend. The moon cycle has begun, and we have an empty seat to fill."

"Fill it we will." Pontifex smiled wide. "However, I think you'll agree just because we're slightly behind schedule doesn't mean we should abandon our long standing traditions and procedures. Our laws, Tyrell, were written to protect us from hasty decisions. Let us interview your candidate and bring him before a vote of the representative—as is the mandate for the Synod— before we swear him in."

A light clapping followed.

"Our laws," shot back Sodador, "were written to protect us from a council chair who abuses his power."

Pontifex looked hurt. "Are you accusing me of something, Sodador?"

Sodador opened his mouth, but Tyrell raised his hand to stop him. "Our young councilor accuses you of nothing, Lord Pontifex. He merely speaks of the conventions of balance." The elder statesmen turned to the assembled vedalken standing above him on the spiral. "As you all know, good citizens, the Synod is a council of four members. Though there is rarely a conflict of opinion, from time to time it becomes necessary to break ties when the council members do not agree. It is at these times that the council chair casts a second vote." Tyrell spun as he spoke, making eye contact with each and every one of the elected representatives as he did. "Currently, there are only three members on the Synod. That is why you have been called here for this most unusual meeting. Many of you have never before set foot in this assembly hall. Many of you will never again be compelled to do so, but today is different. Today you must fill the fourth seat by wielding a single collective vote that will be cast in the event of a tie."

Pontifex spoke in turn. "Because of the unusual circumstance which has brought you all here today, you have been given a rare glimpse into the workings of the Synod, and how we—" Pontifex indicated the other members and himself— "take into account the concerns and needs of the entire vedalken empire." He nodded his head, smiling up at the representatives. "I, for one, am most excited. It is not every day that you get to witness the governing council at work, much less participate in the ruling of your own sovereign body. I'm sure you all are as excited by the prospect as I am, but I must take this opportunity to speak to you of the grave importance of the decision we are all about to make."

Lord Pontifex stood up straight, his smile fading into a look of stern seriousness. "Weigh your vote very carefully, for whomever you chose to fill that empty seat will rule on the Synod for life."

*　*　*　*　*

Memnarch ambled from his laboratory. The work he did outside Panopticon was easy enough, but the journey to the soul trap fields and back would take him considerable time—time he would have to spend away from his infusion device.

With serum storage tanks attached to his frame, it would take him even longer. The contraption kept him fully lubricated, but its bulk and weight slowed him down. No matter. He enjoyed his trips to the soul traps. Better to enjoy the work than to try to finish it in the least amount of time.

Besides, the metal tanks made Memnarch feel as he had before, when his body had been all metal. Perfect, the way it had been created.

"Do you think Memnarch has forgotten?" The Guardian shook his head. "Of course you do not."

The lift stopped and the doors slipped open. Memnarch was greeted with silence as he looked across the empty staging area at the base of Panopticon. Before, there had been a hundred levelers arrayed here.

"Malil has taken them all," he said. "He takes his duty seriously."

The bulbous, crablike Guardian of Mirrodin scuttled from the lift then from his tower. The dimly lit interior was replaced by the blinding blue-white light of the mana core. High above the floor of the interior, the power core of the entire plane hissed and crackled with energy.

"Sometimes Memnarch misses the darkness. Yes. Yes. It is much easier to work with a constant source of light. Still, the convergence of the moons was a spectacular event, a spectacular event." He stopped for a moment, putting one of his fingers to his lips. "There is a minor convergence happening now," he said. "Do you remember when the first moon shot from the core of the plane?"

Memnarch moved on, shaking his head. "No, I suspected you would not. You were not here for that. Or for the next one." The Guardian scowled. "Or for the next one. Or for the next one after that. Come to think of it, Mirrodin was always dark when you were here. Oh, how things have changed."

Memnarch could see the tall chrome spires of mycosynth up ahead, touched at their bases with tarnish. They reached high into the sky, climbing from the ground up toward the mana core. Forests of these pointy towers dotted the interior of Mirrodin from one side to the other. From Panopticon, Memnarch could actually see how they curved with the slope of the round plane.

The Guardian wasn't interested in these structures. They represented all that was wrong with Mirrodin now.

"True," he said as he approached the nearest of the columns, "they are not the problem, but they are a symptom. Memnarch does not like the symptoms."

Inside the forest of mycosynth, Memnarch stopped and knelt. Below him, dozens of little furry creatures scurried around, stopping when they encountered the large, diamond-shaped boxes, covered in mossy verdigris, spaced several meters apart.

"You would be proud of these, Master Karn," he said, reaching down to examine one of the boxes. "These devices are Memnarch's own creation. His own creation. We call them soul traps, and they keep Mirrodin populated." Gently brushing aside several of the furry little creatures, the Guardian probed the sides of the diamond. It was soft, fleshy to his touch.

"This too," he said poking the soft sides of the contraption. "This is a symptom. If only Memnarch knew what caused the symptoms, we could study it. Understand it. Cure it."

Memnarch looked down at his own arm. The flesh there was soft and supple, just like the sides of the trap and the furry beasts running around on the floor of Mirrodin.

"It infects us all. It corrupts perfection." Memnarch gritted his teeth, squeezing his fists together until this arms turned bright red. "It makes a mockery of all that the Creator built."

Memnarch's body began to shake. "This is not how Memnarch is supposed to be. You created Memnarch in your image, and now Memnarch is…is…" He held his arms up, opening his whole body to the rays of the mana core.

"This!"

The bright blue-white light seared into Memnarch's eyes,

and tears ran down his face. Except for the electrical hiss the mana core gave off, the rest of the interior of Mirrodin was silent.

Finally the Guardian let his hands fall to his sides. A floating patch of orange filled his vision. For a moment Memnarch lost his connection to the solid world. Vertigo filled his head, and the Guardian lost his balance. He stepped back to catch himself, and his foot landed on something soft. He heard a popping noise and slipped.

Memnarch fell. All four of his legs folded underneath him, and his serum tank made a tremendous clang as it hit the ground.

"Why is Memnarch being punished so?" he moaned.

The Guardian rested on his side, not moving. The burning orange sphere obscuring his sight slowly drifted away, and Memnarch looked out at a puddle of red fluid covering the ground around him.

"Blood? Do we see blood?"

Lifting himself to his feet, he examined his body. His entire side was slick with blood, but he felt no pain. Poking and prodding his partially fleshy limbs, Memnarch searched for wounds, but found none.

On the ground, near his feet, the furry little creatures scuttled around, avoiding the bloody mess as best they could.

"Our grendles? Have our grendles turned completely to flesh?"

Memnarch bent down and picked up one of the crushed, furry creatures. A feeling of overwhelming sadness crept over him, and he shook his head as he looked down at the dead creature in his hands.

"Is this what will happen to Memnarch?"

* * * * *

Drooge held up a finger. "By itself, the helm will aid you in battle. Your blows will strike harder. Your moves will be faster. In concert with the Sword of Kaldra and the Shield of Kaldra, it will do much more."

"The Sword of Kaldra? What's that?"

Drooge lifted his massive hand and pointed to Glissa's hip. "The blade you took from Chunth."

Glissa pulled her hand back. "You mean it's part of a set?"

"Yes. More appropriately, it is part of a key."

Slobad's ears perked up. "What does this key open?"

"It is not so much a key to open something as a key to activate a powerful being."

Slobad's ears picked up. "Artifact, huh? Where we find this powerful artifact? "

"Not an artifact."

Slobad slumped, disappointed.

"You must travel to the swamps of the Mephidross," Drooge continued. "There you will find the Shield of Kaldra." The troll held out his hand. "May I see your sword?"

Glissa looked hesitantly at Slobad then at Bosh. The golem stood silently behind her, as he had during the entire interview, ready for anything. The sight of her hulking friend calmed Glissa's nerves, and she pulled her sword from its sheath, handing it to the troll.

Drooge ran his fingers over the blade's hilt, examining the etchings and runes inscribed there. "You see this," he said after a moment, turning the handle toward the trio and indicating a circular groove. At the center of the groove, the same circular rune broken into five parts had been inscribed. "This is where the sword's hilt will attach to the shield when you find the last part of the Kaldra Guardian."

"The Kaldra Guardian?" asked Slobad.

"Yes," replied the troll. "The guardian is an avatar, a very powerful one. Once you have all three pieces, you must assemble them, and the guardian will come to life."

"Wait," said Glissa. "If the trolls knew about this being before, why didn't Chunth just tell me about it?"

Drooge pawed his crutch. "You were not ready."

"Not ready?"

"You did not believe Master Chunth. Now that you know your destiny, you are ready."

"I still don't understand what it is I'm destined to do."

The troll smiled. "One step at a time," he said. "Your journey will be long. Do not try to do it all in one day."

A loud boom echoed through the Tree of Tales, and for the first time since they'd arrived, the trolls in the bleacher seats stirred. Lumbering up from where they were seated, the entire troll clan separated into four groups, filing from the room in an orderly fashion.

"What is that? What's happening?" asked Glissa.

Drooge placed the casket back inside the cabinet and shut the door. "The Tree of Tales is under attack."

* * * * *

Malil stood atop his personal leveler. The power of the serum still held him tightly in its grasp. The world had coalesced, and he had come back to Mirrodin just as Memnarch had told him he would. But the world to which he returned was different now. He understood better the way things worked, but that wasn't what had changed.

Before him, arrayed and ready for battle, were nearly a hundred other levelers, each of them under his command. He looked out on them with a measure of pride. It was odd, this sensation.

Many times before Malil had stood in just this place, but never once had he felt . . . anything.

Now his mind raced. They had tracked the elf to the Tangle, to this very tree. The leveler army had surrounded it. Malil had had the foresight to bring along two crushers—mammoths with curved horns on their heads and a single huge cylindrical wheel in front, capable of rolling over nearly anything and squashing it completely flat. In the past, he'd used these creations mostly to level human villages or flatten patches of razor grass. Now these behemoths were both assaulting the tree. Each of the artifact creatures took turns backing up and rolling forward, smashing headlong into the base of the tree. The pounding noise they made sounded musical to Malil.

The first crusher clanged into the tree again as the other pulled back for another run. The vibrating note of the last attack had almost fallen to silence when a flood of green oozed from the tree.

At first Malil thought it might be some sort of organic fluid. He had seen Memnarch bleed before, had even seen the humans and elves bleed when they were caught between the scythe blades of a leveler. Maybe this tree was bleeding.

The green fluid began to strike the levelers and the crushers, and Malil knew this was no fluid after all.

"Trolls."

Levelers were hurled away from the advancing green tide. The crushers stopped their attack, covered by a host of trolls.

"Kill them," shouted Malil, and the rest of the leveler army moved in, tightening the noose around the tree and the trolls.

* * * * *

"What we do?" shouted Slobad. "Levelers have us trapped, huh?"

"We're going to fight," said Glissa. She gripped the hilt of the Sword of Kaldra and took a step forward, but Drooge's crutch bared her way.

"Your path does not lead out this door," said the troll chieftain, indicating the arched front entrance to the tree. "It leads to the center of Mirrodin."

"Wherever I'm supposed to go, I can't get there if I don't get out of this damned tree. We have to fight. We have no choice. Besides, your trolls could use the help."

The elf pointed out to the battle raging just a few yards from them. The forest beasts had torn many of the artifact creatures to bits. Piles of metal parts littered the ground, but among them were the fallen forms of several trolls.

"My trolls can take care of themselves," replied Drooge. "Now you must take care that you do not too easily play into Memnarch's hands."

"You think this army is here to find me?"

"I do not think," replied Drooge, "I know. Now, follow me." Despite his missing leg, Drooge moved faster than she'd ever seen a troll go, and Glissa struggled to keep up.

Glissa looked down at her sword. "Wait! Where do I find the last piece of the Kaldra Guardian?"

The troll did not turn, continuing to lead Glissa, Slobad, and Bosh from the Tree. "You must find Geth. He has what you are looking for."

Glissa looked to Slobad. "Geth again."

"Crazy troll can't find 'nother shield?"

Glissa shook her head. "You're the one who was so excited about a new artifact to tinker with." She shrugged. "Guess we head back to the Vault of Whispers. If we'd only known last time, we could have saved ourselves a trip."

Drooge, standing taller than any except Bosh, looked each of them in the eye then returned his stare to Glissa. "You must get to the Mephidross quickly. Do not stay here and fight, or the sacrifice of these many trolls will be in vain."

* * * * *

Pontifex lowered his wide-headed halberd and lunged at Marek. "These are trying times, my friend."

The vedalken elite guard commander parried the blow then countered, pushing Pontifex back a step.

"Well done," complimented the vedalken lord. He steadied himself then began weaving his blade in a series of practiced patterns.

Marek watched the tip of the halberd as it moved through the air.

"I knew the probable outcome, but I hadn't expected such a unanimous vote." Pontifex continued moving his weapon, attempting to lull his opponent with its gentle motion.

"Does that really matter, my lord? If the representatives vote with one voice, there is no difference between approval from most and from all. The outcome is the same." Marek kept his guard up.

"True, true," replied Pontifex. He watched Marek follow the hypnotic pattern of the blade. "Still, this sort of thing could lead to very dangerous changes inside the empire." The vedalken lord struck. His blade moved forward, but instead of moving back, following the pattern, he lunging farther, catching Marek off guard. The blade spanked off of the warrior's shoulder pad, and Pontifex pulled back. Marek went down, trying to dodge too late.

"Well done, my lord," said Marek, looking up at Pontifex from the ground.

Pontifex placed the butt of his weapon on the ground and extended three hands to Marek. "Thank you," he said, and he helped the warrior back to his feet.

The two placed their halberds in a rack against the wall, and Pontifex grabbed a towel to wipe the sweat from his gleaming, bald head.

Marek scratched his chin. "Forgive my ignorance, my lord, but what sort of dangerous changes?"

Pontifex took a deep breath. "If the representatives get a real taste of power, they may try to be part of the Synod on a more regular basis. If that happens, the council will lose some if not most of its power, and that we cannot have." The vedalken lord stood up. "Perhaps more disturbing would be the possible erosion of my authority. If the representatives think they can challenge everything I do with a vote, I will be forced to take more drastic measures. And if they are successful . . ." Pontifex let out a laugh. "Can you imagine the chaos that would ensue if every decision I made had to be voted upon before it could be enacted. Really! The damage caused to the empire by such a process would be an irrevocable disaster."

A knock came at the door, interrupting the vedalken lord.

"I won't have it," he said to Marek in a whisper. He straightened his robes and turned to the door. "Enter."

The door slid open. Sodador and Tyrell stepped through, followed by a third vedalken—the newest member of the Synod.

"Orland," said Lord Pontifex, "what an unexpected surprise."

The third member nodded then stepped forward.

Pontifex looked him over.

The vedalken had a slight build, even for his relatively frail race. His four arms were long and skinny and seemed out of proportion to his short body. Pontifex drew himself up to his full height, noting that he overtopped the man by nearly an entire head.

"Lord Pontifex," said Orland, "it is my honor and privilege to stand before you as your equal and colleague. Thank you for allowing us an audience."

"The pleasure is all mine," replied Pontifex. "Please, come, sit down." He guided the other three councilors to form-fitting, high-backed chairs surrounding a sturdy table.

When all of the men were seated, Pontifex cleared his throat. "To what do I owe the honor of your visit?"

Orland opened his mouth to speak, but Sodador cut him off. "Forgive us, Lord Pontifex, but this is official Synod business." He looked at Marek. "Would you be so kind as to excuse the commander?"

Pontifex scowled. "Might I remind you, Sodador, that you are inside my personal chambers. Marek is an honorable man, and my trusted servant. While there are guests, I require a bodyguard."

"Oh, please!" spat Sodador. "We are no threat to you."

"This is official business," interjected Tyrell. "How can we be expected to speak freely if we have an audience?"

Orland looked at Marek then turned to both Sodador and Tyrell. "Gentlemen, please. Lord Pontifex has been gracious enough to allow us into his chamber. We should respect his wishes."

Pontifex looked at the new councilor. Perhaps this one could be of some use after all. "Thank you, Councilor Orland." He smiled. "As you were saying?"

"Yes. We have come to you at my urging. I realize the circumstances surrounding my appointment to the Synod were unorthodox. I want to make sure that my presence in the decision-making process is not seen as an invasion."

"My dear Orland," Pontifex said, "whatever would make you think such preposterous things? The representatives voted in a legal assembly. The outcome is indisputable."

Orland nodded. "Precisely, but if I were in your position, I might feel as if I'd been fooled."

Sodador and Tyrell squirmed in their seats.

"I've come to you on a mission of diplomacy," continued Orland, "to make available to you my services—as a token of my respect and dedication to the greater good of the vedalken people."

Pontifex was puzzled. "What do you have in mind?"

Orland smiled. "Helping you catch the elf girl, of course."

CHAPTER 7

Glissa followed Drooge through a winding passageway inside the Tree of Tales. As they ran, they descended. The clank of Bosh's feet on the metal ground filled the passageway, drowning out the sounds of battle from above.

The tunnel twisted and turned then abruptly ended around a corner at a set of stairs leading up.

"This is where I must leave you," said the troll chieftain. "Good luck to you, and good speed." Drooge nodded to the three, then ducked back down the passage.

"So we go up again, huh?" said the goblin.

"Guess so," replied Glissa. "Any idea where we are?"

Both Slobad and Bosh shook their heads.

"There's only one way to find out." Glissa pulled her sword from her sheath and climbed the stairs.

The goblin and the golem followed.

The stairway led up into a dark cavern. At the opposite end, a small opening let in light, and with it the sounds of battle.

"Come on," Glissa led the others to the opening and looked out. They were near the edge of the Tangle inside a narrow cave at the base of a very large tree. The army of levelers covered the ground before them, but their attention was focused the other direction, on the Tree of Tales. Near the middle, riding on a leveler, was the metal man Glissa had seen inside Mirrodin.

"Memnarch," she said.

Slobad jumped. "Where?"

"Right there," replied the elf. "Riding that leveler in the middle."

The goblin squinted. "How do you know, huh?"

Glissa shrugged. "We saw him on the interior. Don't you remember?"

"Yes, but . . ."

"But what?"

"Goblins never seen Memnarch before," replied Slobad. "You tell Slobad this tree him, Slobad believe crazy elf, huh?"

Glissa turned to the golem. "You've seen Memnarch, right Bosh?"

The golem nodded. "Yes, I remember the Guardian."

"Well?"

"Well, what?"

"Is that him?" Glissa stuck her arm out, pointing to the metal man riding atop the leveler.

"It looks like him."

Glissa punched the goblin in the arm. "See, I told you."

"But it is not," finished Bosh.

The elf let her jaw drop open. "What? You just said it looked like him."

"It does. It looks as he did when he was first created," said the golem.

"But?"

"But he does not look like that any more. At least, he did not when I saw him last."

Glissa was frustrated. "Well, if it's not Memnarch, then who is he?"

The goblin and the golem both shrugged.

"Not matter, huh?" said Slobad. "Metal man introduce himself soon. Slobad not want to meet him. Not here, huh? "

"Good point." Glissa examined the open field before them. The fighting was taking place only a few yards from the opening to their cave. "Everything is focused on the Tree of Tales," she said back over her shoulder. "If we sneak out and head back into the Tangle, we might be able to avoid them."

"That wrong way, huh?" said the goblin. "Mephidross that way." He pointed out over the battlefield.

Bosh's booming voice filled the cave. "That way gets us killed."

"You took the words right out of my mouth." Glissa took a step forward.

The goblin's tone turned sulky. "Lots of danger in the Tangle, huh?"

"There's lots of danger everywhere." Glissa pointed to the Tree of Tales. The trolls appeared to be in retreat, backing away from the levelers up into the Tree of Tales. Memnarch's army followed. "This isn't the time for argument. The battle will be over soon, and we will lose our chance." She waved her companions forward. "Follow me."

The elf snuck out into the light of day. Crouching, she slipped up next to the huge tree and peered around. She watched as the trolls disappeared from the battlefield. Most of the levelers followed them in, and finally, the silver man who looked like Memnarch entered the Tree.

"Now's our chance," she said, turning around.

"Duck!" screamed the goblin.

Glissa needed no more encouragement. Crouching, she somersaulted away. The crisp ringing sound of a metal blade hitting a metal tree vibrated through the air, and the elf came up on her feet. Before her stood a trio of levelers, one of which had just tried to take her head off of her shoulders.

Glissa brought the Sword of Kaldra around her back and over her head. Grabbing hold with both hands, she brought it down on the offending leveler. The creature's scythe blade came clean off, clattering to the ground.

Behind her, Bosh brought his fist down on another of the creatures, smashing it flat with a musical clang, but the third leveler was nowhere to be found.

"Where'd it go?" asked Glissa. She took a step back, wary of the fact that the artifact creature in front of her was still deadly even without its scythe claw. She scanned the near distance. "There!" She pointed deeper into the Tangle.

Heading away from them, through the trees, was the third leveler—and it had Slobad firmly in its grasp.

Glissa glanced up at the iron golem. Bosh lunged forward, bringing his huge fist down on top of her.

"Bosh—" she shouted, diving away to avoid the wrecking ball aimed at her head.

The golem's fist bashed the crippled leveler to a pulp beside its already flattened friend.

"You should pay more attention," said Bosh.

Glissa got up, dusting herself off. "I'll try to remember that. Now, come on! We've got to stop that leveler before it rips Slobad to pieces."

She took off at a run, jumping over fallen bits of metallic debris. Bosh clomped along behind her, moving slower but covering longer distances with each stride.

"Well," she said, "at least we're headed the right way."

* * * * *

Malil looked down at a beaten and bloody troll. Unlike many others of his kind, this one seemed to have a quicker recognition, a sharper intelligence that showed in his eyes. He had also held a staff, which led Malil to believe that this was indeed their chief.

"I don't like to see you suffer, troll," he said. "If you tell me where the elf girl is, I will leave here, and you and the rest of your tribe can go about your lives."

The troll glared back. "I do not know of whom you speak."

Malil leaned back then swung his leg forward with all of his might. His metal boot clanged against the creature's hide, and the troll doubled over, spitting out a large glob of sopping red and black paste.

Over the course of the past few days, Malil had experienced much—new wisdom and strength, pride and pain. Now he was experiencing something else—anger.

"Tell me, troll," he said picking up the creature's staff. "Do you have a name?"

"I am called Drooge."

"Drooge. That is an interesting name. Does it have any cultural significance?"

The troll chieftain nodded painfully. "It means 'gift giver.' "

"Gift giver?" Twisting the staff in both hands, Malil swung it down on Drooge, hitting him squarely in the temple.

The troll staggered under the blow. He struggled to lift himself off the ground, but his hands slipped in a pool of his own blood, and his chin hit the floor of the Tree of Tales with an undignified slap.

"Well, Drooge," said Malil, bending down to look the troll right in the eye, "I have a gift for you."

Drooge looked suspiciously at the metal man.

"I will give back to you your life, which you have forfeited by harboring the elf girl." Malil rose. "All you have to do is tell me where she is." The metal man gripped the bone staff in both hands. "However, if you are ungracious enough to refuse my gift…" Squeezing with all of his might, he bent the tips together, forcing the withered crutch to snap in half, shattering it, showering the prone troll with the shards.

Drooge cowered, protecting his face with his arm. Sharp bits of the staff embedded themselves in his tough skin, and he bled.

"I do not know who you are," said the troll chieftain, "but I cannot help you." He lowered his head.

Malil turned to one of his levelers, pointing with the sharp fragment of the staff still clutched in his hand. "Bring me three of the trolls," he said then turned back to Drooge. "I'm sorry that you didn't appreciate my gift. Perhaps this one will be more to your liking."

Three trolls were herded into the open room, prodded forward by a trio of levelers.

"You creatures really are remarkable," said Malil. "Your ability to heal is something to be envied. If I were capable of being wounded, I would covet what you have."

The metal man walked over to the prisoners. A series of fresh wounds crisscrossed their bodies. But already, the dried blood and puckered skin was beginning to heal. They would still have scars from this battle, but they quickly shrugged off wounds that would kill a human or an elf.

"Even though you can heal so very quickly," he said, lifting the remaining bits of Drooge's crutch into the air over the first of the three prisoners, "you can still be killed." He drove the shattered bit of bone into the back of the troll's neck.

The creature's eyes opened wide, and it let out a gurgle. Blood poured around the sides of its neck and down its chest. It grasped at its head, trying to pull out the broken staff, but Malil held firm, forcing it in deeper with another shove.

The troll looked up at Malil. A light of understanding crossed its face, then it closed its eyes and fell lifeless to the floor.

The metal man released his grip on the bone as the dying creature fell. "If you don't want to bargain for your life," he said to the troll chieftain, "perhaps you will bargain for theirs."

Drooge lifted one hand from the floor, showing Malil his exposed palm. "Enough," he said. "I will tell you what you want to know."

* * * * *

Pontifex stepped from the blue lacuna into the blinding rays of the mana core. It was an inspiring sight—this tremendous sphere of power. He thought back to the first time he'd seen it, how awed and terrified he had been. The thought made the vedalken lord laugh. That day had changed his life. He had conquered that fear, used it to his advantage—now he sat at the head of the Synod and had the ear of Memnarch himself. The crushing terror that held other, weaker creatures back had transformed him.

He smiled.

He controlled an empire and had the ear of a god. He should be happy with his accomplishments.

His smile faded.

He was not.

Though he had worked hard to climb so high, he had to work even harder to keep what he had. The vedalken lord shook his head. Wasn't life supposed to get easier? Wasn't he supposed to reap the benefits of his labors as he grew older instead of defending himself against constant assault and ambush?

Pontifex glided over the mosslike ground, weaving in and out of the mycosynth monoliths as he headed toward Panopticon. He admired the strangely shaped towers that rose from the ground toward the mana core. They seemed to reach for the light and power above, as if they were humanoid creatures, lifting themselves up on their tiptoes. The image was oddly beautiful.

The journey through this forest would have taken him an eternity on foot. Travel on the interior of Mirrodin was arduous work, made harder by the mossy ground covering that stuck to ones feet and the dense growth of chrome mycosynth spires. Covering the same distance here took twice as long as it did on the surface.

Pontifex's trip was made easier, and swifter, by the aid of a new device. The vedalken lord now stood on a diamond-shaped disk. It hovered above the ground on a "cushion" that allowed the device to float and glide, touching nothing but air.

The most ingenious part of the artifact was the control built into the handlebars that Pontifex now gripped in two of his hands. By applying subtle pressure, the rider could increase his forward speed. The rider really only had to squeeze and lean in the direction he wanted to go.

This left Pontifex free to contemplate the recent turn of events and how he would deal with them.

The situation with Orland would be touchy. It was still too early to tell if he could be brought into the fold and turned into an ally. For now, it was better to not trust him. Having him along on the hunt for the elf girl would also prove tricky, but it did provide Pontifex with the ability to work on him—to discover his weaknesses and assets.

Better to have your enemies close, he thought. Easier to kill them.

The other part of this conundrum was Memnarch's servant, Malil. The metal man could destroy everything the vedalken lord was working for. If Malil managed to catch this elf, Pontifex would be without a bargaining tool. This upstart could conceivably drive a wedge between the vedalken lord and Memnarch. Indeed, he'd already managed to step in between on two occasions.

Pontifex knew that the metal man was on the surface, chasing the elf. This might be the vedalken lord's last chance to get Memnarch's full attention without Malil interfering. He could reestablish his connection with his god and perhaps deal a blow to Malil at the same time.

The Guardian's observatory loomed up before Pontifex, and he eased off on his grip, bringing the hoverer coasting to a stop at the base of Panopticon. The gleaming fortress was a sight. Its polished chrome surface reflected the blue-white light of the mana core. The sharp corners where the walls came together intensified that light, bursting forth with a million tiny stars that were so bright they were painful to look at.

To Pontifex, the most impressive things about the tower's exterior were its perfect lines and unwavering straightness. Panopticon rose into the air nearly to the same height as the mana core, yet its walls were unmarked by blemishes, bends, dents or even seams. The whole fortress was perfectly straight, with no signs of wear, no indication that its gargantuan frame was made from anything but a single, contiguous piece of metal. Its structural perfection was astounding.

Pontifex pulled himself away from the sight and stepped through the portal.

Inside, the tower seemed eerily quiet. The regular humming of levelers and other beasts was noticeably absent, and the silence unnerved Pontifex. As he stepped onto the lift, he was grateful for its whirring and buzzing.

The vedalken lord traversed the observation room, wound up the spiral walk, and reached for the blood-red crystal in the pedestal. Before he touched it, the door opened. Pontifex took a deep breath, straightened, and entered the chamber.

"What can we do for you, Pontifex," said Memnarch.

"My lord," he replied, dropping to the floor to bow.

"Please, spare us the irritation of listening to you mumble into the floor. Get up off your knees."

Pontifex looked up at Memnarch. The Guardian was standing before him, gazing down intently with all six of his enhanced eyes, each now covered in a dark blue lens. Pontifex nodded and stood up.

"Thank you."

"Now what brings the vedalken lord to see Memnarch?"

Pontifex had rehearsed a speech, but standing here, before the Guardian of Mirrodin, his words failed him. Somewhere his relationship with Memnarch had gone awry. He couldn't pinpoint the moment in time when Malil had interceded, taking away from Pontifex the attention of his god. Nonetheless it had happened, and though he ruled the vedalken empire and was the father figure to an entire race of people, right now, before this divine being whom he loved with all of his heart, Pontifex felt like a child.

"I . . . I . . ." stuttered the vedalken. He looked up into Memnarch's eyes. "I have come to ask for your blessing."

"You want Memnarch's blessing? For what?"

"To seek the elf girl."

Memnarch shook his head. "We do not understand. Have we not already charged you with finding her and bringing her to Memnarch?"

"Yes, my lord, you have."

"What is the problem?"

Pontifex closed his eyes, unable to look the Guardian in the face. "You have sent your servant Malil to find her."

"Yes, Memnarch has sent Malil to capture the elf girl," affirmed the Guardian.

Pontifex, his eyes still closed, took a deep breath. The fear he had so many times before conquered now gripped his chest, threatening to hold him back, keep him from saying what he needed to. Finally, he spoke.

"Does Memnarch not believe I can catch the elf?"

Memnarch placed a hand on the vedalken's shoulder, and Pontifex opened his eyes.

"We understand."

The vedalken lord smiled. Only after hearing these words did he realize how tense he was. His shoulders were near his ears. His heart was racing, and his four armpits were damp with sweat.

"Memnarch needs the elf girl before the green lacuna," continued the Guardian. "You and Malil must look for her at the same time."

Pontifex nodded.

"It is a simple matter of mathematics," explained Memnarch.

"But—"

The Guardian cut him off. "There is no room for pride here, Pontifex. We must have the elf girl."

"Why is she so important?"

Memnarch turned and pointed out the window. "Can you see the disease growing within Mirrodin?"

"Disease?"

"We can. We see the degradation of perfection." The Guardian sidled over to the window. "Come."

Pontifex followed.

"Can you see the mycosynth?"

"Of course."

"Do you know what causes these blemishes?"

Pontifex thought for a moment. "Why do you call them that?"

"Because that is what they are. They were not here when Mirrodin was created."

"No?"

"No, indeed. At first we thought they were no more than a little tarnish, nothing that a good polishing could not fix, but they have grown to what you see now. Towering monoliths of disease. They are a symptom of Mirrodin's sickness."

Pontifex had always thought of the mycosynth as something much like the trees in the Tangle or the razor grasses of the plains. They were simply part of the plan. But if they weren't . . . The vedalken lord followed back the path he had taken from the blue Lacuna to Panopticon. It was littered with mycosynth.

A chill ran up his spine.

"So the mycosynth are killing Mirrodin?"

"Yes. Yes."

"What does this have to do with the elf girl?"

"She has something we need. Something inside her," explained Memnarch. "We must have it."

"What does the elf girl have, my lord?"

"A piece of divinity," said Memnarch, not looking away from the window. "A gateway to another plane of existence. Memnarch wishes to cross over, to acquire this gateway."

"You wish to procreate with her, my lord?"

"No, Pontifex," scolded the Guardian. "We wish to make her part of our being. To use her to become more."

The vedalken's jaw dropped. "Please, my lord, I beg you. Take me."

"What?" Memnarch turned to glare at Pontifex.

Pontifex dropped to his knees. "Please. You must. I will do anything. I will sacrifice myself and all of the vedalken on

Mirrodin if that is what it takes." He grasped at his god's crab-like legs. "I am ready. My Guardian. Use me. Make me part of your being."

Memnarch stepped back, and Pontifex fell forward, landing on his belly without the Guardian's limb for support.

The Guardian looked down with a disgusted look on his face. "For all that you vedalkens cherish knowledge," he said, "you have such a limited understanding of how things work."

Pontifex let his forehead rest on the ground. His world was crumbling. First the Synod and now his god had lost faith in him.

CHAPTER 8

Glissa was surprised by the speed at which the leveler made it through the trees. The heavy underbrush was making it difficult for her to run. She very nearly fell flat on her face a number of times. It seemed ages since she'd been on a hunting party.

Even with her rusty recollection of how to move through the Tangle, she kept up a good pace. How then could this leveler outpace her?

Deeper and deeper into the mass of metal trees they flew. As the canopy grew thicker, Glissa had been forced to let Bosh fall behind. He could take care of himself. Slobad was a different matter.

For the past several minutes, Glissa had been steadily losing ground, relying on long clearings to give her a glimpse of where the metallic beast was heading. Here, though, near the deep center of the forest, such clearings were few and far between. The elf wondered if she'd lost the trail.

Leaping over a stump and ducking around a tangled bramble of razor vines, Glissa stopped to listen. Closing her eyes, she slowly isolated all the sounds around her, tuning them out one by one as she had done while hunting with the other elves. The sounds of wind and rustling foliage went first. Then the scampering of vermin and small game. With an uncanny accuracy, Glissa pinpointed two larger creatures within just a few yards from where she was standing. From what she could tell, one was a vorac, walking on three legs with a limp. The other—

Glissa's eyes popped open. "A wolf."

Gripping the hilt of her sword, she slowly turned to stare into a pair of brilliant yellow eyes, slit down the center by brown, almond-shaped pupils. The creature took two casual steps toward her, coming up within an arm length.

Glissa looked up at the beast. The bottom of its jaw started where the top of her head left off. Its shoulders, neck, and legs were covered in dappled brown and gray fur. Its face and shins were much like her own, covered in tarnished metal that ended in spikes, several of them broken or worn completely to a nub. Patches of pink skin showed through bare spots and along what Glissa assumed were the remnants of old, healed wounds. Four very large, very sharp tusks jutted from the creature's mouth, each tipped in silvery metal.

"Looking for something?" asked the wolf.

Glissa was amazed. "Who are you? What do you want? You talk?"

The wolf began to circle the elf, still keeping an eye on her as it moved. "Yes," it said. "So do you."

"I'm an elf," replied Glissa. "You're a . . . a—"

"A wolf." The creature completed her sentence.

"My father used to tell me tales about wolves, but I've never seen one. At least, not until now." She followed the creature around as it circled, keeping her shoulders squared to the beast. "Are you real?"

The wolf chuckled. "Yes. Very much so."

"I thought wolves were just made-up creatures. Things parents told their children about to keep them good."

"Well," observed the creature calmly, "either you're having some sort of hallucination, or I'm really here."

"Did Memnarch send you?"

"Who?" The wolf continued to pace.

"Or the vedalken?" Glissa gripped her sword, ready for a fight. "Did Pontifex order you to kill me?"

"No one orders me to do anything."

Glissa narrowed her eyes. "I don't have time for this. If you're going to try to kill me, get on with it."

The wolf cocked its head. "I haven't decided yet if you deserve to die or not."

Glissa drew her blade from its sheath. "That doesn't help me."

"I don't suspect it would." The wolf stopped its pacing. "Why are you here?"

Glissa's fear and awe of the mythical creature standing before her gave way to another kind of terror. "Slobad! I'm trying to find my friend. A goblin who was abducted by a leveler."

"A leveler? You couldn't catch a leveler this deep in the Tangle?"

Glissa scowled. "Listen, I don't have time to discuss with you the finer points of forest tracking." She held out her sword. "If you've seen him, now's your chance to tell me."

The wolf stepped back in surprise. "Are you threatening me?"

"Only if you're threatening me."

The wolf tilted its chin, looking across its long nose at Glissa. "Perhaps we got off on the wrong foot. My name is Al-Hayat." The wolf made a shallow bow with its front legs.

Glissa stared. "Al-Hayat. That was the name my father used to give to the leader of the wolves. You *can't* be . . ." She shook herself. "My name is—"

"Glissa. Yes, I am aware of who you are."

"Look, Al-Hayat, if that's really your name, if you know where my friend is, then please tell me. If I don't get to him soon, he'll likely be dead."

The wolf nodded. "You know not how true are your words." Al-Hayat pointed toward a mound of tangled brambles around a fallen tree. "The goblin has been buried. He is under that stump."

* * * * *

Memnarch unhooked himself once again from his infusion device. Serum flowed freely through his body, and he was at peace again. This was the third time he'd taken the serum on this day.

The Guardian crossed to where his scrying pool had been. The events in the recent past had spurred him to improve upon his viewing techniques. One pool would not be enough to keep track of the comings and goings of all the players.

So far, everything was on track, but he needed to collect more data, so he had recently installed this new device—the Eye.

Constructed from a magical alloy called Darksteel, the Eye was nearly indestructible. The device was the most technologically advanced and magically sensitive creation Memnarch had ever produced. Because of the impervious nature of Darksteel, it had to be created and forged in the very same moment. Once the metal solidified and the magical spell that fused the molecules together subsided, Darksteel was harder than anything in existence. It couldn't be cut, carved, etched, melted, or even scratched. Consequently, Memnarch had found only limited uses for it, though weapons and armor for his servants could be forged from it.

The Eye was the most complex item Memnarch had ever created from Darksteel. It had taken him several long moon cycles just put together the frame.

In appearance, the Eye was very much like his scrying pool, but it provided six times the viewing pleasure. What was the sense of having six enhanced eyes if he couldn't use them all at the same time?

On the outside, the Eye looked like two three-sided pyramids fused together to form a dark, towering, elongated diamond. One side lay open, providing Memnarch access. But once inside, the door closed, and each of the six surfaces lit up with a magical spell, allowing Memnarch to see into even the remote corners of Mirrodin—all at once.

In the center of the Eye, a console rose from the floor which allowed Memnarch to adjust what he saw. Each of the mirrors was tuned to the eyes of a particular creature on the surface, or sometimes in the interior, of Mirrodin. By attuning his mind to the Eye, Memnarch could see different parts of the plane, viewing things through different servants' eyes. Though he had six mirrors, he had many more eyes with which to see.

One of those mirrors was connected permanently to Malil. What the metal man experienced, so too did his creator. Memnarch looked into that mirror now.

"He has become more cunning," said the Guardian. "More violent too. Memnarch thinks he must be fighting the serum. A natural reaction. You remember when we first tried the serum. Yes, yes you do. Memnarch never fought the new power. Memnarch surrendered." The Guardian scanned his attention across the other mirrors. "He will learn to embrace the gift, or it will destroy him. We shall see."

Four of the remaining five mirrors showed him images of the razor grass planes, the swamps of Mephidross, the mountains in the

Oxidda Chain, and the Tangle. The pictures darted and moved, projected back to Panopticon through the eyes of the myr, humanoid creatures with birdlike heads and well-articulated limbs. Some of them were made of precious metals—gold, silver, and platinum. Others were made from iron, lead, or even nickel, but all of them were developed by Memnarch solely for the purpose of providing him with the tools to observe his grand experiment. They were programmed to watch, and they did their jobs well.

The last mirror showed the placid Quicksilver Sea rolling gently around the mushroom-shaped fortress of the vedalken—Lumengrid. Memnarch passed over this image. In time, the fortress would play an important role in his plan. For now, though, his attention was focused on the Tangle.

* * * * *

"What!" Glissa ran in a circle around the fallen tree, trying to look for any indication of fresh digging. "How could he be buried under that stump?"

Al-Hayat explained. "He wasn't abducted by a leveler, as you thought. He was carried off by a beetle who plans to use his soft flesh to feed its offspring."

Glissa's heart leaped. That's why she'd lost sight of him. He was underground, but how long could he survive down there?

Sure enough, as she came around the back side of the brambles, she saw a large pile of freshly disturbed ground. Metal shavings and big chunks of heavy minerals had been discretely piled up behind the stump.

The elf dropped to her knees, but razor sharp vines hung over the pile, making it impossible for her to reach it without cutting herself to ribbons. Standing back up, she lifted her sword and hacked down on the vines.

Sharpened brambles parted before her blade, but when she pulled back for another swing, they popped back into shape. Her blade could hold them down or cut off little shreds, but it would never be able to clear them all away. Her weapon was useless.

A heavy pounding shook the ground. From around a tall tree stepped the iron golem, Bosh.

A glimmer of hope entered the elf. "Help, Bosh, quick," shouted Glissa. "Slobad's trapped under this stump."

Without a word the golem took hold of the entire pile of debris, lifting free not only the fallen tree but the brambles as well.

Glissa dropped once again to the ground and began digging away the piled-up earth. The metal shavings cut the fleshy parts of her hands, but she frantically pawed at the ground. Though she pushed and pulled with every ounce of strength she had, the pile remained nearly the same size. She wasn't even making a dent.

"Bosh, help," she shouted. "He's going to die if he doesn't get some air."

A large furry paw came from nowhere, knocking Glissa to one side.

"What the—" The elf looked up at Al-Hayat.

"Leave this to me," he said, and the wolf began to dig.

Glissa got to her feet and dusted herself off. The wolf dug swiftly into the mound of loose earth, tossing it away many times faster than the elf ever could have hoped to. Al-Hayat stuck his great snout into the hole and pulled it back out— Slobad's limp body dangling between his front teeth. The goblin was covered in scrapes and bruises.

Once again, Glissa's heart dropped. "Is he—?"

The wolf lowered the goblin to the ground, and Glissa rushed to his side. Placing her hand along his neck, she felt for a pulse.

"He is still breathing," said the wolf.

Glissa nodded. "He's alive, but just barely." She turned to Al-Hayat. "Can you help him?"

"Me? What makes you think a wolf can cure a dying goblin?"

Glissa turned her attention to Slobad's unconscious body. "Until only a minute ago, I thought wolves were just stories." She shrugged. "If you're a make-believe creature, who says you can't heal a goblin?" She shook her head. "Now I really do sound like a crazy elf."

The wolf gave a throaty chuckle.

"You're right."

Stepping over both the kneeling elf and the prone goblin, Al-Hayat pushed his muzzle into Slobad's belly. The great beast growled, a deep, resonant sound that shook the ground and the goblin.

Tiny motes of light coalesced around the wolf's face, growing in size and number as they circled. The twisting mass of magical energy formed a brightly lit ring that circled Al-Hayat's head. The wolf went silent, and the ring dropped from the air as if it were suddenly pulled to earth by gravity. The light seeped into the goblin's skin, and the forest creature stepped away from his patient.

"I have done all I can do," he said.

Slobad's body jerked, followed by a tremendous hacking cough. Metal shavings and small chunks of mineral sprayed from the goblin's mouth, and he sat up.

"Where Slobad, huh?"

Glissa gathered him up in a huge embrace. "You're in the Tangle, running from a band of levelers who just attacked the Tree of Tales."

Slobad nodded. "Whew," he said, "Good. Goblin dozed off, huh? Dreamed Slobad eaten by giant bug."

CHAPTER 9

Glissa held Bosh's hand in both of her own. It was so big, she could hardly get all five of her fingers around one of his. Carefully, the elf pulled shards of razor vine from the fleshy parts of the golem's palm.

"It hurts," said the golem.

"I'm sorry," replied Glissa. "If I had realized that the fleshy parts had spread so far, I wouldn't have been so quick to ask you to move that stump."

"If you hadn't, Slobad would have died."

Glissa smiled. "You're right. You did a brave thing, Bosh, especially knowing that you'd get hurt." She pulled another large chunk of razor vine from his palm. The wound was deep, and Bosh's hand filled with blood.

"What is that?"

"Blood," said Glissa.

"What does it do?"

"It keeps people alive."

Bosh looked at it intently, tipping his hand from side to side and letting it swish around. "Does it keep me alive?"

Glissa thought about it. She didn't know. In elves, blood coursed through their veins, feeding their body and keeping their insides clean. In a metal golem, there were no veins, no need to feed anything.

Finally she said, "I'm not sure Bosh, but until we find out, it's best that you keep as much of that—" she pointed to the pool of blood in his hand— "inside of you as possible." She pulled the last bit of metal from his flesh. "Let's wrap it in a vine for now, see if we can't get it to stop."

Glissa went to a nearby tree and pulled down several rope-like vines with wide leaves attached to them. As she turned, she caught a glimpse of Al-Hayat and Slobad. The wolf had curled up on the ground, and the goblin had climbed onto the forest creature's fur. Both seemed to be sleeping peacefully.

After tying a quick bandage around Bosh's hand with the vine, Glissa walked over to the napping pair.

She watched them. This wolf, a creature she had thought all of her life to be something of fantasy, had appeared and saved the day. Had that taken place only a few months before, she might have been surprised. Now nothing seemed impossible.

Al-Hayat's ears twitched, and the great four-legged beast lifted its head.

"You're awake," said Glissa.

"I never really sleep," replied the wolf. "It's not a luxury I can afford."

The elf knelt down in front of Al-Hayat's muzzle. "Can I ask you a question?"

"You just did."

The elf smiled. "No, I mean, I grew up in the Tangle, hunting and ranging all around in the forest. How come I never ran into one of your kind?"

"We have become very good at hiding," he said, with a sigh. "As well, I am one of only a very few."

"Why aren't there more?"

"There were," replied the wolf. "The pack has dwindled with

every moon cycle since I was but a pup. Many have been killed by hunters or levelers. Now the remaining few are scattered around the forest, for our own protection. It's harder to kill us all if we don't stay bunched up." The wolf looked down at the sleeping goblin then back at Glissa. "Unlike most other beasts in the forest, wolves stay with their mates for life, so there are fewer and fewer young ones each year."

"Where's your mate?"

The wolf let out a low growl. "She was taken from me last moon cycle." The words were obviously painful for Al-Hayat.

"I'm sorry," replied Glissa. Her curiosity was piqued, but she didn't want to push the subject any further. "May I ask you another question?"

"Ask as many as you like."

"Why, if you distrust others so much, did you show yourself to me?"

"What makes you think I distrust others?"

"You hide from the elves so well they think you're nothing more than a legend. If I were only one of a few, I wouldn't trust anyone either. Better to keep my distance and stay alive."

"A wise choice."

"Then why did you help us?"

"Because the fate of the wolves doesn't have to be the fate of all."

Glissa was confused. "You sound as if you've given up on your own kind."

"Not given up," replied the wolf. "I merely accept a likely eventuality. I understand that one day there may be no more wolves on Mirrodin."

Glissa tried to put herself in the wolf's place, She shuddered at the thought of all the elves being extinct. What if she were the only one left?

"That's a horrible thing to live with."

Al-Hayat smiled. "No one said it was easy being a wolf. But you're right, and that is why I came to you. I tire of hiding, of waiting for the inevitable end. Better to do something, even if I fail, than simply sit still. That's no way to live—alive but without hope or options." The great beast let his head fall back to the ground, blowing out air through his nostrils and sending up a plume of dust. "I no longer wish to be afraid."

"So I just happened through your part of the Tangle in the moment when you decided to end your hiding?" Glissa scratched her head. "Maybe my luck is changing."

"I wouldn't be so sure of that," said the wolf.

A chill ran down Glissa's spine, and she drew her sword, spinning around to scan the area.

Al-Hayat laughed so hard he tossed Slobad into the air. The sleeping goblin awoke mid-flight, landing in the soft fur only to be tossed back up again.

"Hey," screamed the groggy goblin, "stop that."

Glissa scowled. "What?"

"I'm sorry," replied the wolf, "I didn't mean to alarm you."

Glissa looked around cautiously, glancing up at Bosh.

The iron golem shook his head. "I see nothing."

Certain that there were no levelers or unfriendly beasts around, the elf turned back to the wolf. "So what then?"

"I merely meant that you shouldn't take my appearance as luck," said Al-Hayat, still chuckling. "I have been stalking you since you arrived in the Tangle."

Glissa sat down hard on the ground. "Why is it that everyone knows where I am and what I'm doing?" The elf picked up a pile of metal shavings and tossed them at a tree. "*I* don't even know what I'm doing. I wish someone would tell me where he gets his information. At least then I'd know if I'm on the right track."

Slobad climbed off of Al-Hayat and sat down beside her. "Slobad think you on right track, huh?" he said.

Glissa looked own at the bruised goblin. "Thank you."

"No problem."

Al-Hayat stood up and lowered his face to Glissa's. "I too think you are on the right path. That is why I am here. That's why I joined you."

Glissa shook her head. "How did I get here? One day everything was fine. I had parents, lived in a village with other elves, had friends." She threw another pile of metal shavings. "Now I'm on the run, following some destiny that I'm not even fully aware of, looking for the creature responsible for my family's death, talking to a creature who those same parents had told me was nothing more than the creation of an overactive imagination."

"And you have friends," boomed Bosh.

"Yes," added the goblin.

Glissa looked up at the wolf. "You too?"

Al-Hayat smiled. "I'd be honored to be your friend."

* * * * *

Malil sat atop his leveler. The wind whipped around his head. Arrayed before him, traversing the plains of Mirrodin, was the remainder of his leveler squad.

They were headed to Mephidross.

What a dark, dank place that was. Malil didn't know when he started feeling this way about the swamp. He didn't remember having any opinion of the place at all when he'd been introduced to it.

Things had changed.

Not in Mephidross but inside Malil. Things were different

now. He couldn't say for certain exactly how, but they were. It wasn't so much that there were specific obstacles he faced, things that made his life more difficult. No, it seemed to him that everything looked the same, felt the same, but now the edges were blurred.

Before, he had known exactly where his loyalties lay. He had been created by Memnarch. He owed his life and his allegiance to his creator, and simply serving the Guardian had been enough. Now, though, Malil felt . . . well, he wasn't sure exactly how he felt, but he knew it was different.

Things seemed clearer than before. He understood how the world and the systems within it functioned as a unity. But with this new knowledge came more confusion. He didn't understand his own place within Mirrodin. Would he forever remain the servant to Memnarch? Was that the entire purpose of his life? Or was there . . . something more.

For all his new-found clarity, Malil felt more confused. Maybe with more serum, he'd be able to figure all this out. The dose he'd taken had only scratched the surface—cleared away enough of the debris to capture his interest. But now the glimpse of the bigger picture he'd been given was driving him mad. He needed more.

That was the problem.

The only place he could get more was Panopticon. But if he went back to the interior, he'd have to report to Memnarch. To do that he needed to have the elf girl.

How could he be expected to concentrate on finding the elf girl if he didn't get more serum?

Malil repeated this mantra to himself as he and his levelers approached Mephidross.

* * * * *

The open plains stretched out before Bosh, Slobad, Glissa, and Al-Hayat. To the iron golem, the rolling hills, pieced together from huge sheets of colored metals, had always seemed a hospitable and welcoming place. Everything fit together in an overly organized fashion.

Bosh liked that.

Lines made sense to him. It was the curves and the unpredictable creativity of flesh creatures that he didn't understand. Better that things fit inside a box, made sense, followed strictly designed rules.

Now it no longer worked that way. Once the creator had left—was compelled to leave really—everything went to the nine hells. Now Bosh too was turning to flesh.

Bosh looked out to the East as the group walked. The wind whipping through the tall razor grass made high-pitched whistles that rode off into the distance. In some places, the iron golem recalled, you could hear that sound from miles away. Up close though, when the blades of grass touched each other, you could hear a subtle, tinkling chime. Combined with the whistling, the two sounds together created a noise unlike anything else on Mirrodin—an unintentional music.

The group of friends traveled in the valleys of the sloping hills. This time of year the moons were nearly aligned, so if they weren't in the sky, they were on the other side of the world, leaving parts of Mirrodin black and cold. The alternative wasn't much better. When all the moons were overhead, color began to wash out. The metal plates of the plains reflected back black, white, blue, and red, making everything look brown and ugly.

During a convergence, it was hot as well. All those moons—or suns, as the leonine persisted in calling them—pouring light down onto the open ground made a metal golem uncomfortable, especially those parts of him that had become flesh. Now was one of those times. The exposed fleshy bits on Bosh's arms and torso were turning a bright red, and they tingled.

"Is flesh always so bothersome?" he asked, scratching a patch of skin.

"You get used to it, huh?" replied the goblin, who was riding on his shoulder.

"Does it get easier?"

"Oh yeah."

"That's good to know."

Glissa, riding on the back of Al-Hayat, pushed a finger into the reddened flesh near Bosh's collar. "We should cover you up. You're getting moonburn."

"Moonburn? What is that?"

"It's when you stay out under the moons too long, and your skin gets too much moonlight."

"Too much moonlight?"

"Skin isn't like metal," explained Glissa.

"I am finding that out." Bosh held up his bandaged hands.

"Yeah, well, razor vines aren't the only thing that can damage flesh. Moonlight can too."

"How?" asked the golem.

"Yes, how?" The wolf sounded curious as well.

Glissa looked up at Slobad.

"Don't look here, crazy elf. You said it, huh?"

"Well," the elf grabbed her chin, thinking hard. "You know how when the moons are in convergence, the plates of the plains get hot?"

Bosh nodded. "Yes, my frame can get hot too."

The elf lifted her finger in the air. "Right. Why is that?"

Bosh shrugged, nearly tossing Slobad from his shoulders. "I do not know."

Glissa frowned. "Well, I don't know either, but it happens, right?"

Everyone nodded.

"Well, skin gets hot too, only when it gets hot, it—"

"Expands," interjected Bosh. "I understand. It is just like metal."

"Not exactly," said the elf.

Bosh looked out over a barren patch of plain, where there was no razor grass. The hexagonal plates that formed the ground were bowing up, like bubbles in a swamp. The iron golem pointed to them.

"See," he said, "just like that."

Everyone looked.

"What's happening there?" asked Al-Hayat.

"You not know?" asked Slobad. "Slobad think magical beasts know everything, huh? "

The wolf looked up at the goblin. Glissa thought she detected a sneer on his lips. "I've never been out of the Tangle. I've never seen anything like that before."

"Oh," grunted the goblin. "You just like crazy elf when Slobad find her, huh? Don't worry." He hitched his thumb toward his chest. "Goblin teach you everything, huh?"

"It is caused by the convergence," explained Bosh, ignoring Slobad. "The metal plates expand when they are hot. Since they are joined so tightly, they have no room to move. They bend." He nodded to the section of plain he had pointed to earlier. "Like that."

"Oh," said the wolf.

"Yes, but that's not what happens to skin." Glissa seemed frustrated.

"It gets hot," said Bosh.

"Yes, and when it gets hot, it burns, like fire roasts meat."

Bosh nodded slowly. "So the moonlight cooks flesh."

Glissa shrugged. "Well, yes."

"I do not want to be cooked," said the golem.

"Golem not taste good anyway, huh?" chirped Slobad.

Al-Hayat let out a low growl. "Maybe not," he said, lifting his muzzle toward the sky, "but someone is willing to test your theory, goblin."

Bosh followed Al-Hayat's nose to a patch of dark blotches in the sky. "What is that?"

Glissa strained her eyes against the glare of the moons.

"It looks like a pack of large plains birds or a group of small dragons."

"They're artifact wings with vedalken riders," answered the wolf.

"Hey," squealed Slobad, "how you know what vedalken looks like, huh?"

The wolf kept his eyes on the slowly growing forms ahead of them. "I have fought with them before."

"In the Tangle?" asked Glissa.

The wolf nodded. "But out here, we have no trees for cover."

Bosh stopped moving and lifted Slobad from his shoulder. "No," he said, "but they do not have their sea or their fortress." He turned to look at the wolf. "And they do not know about you."

CHAPTER 10

Pontifex flexed his fingers. First in his right hand then his left. Between them, he gripped the handle of his hover guard glider. It was a simple device, not unlike the unmanned aerophins. A lightweight, hollow frame was constructed in the shape of a bird's wings. Between this frame was stretched a fine woven-metal fabric that billowed slightly in the wind. The whole thing was attached to the rider's back with a set of straps and a buckle.

To Pontifex's left rode Marek, to his right, Orland. Behind the three followed four dozen of Marek's finest elite guardsmen.

Pontifex looked to his left. "Do you see them?"

Marek nodded. "The human woman doesn't appear to be with them."

"That doesn't matter now," replied the vedalken lord. "We're after the elf girl."

"The Guardian will be very pleased that we've brought her in," interjected Orland. "The vedalken people will be well rewarded for our service."

Pontifex smiled. "Yes. Yes indeed."

"My lord," said Marek, pointing down at the group of foot travelers. "They have some sort of beast with them."

Pontifex narrowed his eyes. The reflection of the moons' light off the metallic plain made it hard to pick up shapes and impossible to distinguish colors. It did, however, appear as if the elf rode atop some large creature. "If she thinks she can outrun us with her mount, she's mistaken."

Marek nodded. "What should you have us do?"

Pontifex glanced back at his troops then looked back down on the elf girl and her party.

"We split up," he said. "Marek, you take two dozen warriors and swoop around behind them." He hitched his thumb over his shoulder toward Orland. "The councilor and I will keep the rest of the men and hold here. When we see you're in position, we'll swoop down from both sides, surrounding them."

"As you wish," Marek placed his fingers to the front of his mask in a salute to Pontifex. "My lord." He did the same to Orland. "Councilor." Then he was off.

Pontifex looked at the warrior with resentment. When he saw the smile on Orland's face, he changed his mind. Marek was smart. He had learned from Pontifex, and this gesture of recognition to the new councilor would set the man at ease, making him easier to manipulate—or kill—when the time came. A feeling of tremendous pride filled the vedalken lord, and he smiled. Without even a word, his trusted bodyguard had picked up on the plan and played along perfectly.

Lifting the handle on his glider toward the clouds, Pontifex rose higher and made a gentle curving turn.

"Where are we going?" asked Orland, beside his leader.

"Nowhere," replied Pontifex, steering around. "We're circling." He smiled. "Circling our prey."

* * * * *

"What they doing, huh?" asked Slobad.

"Looks like they're splitting up," replied Glissa.

All four intently watched the flying figures as they broke up into two smaller groups. One appeared to be retreating.

Slobad tugged on Glissa's arm. "They leaving. Scared of Slobad and his golem, huh?"

"No," said the wolf, "they're trying to surround us."

Glissa felt panic fill her chest. They were out in the open. The only thing they could possibly use for cover was a large patch of razor grass that looked as if it had been recently mowed down by a gang of hungry threshers. If they ran hard, they could reach a fuller patch of grass, but even if they made it, they'd have to fight both the vedalken and the sharp-edged foliage.

"What do we do?" she asked, more to the heavens than to anyone in particular.

"We run, huh?"

Glissa looked up at the flyers. Already the splinter group was nearly overhead. The other group had completed a full circle and was beginning a second.

"No," she said. "They move too fast. We'll never out run them."

Bosh's voice rumbled in the light breeze. "We might be able to get out from in between them," he said. "That might give us a better chance, if we only have to fight half of them at one time."

"That's a good idea," said the wolf. "Under the glare of the moons, it'll be hard for them to see us. If we stay near the razor grass and stick close together that could buy us some more time."

"Let's go then!" shouted Glissa.

Bosh grabbed Slobad and deposited him once again on his shoulders, then the group was off. Glissa rode Al-Hayat, and Slobad held onto the iron golem's collar for dear life. They skirted the edge of the razor grass field, galloping at full speed.

Bosh's huge metal feet pounded out a drum beat as he ran. Al-Hayat moved silently, with a fluid grace of an organic creature. Glissa squeezed the great forest beast with her knees and clutched handfuls of fur, trying to stay on his back. They narrowly outpaced the metal golem, running beside the small patch of razor grass.

Looking up into the sky, Glissa's heart plunged into her stomach. "They're coming right for us."

The first few strides had moved them past the splinter group of gliders, but the other half had seen them try to run. They dived now to intercept. A deep, hollow whistle followed, louder the closer they came.

"They're going to ram us," she shouted.

Al-Hayat planted his front feet and came to a sudden, abrupt halt. Glissa couldn't squeeze hard enough with her knees, and her rear end lifted off the creature's back. If not for the solid grip she had on his hair, she would have been tossed right over.

Bosh came stomping up right beside.

"Why are we stopping?"

Glissa watched the gliders getting closer. They were almost on top of the foursome. There was nowhere to go. In seconds they would be smashed into the ground or pushed into the razor grass and cut to bits.

"For this," said the wolf. Al-Hayat closed his eyes and muttered something under his breath.

To Glissa it felt as if the wolf were vibrating. She couldn't hear what he said, but she could feel every syllable. Looking into the sky, she could see the gliders, make out their construction, recognize every detail on the warriors' faces. She drew her sword.

"I won't die like this," she shouted, and she lifted her blade into the air.

Al-Hayat stopped his rumbling and opened his eyes. A swirling green ball of energy shot out from the wolf, striking the razor grass field. Like the magic he used to cure the goblin, the spell settled onto the metal foliage in a puddle nearly as large as the creature who cast it, soaking into the ground as if it were water.

The whistling noise the gliders put off grew to a horrific screech, and the vedalken guiding them pulled back, bringing forward charged lances with glowing blue heads. The gliders cast their shadow over the group, blotting out the converging moons. The magical blades swung down on Glissa, Al-Hayat, Bosh and Slobad.

The patch of razor grass touched by the wolf's spell grew up to meet the vedalken's halberds. The sharp blades climbed high over the travelers, reaching farther in the air than the elf's extended blade, overtopping even the iron golem. Glissa felt a warm splash as three of the glider pilots were skewered by the still-growing grass. She ducked her head, shielding herself from anything that might fall from the sky, and hoping that Al-Hayat's magic wouldn't let any of the gliders get through.

Gurgling screams and cries of pain filled the air, as the three front glider pilots were smashed from behind by their comrades, forcing them deeper onto the reaching spikes. The misfortune of the vanguard saved the rest of the flight from certain death, and the remaining pilots pulled up, landing on the plain before the foursome.

The companions wasted no time, engaging the pilots as they unhooked themselves from their artifact wings. Glissa slipped sideways off of Al-Hayat, charging out from under the growing razor grass to slash a vedalken warrior across the gut while his arms were still enmeshed in his backpack.

The wolf followed, snapping up a blue-skinned, four-armed

warrior in his mouth and champing down, making the vedalken look like nothing more than a tasty snack. The warrior's powered lance gleamed brightly, falling from its wielder's hands as he was summarily devoured by the wolf. Its bright blue beam mixed with the colors of Mirrodin's many moons as it reflected off the plain, turning the swirling brown light into something closer to purple.

The sound of metal clashing on metal rose over the plains. Bosh and Slobad came out from under the razor grass. The iron golem pounded a pilot into a pile of broken glider, flesh, and bones, which sizzled on the hot hexagonal plates. The goblin stayed near the golem, taunting the vedalken into attacking, then letting the big metal man do all the work.

For having been backed into a corner, thought Glissa, the opening few moments of this battle were going quite well.

Another heavy shadow passed over the winged warriors, momentarily blocking out the mixed colors of the overhead moons. The temporary shade was accompanied by a deep, hollow whistle.

The second group of gliders had arrived.

* * * * *

Pontifex landed on the plain behind his elite guards. This was preposterous. Three glider pilots killed by a patch of razor grass. Razor grass! Had none of these trained soldiers grown up on Mirrodin? What child didn't know enough not to get caught up in those killing blades?

The vedalken lord shrugged his glider from his shoulders and unhooked his sword from his hip. Unlike most conventional blades, Pontifex's was less like a sword and more like a kris-knife. The sharpened length jutted out from a straight, leather-wrapped hilt, but from there it began to curve. The blade formed an **S**, as if it were a slithering snake, finally ending in a deadly jagged head.

Next to him, Councilor Orland was having trouble unfastening his glider from his shoulders. The clod had obviously never been in battle before, living a soft life inside Lumengrid. Pontifex thought briefly about stabbing the man in the gut, right here on the open plain, while his arms were tangled. But he stayed his own hand. The time would come when he could do that in a much more private setting. Judging from Orland's twisting and wrenching display as he tried to free himself from the glider, it wouldn't be too hard to kill the bumbling politician even if his hands were free.

Marek and his group of gliders would land and join the fight in moments. The two dozen pilots Pontifex had come to ground with were circling the elf girl and her comrades, but their numbers had dwindled. Already six were down, including the three who had been killed by the growing razor grass. The vedalken lord didn't want to have to wade in himself, but if it came to that, he would. Nothing was going to stop him from getting that elf.

Somehow that girl had tarnished his image as a leader of his people. She had stormed through their fortress, committed the sacrilege of swimming in the Pool of Knowledge, and escaped without punishment.

But that wasn't the worst of it.

Somehow that bitch had managed to get between him and his god, had managed to make him insignificant in the eyes of the Guardian. For that she must die.

* * * * *

Glissa fought for her life.

The vedalken carried halberds—long thick blades attached to even longer poles, so that a warrior could reach out and attack an opponent from a distance. The heads of these weapons coursed with power, and two came right for her legs as a pair of warriors leaned in. Her back up against the razor grass field, all she could do was bat them away. Again and again the sharp, glowing blue points came at her, and each time she knocked them away.

Bosh leaned out with his long arms, able to match the vedalken warriors with his reach. Glissa felt the impact as his hand hit the ground, a smashed foe underneath. He swung down with his other fist, punching a guardsmen in the face. The warrior was thrown, loosing his grip on his weapon and falling on his back. Despite the heavy impact, the soldier got to his feet, dazed and shaking his head but still alive.

Bosh lifted his hands back for another strike. Large droplets of blood dripped from between his clenched fingers. Splashing to the hot metal ground, the liquid sent up a short wisp of smoke as it quickly dried. In the strange mixed light Glissa couldn't tell if it was the blue blood of the vedalken warrior or the red blood of the now fleshy golem. The thought of Bosh bleeding to death brought a sudden chill to the elf's spine.

Two more halberds came from nowhere, forcing Glissa to spin to one side. Unlike the other weapons the vedalken had been using, these did not have sharp heads. Instead, they sprouted loops of heavy wire meant to ensnare rather than wound. One of those loops lunged for Glissa, and she narrowly managed to duck under it. The warrior who carried it had a handle near the end of the shaft, and he pulled on it now. The loop tightened just as the elf pulled away.

"What am I?" she shouted. "A wild boar?"

The vedalken answered by lunging in with another thrust of their pointy weapons. These too Glissa pounded away, but this time she managed a counter attack. Not bothering to aim for any one warrior in particular, the elf jabbed the tip of her powerful blade into the throng of blue-skinned guardsmen. The tip momentarily caught on one warrior's robes then tore free, sending her tripping forward.

Losing her balance, the elf lifted up on the tiptoes of her right foot. She could feel her weight dragging her forward. The thought of landing prone before four warriors, all of whom wanted her dead, had absolutely no appeal to the young elf, and she struggled to stay upright. With her left leg held out behind her, she toppled forward.

Skipping once and reaching out, she jabbed her sword point into the nearest warrior, hoping to push herself back and regain her balance. But the head of the sharp weapon punctured the vedalken's armor and slipped through into soft flesh. The creature screamed, turned sideways, and pulled away. The hole in the warrior's armor, now twisted to one side, clamped down on the tip of Glissa's blade, trapping it and dragging the elf farther forward.

Glissa was extended as far as she could go, and she held onto her sword with all of her might. Reaching over, she grabbed the pommel with both hands, letting her toe slide across the hot metallic ground as the vedalken pulled back. Warrior and elf moved as a pair, the tip of Glissa's sword still lodged in the vedalken's chest.

The injured fighter struggled to free himself, flailing all four of his spindly arms. Blood now covered the blue ornamental robes he wore over his armor—looking like a dark brown stain on light brown robes in the mixed light of the converging moons. Then his struggles slowed, and he looked at the elf through his visor.

His eyes were sad, even frightened, and Glissa felt a pang of pity.

The warrior collapsed, dropping to his knees. Glissa was yanked forward, and she watched the ground come up toward her face. This is it, she thought.

Something grabbed hold of her left foot, still lifted high in the air, and she was tugged back. She watched two halberd blades and a heavy wire loop strike the ground. The enchanted weapons cut into the metal plates of the plain, leaving huge gouges beside the dying vedalken—right where she would have been lying facedown.

Coming to ground on both feet, Glissa turned back to see her savior—Slobad. His bony hands were wrapped around her ankle, but he lost his grip and fell backward from the force of his tugging her free of the dying vedalken. She wanted to thank him, but there wasn't time. More warriors pressed in.

* * * * *

Marek came to ground right beside Pontifex. His two dozen glider pilots landed closer to the melee. The elite guard commander shucked his glider wings and crossed to the two vedalken Synod members.

"Councilor," he said to Orland, bowing his head slightly. He turned to Pontifex. "My lord, we were to pin them between the two groups. I fear I have failed you."

Pontifex shook the comment off. "Nonsense. You flushed them right into our hands."

Marek nodded.

Pontifex looked over his bodyguard's shoulder at the fighting. The elf and her companions were still backed up against the razor grass field, but the vedalken warriors had made little progress in capturing Glissa.

Pontifex gripped his sword tightly.

Marek took another shallow bow. "I bid you farewell," he said. "I will capture the elf and bring her to you." The warrior turned on his heels and marched toward the battle.

"Kill her," said Pontifex, his teeth clenched.

Marek stopped in his tracks.

Orland turned to the vedalken lord, a look of utter astonishment on his face. "Kill her? You can't be serious?"

Pontifex grabbed Orland by the collar of his robes, forcing the gangly politician's visor up against his own. "Quite."

Marek stepped closer. "Are we not to return the elf girl to Memnarch?" He paused. "My lord?" he added late.

Pontifex glared into Orland's eyes. Not letting the councilor loose, he spoke to Marek. "Plans have changed," he said. "The Guardian no longer wants her."

Orland shifted his eyes. Pontifex followed his gaze to Marek. "He's not going to help you," he shouted at his captive.

"I am not your enemy, Lord Pontifex," claimed the councilor. "Please, let me go."

Marek stood watching the scene. Pontifex could see him from the corner of his eye. "What are you waiting for, Marek?" he said. "Go kill the elf girl."

Marek nodded. "As you wish, my lord." This time he was more forthwith with the title. "But I would not be doing my duty to you if I did not ask you to reconsider."

Orland squirmed in Pontifex's grip. The vedalken lord, using his superior height, lifted the councilor up off of his footing, forcing the politician to stand on his toes or be strangled by his own robe, now bunching around his neck.

"Thank you, Marek, but no little elf is going to get between me and the Guardian of Mirrodin." He shook Orland. "Neither is an *elected* Synod councilor." He finally took his eyes off of

Orland, loosening his grip on the man's robe and letting him get his feet back under him. "Kill her."

Marek didn't even blink before he turned and sprinted toward the melee. Pontifex watched him as he rallied his men and headed off, following his orders to the letter.

"He's good, Marek is," he said to Orland, who was now trying to sooth his damaged throat. "Very good."

CHAPTER 11

Blood covered the plain. Nearly a dozen vedalken lay dead or dying on the ground—half the number who had swooped from the sky to press Glissa, Slobad, Bosh, and Al-Hayat back against the razor grass field.

Glissa herself had received nasty cuts on her cheeks and one across her breast. They stung and bled, but they weren't painful enough to distract her, so she ignored them. Slobad was the same. He'd taken a thump to the head, but that was about it, as the small goblin did his best to stay away from the sharp ends.

Al-Hayat, on the other hand, was bleeding from the nose and throat. The wolf fought on, grabbing away halberds with his teeth, chewing soldiers to bits, bowling warriors over where he had the chance. He stood at the front of the foursome, growling and pushing his fur out to make himself look even bigger than he already did.

Lunging forward and snapping his teeth closed, the great forest creature reached out and caught another one between his wicked fangs. The vedalken gurgled out a cry, and the wolf began shaking the blue-skinned creature from side to side. Blood sloshed in a fan-shaped wave out across the other warriors, and the guardsman let out a scream more desperate and frightened than any Glissa had ever heard.

Al-Hayat stopped shaking, and the vedalken hung limply from his teeth, unmoving, no longer screaming.

Then the next wave of glider pilots arrived. Glissa had seen them land, had felt their shadow cross over the battle, bringing with it a deep pit that sank to the bottom of her stomach. But now they were here, pressing into the fight from the back of the vedalken line.

The four-armed warriors were pushed forward, right into Al-Hayat. The wolf bit the head off of one warrior, but the crush of blue-skinned bodies was just too great, and the forest beast had to retreat.

The warriors continued on, running into Glissa next. Despite her quick blade, she wasn't as fast as Al-Hayat, and she too had to take steps back. Her heel came up against the sharp stalks at the base of the razor grass, and without looking behind her, she knew she'd run out of room. There, at the foot of the iron golem, standing beside the bloodied wolf and the bruised goblin, she made her final stand.

"Any ideas?" she shouted above the sound of metal on metal.

"I could stomp through the razor grass," said Bosh.

Glissa glanced up. The golem was covered in blood, which blended into the color of his partially rusted hide in the strange light.

"No," she said, "we'd get killed faster that way. How about you?" she asked Al-Hayat. "Got any magic that can get us out of this?"

The wolf snarled. "Not in this particular predicament—"

The great forest beast's words were cut short when one of the vedalken warriors managed to wrap the looped wire from his containment halberd around the wolf's neck. Al-Hayat struggled, lifting the warrior on the other end off of his feet. The wolf nearly got loose, but three more vedalken came to their comrade's aid, and the lasso tightened. With great difficulty, the four warriors pulled the wolf to his knees, his snout to the ground.

Glissa took a step forward, hoping to free her friend. A loud pop echoed off of the razor grass, and she had to dodge out of the way as a metallic web unfolded over her head. Someone from the back of the vedalken line had fired a net, shaped like a spider's web. The ends were weighted, and when it unfurled, it formed a glistening metallic dome that settled over Bosh, Slobad, and Glissa.

Her back against razor grass, the only place to go was toward the vedalken. Glissa stepped out from under the net, barely missing being entangled, but Bosh and Slobad were not so lucky, and the iron golem was trapped, the goblin between his feet.

With a desperate hack, Glissa swung at the still crowding warriors. They were packed so close together it was difficult for them to move, and the elf's blade slashed right through two clear visors, releasing a flood of serum onto the hot ground.

The move had bought her a few precious seconds, and she cashed them in now. Turning around, she brought her Sword of Kaldra down on the webbing holding the golem. The blade slipped swiftly through the woven metallic fibers, cutting a gash in the net the height of an elf.

Slobad saw the webbing separate, and he made a dash for the opening.

"Hurry," shouted Glissa, then she turned.

A thick wire dropped down over her shoulders, and Glissa felt her arms get pinned to her sides. The force of the lasso closing around her knocked the wind from her lungs. She let out a scream and dropped her sword.

Another lasso closed around her neck, and Glissa was pulled

forward onto her belly, face down on the hot plain. Twisting to her side, she looked up at her friends.

Al-Hayat was pinned to the ground by a gang of vedalken warriors. Bosh struggled with the net, but it too was controlled by the glider pilots, and despite his great strength and obvious size advantage, the iron golem had nowhere to move. Worse, Glissa could see that the vedalken had pulled the net so tightly around Bosh, it was digging into his fleshy shoulders, cutting large gashes and causing him to bleed.

Slobad had managed to make it out the hole Glissa had put in the net, but he'd been caught and was held face down on the ground by two warriors—the pointy ends of their halberds firmly against his back.

"What do you want from me?" Glissa shouted. Held to the ground as she was, she couldn't see her captors.

No one replied.

* * * * *

Marek watched his troops capture the elf girl. In the face of heavy losses, they had done a fine job showing restraint. It would have been much easier to kill them all. Before the mission had begun they had been given strict orders to keep her alive. Only Marek knew of Pontifex's change of plan. It would be up to him to carry out the new orders.

As he pushed his way through his troops to where the captives were being held, Marek ran through his options. If he did what he'd been told, gave the order and executed the elf girl, he'd be acting in direct opposition to the wishes of the Guardian. True, he'd never met the being Pontifex referred to as his god. But he had seen Panopticon, and he felt certain there was someone powerful inside. He had seen enough evidence, and he didn't doubt the consequences of crossing such a creature. To make matters worse, Marek had a healthy suspicion that the Guardian could see almost everything that took place on Mirrodin. And though Pontifex had given the order to terminate the elf girl's life, it would be Marek who would do the dirty work—something the captain of the elite guardsmen felt certain would not go unnoticed.

On the other hand, Pontifex would certainly punish him for disobeying his orders. His life would be forfeit, and the best he could hope for would be to desert and try to find another place to live. This thought almost made the warrior laugh. Who would have him? The human wizards? Not likely. He'd been responsible for enslaving and oppressing too many of them. He doubted they would greet him with open arm. No, that way too led to death.

He stood now over the prone elf girl. Marek had seen her before, but never up so close. She seemed so frail now, held helplessly to the ground. He leaned down and looked her in the eye. Despite her disadvantage, she looked defiantly back at him, a fire in her eyes. Her determination and conviction in the face of certain death unnerved the warrior. How strange, he thought, that even at the end, pinned to the ground and held by two lasso halberds, she could muster enough courage to frighten him. Would he go the same way?

"Who are you?" asked the elf.

Marek unhooked a one-handed axe that had been strapped tightly to his thigh. Its sharpened head reflected a riot of colors. "Who I am is unimportant," he said. "All you need to know is that I'm here to kill you."

"Rather unsporting of you," the elf spat. "Killing an unarmed elf held to the ground by a pair of your henchmen."

Marek nodded. "I agree," he said, "but you were hard to catch. I've had enough of sport." The vedalken captain of the guard lifted his axe in the air. "Goodbye," he said, and he brought the axe down with all his might.

Even as the blade whistled toward the ground, the elf maintained eye contact with him. The closer her death came, the more determined and confident she looked. Finally, Marek couldn't take it, and he closed his eyes. His axe connected, and a heavy ringing sound echoed out, followed by the general cacophony of battle and the telltale clang of weapons crashing.

That wasn't right.

Marek opened his eyes. Standing before him, her sword hooked under the blade of his axe, stood the human wizard woman—Bruenna.

"Hello, Marek," she said.

* * * * *

Glissa stared up at the vedalken warrior with the axe. She hated this man. She had never before met him, but right now he represented everything that was wrong in the whole world, and she wanted him dead.

His blade descended on her. She was defenseless; all she could do was watch and hope that her hatred was enough to strike him down.

The air before her face began to waver and something materialized, blocking her view of the vedalken. The axe crashed into the object and was turned aside. Glissa twisted to see Bruenna standing over her. A sudden rush of relief filled her whole body, and the elf laughed nervously. She might live to strike down the vedalken after all.

Then the brief euphoria over being saved suddenly gave way to fear. Watching her friends be captured and held down like animals had so infuriated her that she hadn't had time to be scared.

Now, however, she was terrified.

The sounds of battle filled her ears, and Glissa felt the vedalken holding her to the ground release their grip. Rolling up to her feet, she wriggled free of the two lassos. All around, they were surrounded by human wizards. Bruenna's tribe had appeared as if from nowhere, and they fought now with the vedalken warriors.

Glissa scrambled to her sword, still lying on the ground where she had dropped it, and she crossed to Al-Hayat. With two quick slashes, the wolf was free. Turning, Glissa narrowly missed being decapitated by a flying halberd. Blocking the attack with some difficulty, the elf managed to scramble in under the reach of the long weapon. The shaft struck her shoulder, and it stung, but the blade waved harmlessly in the air behind her. Bringing the point of her sword up before her, she jammed it home, puncturing the vedalken's gut. The blade slid cleanly through, popping out the other side, and the warrior went slack.

Glissa had to place her boot on the vedalken's chest to get enough leverage to pull her blade free. The Sword of Kaldra came out with a sloshing sound, and the elf whipped it sideways, tossing the blood from the steel. Then she turned to free the goblin and the golem.

She was too late.

The vedalken were outnumbered two to one by the humans—and they fled toward their gliders. Bosh was now pushing the remnants of the net off of his head as he bent down to pick up Slobad, who, though the warriors holding him prisoner had fled, was still lying flat on his stomach.

The first of the gliders launched into the air, accompanied by the same hollow whistling sound they had made on their way down. Only now the whistle grew higher in pitch, rising to an ear-piercing hiss as it rose out of reach.

One by one the vedalken jumped into the air, flying off in defeat, only half as many as they were when they arrived. The humans let out a collective whoop, giving up pursuit and circling back to tend to the wounded.

* * * * *

Marek saw the humans materialize, and he was grateful. He could back out gracefully, claim defeat and still keep his life. He wondered if the wizard woman Bruenna would understand if he told her how glad he was to see her. Probably not. Marek understood it only because life had always seemed to deal him contradictory roles, and he'd had to make the best of each of them. This situation was no different from many he'd encountered, though he would have been lying to himself if he didn't admit that that was a very close call, so close that it continued to unnerve him as he ordered the retreat. Had he been less distracted, he wouldn't have hesitated. Fewer of his good warriors would had died had they fallen back immediately. As soon as the humans arrived, the battle was lost. As much as knowing how to be a warrior, a commander needed to also know when to fall back—live to fight another day.

Pontifex had taught him that, a long time ago. Recently, it seemed he'd forgotten many of his own lessons. Perhaps the pressures of capturing this elf had taken their toll on him. Marek wasn't certain what it was, but something had changed in the man—and not for the better.

Marek's wandering thoughts stopped as he fell back to Pontifex and Orland.

"My lord," he said. "The humans are too strong. We must leave now and catch them again when we are at the advantage."

"He's right," agreed Orland. "It's time to go." The councilor sprinted to his glider, putting it on with the panicked speed of a desperate man.

Pontifex just stood there, squeezing his fists and grinding his teeth. Finally, he nodded. "We will finish this later," he said, and he slipped the backpack of his glider over his arms.

Marek followed suit, lifting his wings into place then turning to face the humans. He would wait until Pontifex and Orland were safely off the ground before taking off himself.

That was close, he thought, as he listened to the thumping of his heart inside his chest. Too close.

* * * * *

"Where did *you* come from, huh?" Slobad asked Bruenna.

The goblin had looted one of the vedalken warriors for his halberd. The long spear towered over Slobad's squat little frame, making the weapon look even longer and more fearsome. Bosh lifted him off the ground and placed him on his shoulder.

Bruenna smiled. "We've been tracking Pontifex since he left Lumengrid," she explained. "We knew he'd come after you sooner or later, so we followed him. I'm just sorry we weren't here quicker. Those gliders are fast. Our flight spells are not quite so agile as their artifacts."

"Slobad didn't see you, huh? How come you not make us all invisible when we go to Lumengrid, huh?" said the goblin.

"It was a potion left to me by my father, one I've been saving for an emergency." Bruenna shrugged. "This felt like one of those times."

"Well, it's a good thing you arrived when you did, or we would have all been goners," said Glissa. Grabbing Bruenna's hand, she gave it a tight squeeze and looked down at the wizard's once injured leg. "You're all healed."

Bruenna followed Glissa's eyes and nodded. "Not entirely," she said, limping a little on her leg, "but enough." She smiled. "I told you we would provide aid when the time was right."

"Yes. You are true to your word." Glissa cocked her head and looked the human over once from head to toe. "We are truly grateful." She paused. "But I have another favor to ask."

Bruenna nodded. "The only true harm is in not asking," she replied.

Glissa was glad to hear those words. "Would you come with us to Mephidross?"

The sound of that name brought the collected group of human wizards to silence.

"The Dross?" asked Bruenna. "Why would you want to go there?"

Glissa lifted her blade. "To complete the Kaldra Champion." She looked out at everyone standing there in the middle of the razor grass plains. The strange light from the convergent moons painted them in a ruddy orange-brown. "So that we can raise an ally strong enough to defeat Memnarch."

The humans looked dubious.

"So you can exact your revenge for your parents' death?" asked Bruenna.

"No." Glissa shook her head. "So we can all be free of *him* once and for all."

"I don't know." Bruenna looked over her shoulder. "The village will be unprotected. There will be retribution from the vedalken for this."

Glissa nodded. "You have already chosen to take your stand. Now the only question is, are you going to accept the consequences, or are you going to continue to fight for what you believe in?"

Bruenna turned back, the heavy burden of leadership plain on her face.

"You can't go back to being a slave," said Glissa. "We can finish this now. For all time. For all of us."

Bruenna looked at her warriors once again. Glissa could see the looks in the eyes of her human wizards. Many of them nodded to their leader.

Bruenna turned back to the elf. "Very well," she said. "I will follow you to Mephidross."

CHAPTER 12

Memnarch strapped himself into his infusion device and watched the red pinpricks of light float over his body. Funneling the mana, the magical process commenced. His skin flushed, and he felt the familiar fire as the serum burned away the ignorance from his body. The fires he felt would purify him, make him stronger, so that he might be a better servant to his master.

His head buzzed with the pain, and his eyes filled with tears. The light pulsing in from the mana core coalesced as it always did with the first infusion of the morning, and there, arrayed before the guardian of Mirrodin was a vision of the creator himself—Karn.

"Master, you have come."

The vision did not say a word. It wavered in the middle of Memnarch's laboratory, drifting above the floor as if it were a ghost of the liquid metal planeswalker.

"Memnarch has been so lonely—and afraid. It has been so long since your last visit. Memnarch fears you will never return. This place, this plane you created, is beautiful and wondrous. You have truly provided anything a guardian could desire." Memnarch dropped his head. "Except companions. Memnarch had to bring them here himself. All the creatures, except Memnarch himself of course, every one of them was brought here by my soul traps. At first, Memnarch only wanted subjects to experiment with. He wanted to see what made them tick.

"But now Memnarch knows why they work. He has observed their habits, catalogued them all. And he cannot say that the work has been unrewarding. Those who seek knowledge find solace in discovery."

Memnarch stared at the vision. "Though the experiments continue, Memnarch still lacks a companion," he continued his conversation with Karn. "Memnarch has even tried to make the creatures here understand him. The one called Pontifex has been to see Memnarch many times. Many times. If Memnarch wished it, this one would stay here in Panopticon, would stay with Memnarch forever. But that is not what Memnarch wants.

"These creatures, they do not understand. They do not have the capacity for emotion." Memnarch looked up to where the eyes should be in the ghostly image before him. "They are instinctual and predatory, but that is all. They tear each other apart so that they may simply survive another day. Oh, they fooled Memnarch for some time. The systems and rituals they have created seem sophisticated, very sophisticated indeed. But upon further study these things—these complex systems that Memnarch has watched, has hoped would show an understanding, a level of higher intelligence and emotion—have proven just the opposite.

"These creatures, the poor pathetic vermin who populate this plane, your plane, they are nothing to Memnarch. There is no hope of finding a companion among them. They are incapable of love, incapable of providing Memnarch with what he needs."

The guardian sighed. "Memnarch has even tried to build a companion. You have seen Malil." Memnarch chuckled. "Yes, he does look as Memnarch once did—a tribute to you, Lord Karn—and a hope that Memnarch could get what he lacked from a creature just like himself. But it did not work. Though Malil looks like Memnarch, Malil is not Memnarch. No, no. He is a good servant, but he does not suit Memnarch. True. He will do whatever we say and without argument.

"Perhaps that is the problem. Perhaps Memnarch needs conflict in his life." The Guardian shook his head. "No, there is plenty of conflict on Mirrodin. Memnarch has seen to that. It is something else, something lacking."

Memnarch stopped talking as the serum hit the inside of his brain. The fires spread through his skull, and all capacity to speak was taken from him. Then the burning turned to a throb, and he resumed his conversation.

"Forgive Memnarch," he said, feeling a wave of exhilaration run up his spine, making him stronger, smarter, more confident. "But your creation needs you. Memnarch needs your attention, your companionship—your love."

The articulated arms withdrew, and the infusion device reset itself, unlatching him.

"Why do you stay away? Why do you not give Memnarch what he needs?" Memnarch pushed aside the arm straps and stepped from his device. "Why do you not talk to Memnarch when he asks for you?"

The Guardian blinked his eyes. Several of them cleared of tears, and the ghostly image in the middle of the laboratory faded. Memnarch closed the eyes with the clearest view. The image of Karn returned through the blurry eyes, but only partially.

"Do not go, Master," he said, ambling forward on his four spindly metal limbs. He squinted, trying to bring the vision into focus. But by squeezing his eyes closed, he forced the remaining tears from them, and the image of Karn vanished.

"No!" he shouted. "Do not leave Memnarch. You have been gone too long, and you *will* return at once!" Memnarch spun, looking all over his laboratory for signs that the creator had returned. "Do you hear me? I said, *'Do you hear me?'*"

There was no answer.

Memnarch let out a wail. Inside he was alone. In his laboratory, he was alone. On all of Mirrodin, he was alone.

Sadness welled up in his chest. It felt as if a heavy weight had been placed on top of him, one that he couldn't see or ever remove. He had chased the Creator away. Today it had been his harsh words. Before it had been his devotion to his mission, his blind loyalty to do whatever it was that the Creator had asked. He would have done anything for Karn. He *did* everything the master had asked of him. But when he had done those things, it had been because he wanted the companionship and attention from his Creator. When he had been given the role of guardian, he had thought it would bring him praise and acknowledgement from Karn.

Instead, it had left him alone, stranded here on a dying Mirrodin, as his body devolved into flesh.

The sadness in his breast turned to anger. With his powerful legs, he kicked over a table, sending beakers and scientific equipment skidding across the floor. Those items that didn't break in the fall Memnarch hunted down, stepping on each and every one of them until they were all broken into tiny shards. Those things he couldn't break he crushed, smashing them down under his weight until they were flat. Next he turned to the window that looked out on the interior of Mirrodin. Lifting the turned-over table into the air, he hurled it with all of his might. Its four legs collided with the glass. The entire pane shattered, turning the window into a billion slivers, each one looking like a diamond. They fell like raindrops—some of them following the table as it plummeted to the ground far below.

Even this did not satisfy the anger in his heart.

Memnarch spun and grabbed one of the articulated arms on his infusion device. His own arms were small and scrawny in comparison to his enhanced legs, but they held much strength, and he reeled back, ripping the appendage from his device. Sparks cascaded from the broken limb. Bits of broken metal dropped to the ground with a metallic ring.

Without hesitation, Memnarch lifted the shorn arm over his head. It bent at the joint, no longer held in place by hydraulics, and the Guardian whipped it forward, thrashing at the control unit of his infusion device.

The arm's tip whipped over as the arm came down. The point connected with the controls, burying itself deep within the panel. Memnarch pulled it back for another strike, but the sharp edge, stuck inside the device, held firm. The Guardian let out a roar as he yanked again, and the arm snapped, half staying lodged in the controls, the other half coming away in Memnarch's hand.

Again the broken limb came up over Memnarch's shoulder, and again it came down on the device. The Guardian wailed as he pummeled and pummeled some more. Metal bent. Sparks flew, and the machinery withered and died under the assault. With another strike, the serum tanks exploded, flooding the floor of the laboratory with viscous, milky-white liquid. With the next, the power supply was torn out, and the device went dark.

Still Memnarch didn't stop his attacks. Wielding the arm like a flail, he beat his creation until it was nothing more than a smoking pile of rubble. Standing over the ruined device, he looked down, catching his breath and contemplating the impact of his rage.

After a moment, he closed his eyes and let the arm drop to the floor.

"What have I done?"

* * * * *

Pontifex entered the Synod chamber. Far below, Sodador and Tyrell paced the empty floor. Orland, by contrast, reclined on a padded lounger—a new addition to the council hall. The long, curved walls were silent. The packed crowd that had filled the viewing platforms, watching the previous proceeding, had not been invited to this meeting. Save for the four vedalken councilors, the room was empty.

"Lord Pontifex," said Sodador, "we've been waiting for you for some time now."

Pontifex leaned against the railing and looked down at the tiny vedalken below. The height made him feel bigger than life. How he wished he were really that large. He would reach out his boot and smash the others into jelly.

He shook himself from his reverie. "Yes, I'm sure you have."

Orland stood up from his lounger. "Please," he said, "come down and join us. We have much to discuss."

Pontifex brushed aside the invitation with a wave of his hand. "I prefer to stand here, thank you."

Tyrell tossed something to the floor in disgust. "Really Pontifex, your disrespect for this assembly—"

Orland put his hand on the councilor's shoulder, silencing him. "Lord Pontifex has every right to stand where he wishes. We can accommodate his antics."

Pontifex nodded his approval, though inside he bristled. He lifted himself into the most regal pose he could muster. Lord Pontifex had never committed an "antic" in his life.

"Fine, fine," said Sodador, "but perhaps Pontifex would be so kind as to explain his actions to this council."

Pontifex put his hand to his chest. "Whatever do you mean?"

"You know full well what I mean," said Sodador. "You threatened a member of this council."

Orland looked away.

"I did no such thing," said Pontifex.

Sodador slammed his cane into the hard floor. "What sort of fools do you take us for, Pontifex?"

Pontifex chuckled. "Are there different sorts of fools? I was under the impression that there was only one, Sodador."

"This may all be very amusing to you, Pontifex!" Tyrell shouted. The chamber amplified the sound, making it boom off the walls and echo through the hall. "But we take the rulership of the vedalken people very seriously."

"As do I," said Pontifex in a calm voice.

"I think not," said Sodador. "You've always been focused on your own personal gain, impetuously ignoring the will and well-being of the vedalken people."

"The will of the vedalken people?" replied Pontifex. "Since when have the vedalken people had a will? Might I remind you, councilors, that the vedalken empire is not—" Pontifex paused as if the words he was about to say tasted bad in his mouth— "ruled by the people."

"Ah," interjected Orland, "but it could be."

"Yes?" Pontifex laughed. "Then why stop there? Why not just dissolve the government all together?"

"One step at a time, Lord Pontifex," said Orland. "One step at a time."

Though the vedalken lord could hear every word spoken inside the meeting hall, he was too far from the floor to see the look on Orland's face. Pontifex felt certain that the newest councilor to the Synod was smiling from ear to ear. The empire ruled by the people? Were these buffoons serious?

"Are you mad?" said Pontifex. "You're talking about vedalken ruling *themselves*."

"Precisely," said Orland.

"Do you have any idea what sort of mayhem would ensue?"

Orland went back to his lounger. "What you call 'mayhem', Lord Pontifex, others call freedom."

Pontifex was flabbergasted. "Freedom? Aside from the members of this Synod, there are few creatures on this plain who could even handle such a responsibility." He laughed. "Frankly, I have my doubts about you three."

"Your objections have been noted," said Tyrell, "but we are departing from the topic here."

"Oh?" Pontifex rolled his neck, trying to relieve the frustration he felt from having to deal with such imbeciles. "And what *is* the topic of today's meeting?"

Sodador slammed his cane into the ground once again. "Your inexcusable behavior toward another council member."

Pontifex again feigned surprise. "My behavior? I have done nothing even approaching *inexcusable*."

"Then perhaps you'll explain your actions toward Councilor Orland," said Sodador. "I believe you grabbed him by the collar and threatened him."

Sodador looked at Orland, who was now looking at the floor. Then he turned his gaze back up at Pontifex. "What do you have to say for yourself?"

Pontifex looked down on Orland. The young idealist had run to Tyrell and Sodador as soon as they'd arrived home. The newest councilor talked tough, but he had no temperament for real violence. This was a good thing to know.

"Why, Orland," he said, "if the fighting out on the plain was going to make you so uncomfortable, I never would have agreed to bring you along." He rolled his fingers over the railing, gripping it tight. "The battlefield is no place for a soft politician."

Sodador and Tyrell looked at Orland. He shrugged.

"Lord Pontifex," said Tyrell turning away from the other two councilors, "are you denying that you threatened Councilor Orland?"

"Threaten Orland?" Pontifex put both hands on his chest, appearing to be affronted by the notion. "Why, Orland, is *that* what you've been saying? That I threatened you? And to think all I was trying to do was keep you safe from harm's way."

"Don't play your games with us, Pontifex!" shouted Sodador. "You've been opposed to having a fourth member of the Synod since you disposed of Janus. This council has always been ruled by fear and deception. But we're not having that any more. The days of backstabbing and corruption are over. It's time we did things a new way."

"How very admirable," replied the vedalken lord.

"Things are going to change, Pontifex," said Tyrell. "Whether you like it or not."

Lord Pontifex lifted his cape, wrapping it around his shoulder. "We shall see." He turned and exited the assembly hall.

*   *   *   *   *

The rolling hills that had seemed to go on and on, as if they would never end, finally began to flatten out. The interconnected hexagonal metal plates of Mirrodin's plains gave way to a mass of corrupted and tarnished tubes, pipes, and vines. To Glissa it looked like a much maligned and twisted version of the Tangle. Chimneys rose from the ground, belching smoke. Like trees, they had branches and spikes reaching for the sky, but where these same sorts of growths would be whole and green in the Tangle, those in the Dross were riddled with holes and black with decay.

Here, too, everything was shorter. The first time she had been here, Glissa had felt very tall, but as she and her companions entered the darkened area, she realized that a viscous mucous covered the ground, gobbling up the first few feet of anything growing from the earth. Nothing here was shorter than in the Tangle. It just appeared that way because everything was partially covered by the swampy liquid.

The convergent moons of Mirrodin had gone down long ago, leaving the Glimmervoid in complete darkness. Bruenna and the few wizards who hadn't returned to Medev had cast several small light spells to guide the way to Mephidross, but when they arrived, the magic was no longer necessary.

Inside the oily swamp, hundreds of tiny green lights flickered. The resulting ghastly glow didn't light up the night sky, but it did illuminate the outline of the trees and brush. Eerie shadows played over the surface of the thick liquid as the pinpricks of light moved around, covering the Dross in a squirming veil of motion. It was as if the ghosts of all who had lived and passed on were haunting this place, and it set the small hairs on the back of Glissa's neck on edge.

"What makes those lights?" asked the elf.

Bruenna shrugged. "I don't know. Until now, I've made it a point in my life to stay out of this place."

"Good thinking," said Slobad. "Slobad don't like Dross, huh? Gives goblins creeps."

A gentle wind blew out of the swamp, bringing with it the rancid smell of rotting flesh and a light rustling sound.

Glissa stopped just at the edge of the goopy liquid. "I think we should stop for the night. Who knows if we'll find a dry place to camp once we enter."

"Good," said the goblin. "Longer we stay out, better, huh?"

Glissa bent down next to the goblin. "In the Tangle, there are bugs that give off a glow like that. We call them fire beetles."

Slobad narrowed his eyes, looking deeper into the green-lit swamp. "Crazy elf think them lights are bugs?"

Glissa shrugged. "Could be."

Slobad grabbed his chin then, after a moment of thought, shook his head. "Naw," he said. "Slobad don't want beetles, huh? Happier out here."

Glissa laughed. "Okay then." She unhitched her sword from her belt and sat down on the ground. "This is as good a place as any."

Bosh sat down beside Glissa. Al-Hayat curled up not far away and began licking his wounds. Slobad found a soft spot in the wolf's fur, rolling into a ball and falling asleep. Within a matter of seconds, the goblin's soft snoring could be heard over the rustling swamp wind.

Bruenna placed her hand on Glissa's shoulder. "We will set some wards to warn us of danger." The wizard smiled. "Better to get a good night of rest knowing that we won't be eaten while we sleep."

"Good idea." Glissa nodded. "Thank you, Bruenna."

Bruenna and her wizards took off into the darkness.

Glissa turned to Bosh. "I haven't heard much from you lately. How you holding up?"

Bosh looked down at the elf. "I have been better." He held out his hand. Several long wounds criss-crossed his palm and knuckles. Scabs were forming on the older ones, but a few still seeped blood when he moved his fingers.

"Bosh," she said, grabbing a hold of his hand. "Do they hurt?"

"Some," replied the golem.

She touched one of the scabs, and Bosh winced. Glissa pulled in air through her gritted teeth, sympathizing with his newfound pain. "You've got to learn how to avoid getting hurt so much."

"I am trying," he admitted. "When the vedalken attacked, my first thought was to pick you all up and run through the razor grass." He pulled his hand away to poke at a new fleshy patch along his chest and down where an elf would have a ribcage. "I remembered, so I stayed put. We had nowhere else to go, and we had to fight." He gave his hand back to the elf. "What should I have done differently?"

"Well, to begin with," she said, "you need to avoid their weapons as much as possible. Part of fighting is learning to defend yourself. You can't just rely on your metal hide to keep you safe from harm. You have to move, make yourself less of a target."

"What else?"

Glissa thought for a moment. She had to put herself in his place, think like a metal golem, then she could tell him how to think differently. "Okay," she said, having thought of something else. "Smashing stuff."

"I like smashing stuff," said Bosh.

"I know, but that's a problem."

"But I like smashing stuff."

Glissa laughed. "Yes, I know. You don't have to stop altogether, but you need to make sure that what you smash isn't going to hurt you."

"Nothing hurt me before."

"That's the difference. Vedalken who are carrying weapons will hurt when you smash them."

Bosh shook his head. "I do not like being fleshy."

"No." Glissa examined a fresh wound across the top of her hand. It was scabbing up. "Sometimes neither do I." She looked back at Bosh's hand. "But there is one good thing."

"What?"

Glissa pointed to the scabs on the golem's hand. "Now you heal."

Bosh lifted his palm to his face. He examined the dried blood for a long time. "What does that mean?"

"Well," explained the elf, "before when something got broken, Slobad had to find new parts or repair the old ones in order to fix you up."

"Yes, I remember." Bosh slumped. "But he cannot do that now."

"No," said the elf, "but now he doesn't need to. You fix yourself."

Bosh looked puzzled.

Glissa pointed to the scabs again. "That dried blood is your flesh repairing itself."

Bosh looked at it again and fingered the oldest scar. "That was from several days ago," he said. "This healing takes a long time."

Glissa nodded. "Yes, it does. That's why you've got to be more careful about what you hit and what you let hit you."

Bosh shook his head. "I do not think I will ever get used to flesh."

CHAPTER 13

Glissa laid her head on Bosh's lap. It felt as if she had just barely touched her ear to his hard metal leg when the magical wards sounded, and she was on her feet again.

The moons were still down, and the sky was pitch black. The same dull green glow issued from the swamp, but now, instead of there being hundreds of tiny pinpricks of light scattered across the swamp, they were collected together in a tight cluster—standing at the edge of the swamp.

A tingle ran down Glissa's spine, and goose bumps formed all down her arms. "Nim."

There before her stood the decaying husks of nearly a hundred undead creatures. Hunched over, their mouths agape, their knuckles dragging in the muck, the zombies shambled toward the shore. No two looked exactly alike. Each had been a unique human, or possibly elf, during his normal life. What they had now couldn't be called "life." They moved, were animated, but to Glissa these creatures suffered a fate worse than death.

On their backs, in the hunch where their bodies had nearly collapsed from leaning forward, each of them carried a glowing green orb. It was these devices that had lit the swamp, giving it the eerie glow Glissa had seen when they first arrived. Now, with so many collected in one place and with one purpose, the light had intensified—leaving the far end of the swamp in total darkness.

The zombies moved very slowly, a thick, green smoke pouring from open cavities on their shoulders. Their methodical march toward Glissa and her friends was unnerving. It felt like a force of nature. It was so big, so slow moving that you knew it was coming, but there was little you could do to try to stop it. When they entered the ring of magical wards that Bruenna had set, they triggered a loud noise like a huge gong being slammed by a mallet. The alarm went off three times then fell silent.

Glissa pulled her sword and was relieved to see that Bruenna and her wizards were awake and alert. The elf chuckled to herself. Apparently their wards were loud enough to wake the dead.

To her right, Al-Hayat was on his feet. Slobad had taken to his shoulders, his vedalken pike held under his arm like a lance. To her left, Bosh towered over her, rubbing his hands together, the same somber look on his metal face that he always had.

The human wizards were the first to strike. A cloud of wisping blue smoke poured out over the edge of the swamp. It mixed in the air with the nims' poisonous green gas then settled on the advancing monsters, engulfing nearly a dozen of the tattered nim. Where the smoke touched them, whirling person-sized tornadoes emerged, enveloping their victims in cones of spinning wind. The miniature storms lifted the swamp muck into the air, obscuring the nim from view.

As quickly as they started, the tornadoes disappeared, losing all of their momentum and simply falling away. The swamp muck spun on once or twice more before falling to the ground as well in great wet circles. The nim inside were gone.

"Where'd they go?" shouted Glissa.

"Returned to where they came from," replied Bruenna.

"Will they come back?"

"Perhaps," replied the wizard, "but that is something we can worry about when it happens."

Glissa nodded. Better to spread them out, she thought.

Despite their slow march, the nim were now almost upon the group, and the elf gripped her sword tight. The sight of these torn, worn-out creatures unnerved her considerably, and the sooner she could cut them down, return them to their natural place of rest, the better.

Al-Hayat must have agreed because the wolf let out a tremendous snarl and leaped forward, grabbing three nim in one huge mouthful. The forest creature champed down, and Glissa could hear the harsh snapping of bones and the wet slogging of rotten flesh. The wolf shook his head as he had when they fought the vedalken. Only this time, his foe was not so sturdy.

Without a sound, the nim came apart under the assault. Limbs went flying. Arms came off at the shoulders. Legs came apart at the knees, and heads went rolling off into the darkness. Al-Hayat spit out the filth. A mash of rotten flesh and ruined organs covered the inside of his mouth, and he rubbed his tongue against his front teeth trying to dislodge the foul goo.

Meanwhile, atop his back, Slobad rode into battle valiantly, like a knight on a steed. Holding his pilfered vedalken halberd under his armpit, the goblin braced the weapon with both hands and all the muscle he could muster. As the wolf charged in, the goblin skewered a nim on the end of his pike. The magically charged head ripped through rotten flesh, coming cleanly out the other side. With a swift yank, Slobad managed to pull the weapon from the undead soldier's body before it fell, once again lifeless, to the ground.

But when the wolf began shaking his head, the goblin had no way to hold on. Both of his hands firmly gripped around his polearm, Slobad slipped sideways. Refusing to give up his weapon, the little guy allowed himself to slide off of the wolf. Al-Hayat was so large that Slobad had time to gather his feet below himself before he reached the edge, and with a push he leaped, landing safely on the soggy ground, his halberd still gripped in both hands.

Glissa watched the goblin land, could see the streak the head of his blue, charged weapon made as it flew through the air. Then the elf had other things to consider.

The first of the nim made it to her. Having planted her feet, preparing herself for the charge, Glissa let out a whoop and swung down on the first of her attackers. Soft flesh parted, and a zombie came apart right in front of her. A sticky black paste clung to her blade, and she barely had enough time to shake it off before she was cutting into another of the shambling undead.

Beside her, Bosh was testing out the strength of the nims' bodies, gingerly squashing them with his huge thumb. Their soft flesh must have passed the test, because the golem reared back and brought his fist down full force, sending a wave of liquid in all directions.

Glissa felt something cold hit her face. She hoped it was swamp water. The alternative was far too gruesome, and she didn't have time to investigate or get the willies just now. Her blade flashed out before her again and again, taking off limbs and cutting out chunks of flesh.

Nothing short of cutting these foul beasts into tiny chunks stopped them from coming. If they had legs, they would walk. Without legs they would crawl. The squirming mass slowly made its way closer and closer to Glissa, Bosh, Slobad, Al-Hayat, Bruenna and all her wizards. And with each step, they crowded in, forcing the companions to step back.

Behind them was the sharp hill they had come down to reach the edge of the swamp. Moving back up it was difficult, but it provided height—an advantage in this battle. The nim reached out, grasping at the live creatures. Their bony claws were torn from their wrists by blades, halberd, and magic.

Still they came.

The ground turned quickly to a soupy mess of rotten entrails. Fallen nim hit the sloping hill, hydroplaning down the slime, slipping back into the swamp to be gobbled up by the liquid—only to be replaced by more just like them. It seemed as if there was a limitless supply.

Glissa took another step back up the hill. This wasn't the direction she wanted to go. "What do we do?"

"What can we do?" replied Bruenna. "We cut them to shreds. Smash them to bits, but still they come."

Even Bosh retreated against the onslaught. Though his fleshy hands were not harmed by the soft-bodied creatures, the flood of nim was too ferocious, and he fell back with everyone else.

Al-Hayat had taken to swatting the swamp monsters with his giant paw. His claws and fur were covered in filth. Between attacks, Glissa could see him still trying to work the rancid meat off of his tongue and out from between his teeth.

Slobad stayed beside the great forest creature, keeping nim away from Al-Hayat's flanks but also keeping the wolf's body to his back to avoid being surprised himself.

Never before had Glissa felt as if she had scored so many hits while at the same time she lost so much ground. Turning another nim into paste with the flat of her blade, Glissa took a moment to look over her shoulder. While the group retreated they had managed to climb nearly to the top of the sloping hill and back up onto the plains.

The first of the moons was beginning to rise, and the outline of the razor grass fields in the far distance came into her view. Something was not right. Though it was still mostly dark, Glissa could just make out long narrow lines in the fields, as if something had cut its way through, leveling the razor grass to prickly stubble.

Checking back briefly with the nim, Glissa allowed herself a long stare at the plain, trying to figure out what seemed so out of place. Was that a trick of the light or was something moving out there? Then her heart sank once again into the pit of her stomach, and a ripple of fear washed over her shoulders.

"Levelers!" she shouted. "The levelers have found us."

* * * * *

Marek stood before the door to Pontifex's chamber. He closed his eyes and took in a deep breath. Little bubbles appeared inside his face mask, and he drew in air through the serum.

Forcing himself to relax his shoulders, the commander knocked on the door.

"Enter," came Pontifex's voice from inside.

The door slid on its tracks, and Marek opened his eyes and stepped through.

Pontifex was sitting at the long meeting table in his chambers. He had several old, heavy-looking contraptions opened before him. Marek had never seen anything quite like them before. He was aware that such things existed, but they were not very common, and most people lived out their entire lives on Mirrodin without coming into contact with these "books," as they were called.

As Marek got closer, he could see that these books were comprised of dozens of thinly pressed metal sheets, each with different symbols and characters on them. To the vedalken guardsmen, it looked as if the text had been carved or etched into the surface of the metal with either a very sharp blade or a corrosive substance.

On the left side of each sheet, holes had been punched, and bits of wire had been woven through them. It looked to Marek as if the pages had been purposely bound that way, so they would stay together no matter how you handled the package. The warrior nodded as he looked at it. Quite ingenious really.

Marek pulled his eyes away from the contraption. Pontifex continued to look through the book.

"You called for me, my lord?" asked Marek.

"Yes," replied Pontifex, turning the page and examining a new set of runes. "Where is the elf girl now?"

"In the Dross, my lord."

This brought Pontifex's attention away from the book. "The Mephidross? What would she be doing in the Mephidross?"

Marek shrugged. "I don't know, but perhaps Geth could tell us."

Pontifex nodded. "Yes, I'm certain he could." He closed the book. "How soon can you and your men be ready to leave for the swamp?"

Marek smiled. "We're ready now."

Pontifex stood up and put his hand on Marek's shoulder. "You are perhaps the last thing I can truly count on in the world, Marek." He looked through the warrior's helmet, locking eyes with his lieutenant.

After a long moment, Marek looked away. "Thank you, Lord Pontifex. I try."

* * * * *

Malil sat atop his personal leveler as he and his squad of killing devices mowed through the razor grass field. His whole body ached—not a muscular ache, for Malil didn't have any muscles that could feel pain or fatigue. What the metal man felt was desire. He needed something he didn't have, and he was on his way to get it. But first, before he could have it, he needed to capture the elf girl.

After his interrogation of the troll, Malil had come straight to the Dross, and here he had waited. He didn't know how the girl had managed to elude him and his levelers in the Tangle, but she wasn't going to be so lucky this time.

Nearly three full days passed before Malil had gotten word that the one called Glissa had arrived. She was on the other side of the swamp, and she had accumulated more friends along the way.

Some of the story was beginning to come clear. If she had taken the shortest route to the swamp from the Tangle, she would have arrived on the opposite side of Mephidross, the side where Malil had been waiting in ambush. Since she came in from the other side, it made sense that she and her companions had gone through the other side of the Tangle, which would also account for the long wait he'd had to endure.

And a long wait it had been.

In his relatively short life, Malil had never felt time the way he had over the past few rotations. Before he had taken the serum, he had been patient in all things. The movements of Mirrodin went on, and Malil stood his ground, blissfully unaware that there was anything he needed other than to serve his master. Now though, he felt a sense of urgency in everything he did. Time ground on him, taking its toll as the hours and minutes ticked past. Each moment was just another in a long line between right now and when he would taste the serum yet again.

Now that wait was almost over. All that stood between him and capturing the elf girl was a patch of razor grass. His levelers had been designed to level entire fields of the sharp metal reeds without slowing down. That thought brought a brief wave of relief that flooded over his aching frame. The end was finally near. The waiting would be over, and once again he would be granted the clarity of the serum.

CHAPTER 14

Nim flesh splashed from the end of Glissa's sword. The levelers were closing in, and she was trapped. On one side, she and her companions fought with an unending mob of undying monstrosities. On the other, the artifact creatures that had so efficiently killed Glissa's family and best friend were coming on.

"Should we make a run for it?" shouted Glissa. She brought her sword around again, smashing a nim in the face and taking the top half of its head off. The creature lost its balance momentarily then continued up the hill, swinging its bony claws.

"Not enough time," replied Bruenna. She too fought the nim. She used the reach of her wickedly barbed halberd to great advantage, cutting down the undead before they were within reach. The wizard looked over her shoulder. "Even if we had seen them an hour ago, we couldn't have outrun them. They're just too fast."

"Couldn't you fly us from here?" asked the elf between decapitating blows.

Bruenna shook her head. "I'm afraid we didn't bring along enough of the right magic for this situation."

Glissa looked to Bruenna.

The blue wizard shrugged. "Flight just isn't in the cards for us today."

Bosh stepped into Glissa's field of view. Kicking out, he knocked a dozen of the nim backward, sending them tumbling down the slope. But behind them there were more shambling monsters, and these ones packed in so tightly that the falling undead were caught before they fell too far. Landing on their brethren, the kicked nim returned.

"Bruenna is right," said the golem. "We can't outrun the levelers, and even if we could, where would we go?"

Glissa shrugged. "Some place where they're not?"

"Good plan, huh?" interjected Slobad.

Bosh shook his head. "We came here to get inside the Mephidross." He lifted his heavy arm and pointed out over the swamp. The moons were still rising in the sky, but there was plenty of light to see what Bosh was looking at.

There in the middle of swamp, surrounded on all sides by foul liquid, stood the corrupted and pockmarked façade of the Vault of Whispers. It seemed like a long time since Glissa had been inside the fortress in the middle of the swamp. But it couldn't have been more than a couple of moon cycles. Glissa thought about the girl she had been when she had first entered that foul place. She was angry. She wanted revenge for the death of her parents. And she had wanted to set things right, set herself free from the pain of her loss by seeing that justice was served.

She was different now. Discovering that the plane she lived on was hollow had changed her. Discovering that the force pursuing her had a name—Memnarch—had changed her even more. Standing here, on the threshold of the swamp once again, she realized that she still wanted the same things she did when she had been here last. Now she wanted more. Not only did she want to set herself free, but she wanted to free everyone else as well.

Glissa looked up at the golem. "You're right," she said. "Just because it isn't easy to get inside doesn't mean we should stop trying."

Bosh nodded his approval.

The group of elves, humans, goblin and golem was pushed back over the lip of the slope, back up onto the plain. The nim hordes had filled the entire hillside, but the flood of new undead bodies ceased, and the grotesque liquid at the bottom of the hill became still.

"Now that we've decided to stick it out, that just leaves us with one problem," said Glissa after bashing aside the claws of an advancing nim.

"What?" asked Slobad. "That you still crazy elf, huh?"

"How do we fight the levelers and the zombies at the same time?"

No one had time to answer. The levelers broke through the end of the razor grass and charged across the open plain. In the blink of an eye the killing devices were upon them, and Bruenna's wizards turned to face the new threat.

Blue energy arced out over the plain, the light reflected in the metallic plates, catching the levelers across their chests, making their steering sails look green and their silver bodies a dull gray.

The white moon had been the first to rise, leaving the world suited in its natural colors. The next up, not more than a few second later, was the blue. It tainted the white, exaggerating the shadows, deepening the contrast between colors, and bathing everything in a harsh, unflattering light. As the black and red moons rose, colors began to mix and fade, turning everything once again to a ruddy brown.

"This light is making casting magic difficult," said Bruenna.

The elf and the human stood back to back. Glissa fought off the nim, and Bruenna threw spells at the charging levelers.

Sandwiched between the two threats, the allies bunched tightly together. For a brief moment there was a separation between the good and the bad. Though they were squashed between levelers and nim, Glissa knew which way to point her sword. Then both groups pushed in, squeezing between the friends, cutting off allies.

Glissa, Bruenna, Slobad, Bosh, Al-Hayat, and all the human wizards were completely overrun.

Levelers rolled over warriors. Their scythe blades cut down the humans like they were long strands of razor grass.

Nim scratched at eyes, sank their teeth into live flesh, and piled on top of anyone they could reach, using their superior numbers as a weapon.

Glissa fought from side to side, parrying scythe blades to her right and rotten flesh to her left. The three distinct forces swirled and mixed together. It looked like a formal ball, everyone dancing and turning and moving in a great undulating mass.

The nim continued climbing over the lip of the hill, swarming over the plain to get into the fight. Six more came after Glissa, joining the four already slashing at her with their plague-infested claws, poisonous gas rising from their backs. From behind she fought off a pair of levelers. One would strike from the left, then the other would strike a moment later from the right. They took turns, creating a sort of scissoring motion with their sharp blades.

She could only watch as the six shambling monstrosities came on, barely able to keep herself alive without having to worry about more nim. As they closed in, Glissa fought off the urge to close her eyes. She had no control over this situation, and she didn't want to watch the undead beasts tear her apart piece by piece. All the while, as she fought, she knew that sooner or later the sheer numbers would overwhelm her.

That moment had come sooner than she had hoped.

The nim reached out. Glissa dug down deep, trying to make her blade move faster—but she was at her physical limit. Lunging forward, the elf skewered two of them with one blow.

"I'll take you all with me," she shouted.

Her sword was lodged on a bone inside one of the two nim. Slime and rotten flesh covered the hilt of her sword. Yanking with all of her might, Glissa leaned back—and she lost her grip. Falling backward from the force of her pulling, the elf landed flat on her back, looking up at eight nim.

A pair of scythe blades closed just over her face, and for a brief moment, Glissa was grateful for having fallen. If she had been standing when those blades closed down, she would have surely lost half of her left leg—if not more. But that moment passed as the nim closed in.

The first of the undead creatures stepped on her stomach, and Glissa tightened her abdomen to avoid being crushed. Then another stepped on her, and another. The nim were surprisingly light, their bodies made up of little more than desiccated bone and rotten flesh, but they were heavy when all eight of them climbed on top of her.

Pulling her arms up to her sides and twisting away, Glissa curled up into a ball. Three of the nim lost their footing, slipping off and landing easily on the ground. But the others continued to trample her. She was pinned, trapped under the onslaught.

What a funny way to go, she thought, crushed to death by a mob of undead.

The crushing footsteps continued. The weight kept her lungs pinned down, and she had a difficult time breathing. The hard ground underneath was unforgiving, and it pushed back where the nims' feet pushed her down. With each successive attempt, her breath became shallower, and her vision began to narrow.

Everything on the periphery dissolved, and a dark circle began closing down.

Glissa could hear the thumping of her heart in her ears as it labored to keep up with the dwindling air supply. She could feel the soft connective tissues in her body begin to separate and pull away from bone. Pushed past their limit, they were giving way—and so was her life-force.

This was it. She would die here. Her lifeless body would be baked to jerky under the convergent moons, and within a few days the only proof of her existence on Mirrodin would be the stain her corpse left on the interlocking metal plates of the plain.

One by one, the undead creatures stepped off of her. The heavy load lifted. Glissa gasped, swallowing air in giant gulp. Even the fetid swamp gas of Mephidross tasted sweet to her starved lungs. The thumping in her ears faded away, and her vision opened again. Lifting herself up to one elbow, Glissa looked up at a still-raging fight.

The nim who had trampled over her were now locked in combat with the levelers. Their bony claws did little to the armored hide of the killing beasts. Still, the wave of putrid flesh surged forward, throwing themselves fearlessly on the invaders.

Getting to her feet, Glissa found her sword and found Bruenna fighting a pair of levelers. The wizard bashed away attacks from all sides with a practiced ease. Except for the look of utter concentration on her face, the woman's movements were as calm and smooth as if she were doing nothing more taxing than preparing a light spell.

Glissa stepped up beside her friend, engaging one of the levelers.

Bruenna's staff came around and a huge bolt of energy shot from the end. The magic struck the leveler and spread out. Jagged lines of blue power crackled along the seams in the artifact creature's armor, and the leveler stopped dead in its tracks. Its scythe blades seized up, and its steering sail went limp.

Then the buzzing lines of energy slipped inside the creature. It was as if they had been sucked up in a giant breath from the leveler's belly. The device shuddered once, then with a giant clang, things started falling off. Armored plates dropped to the ground. Scythe blades twisted and rolled away, making a satisfying ring as they hit the metal surface of the plain. All the plates and pieces that made up the insides of the leveler suddenly let go. With what seemed a final coughing gasp, the artifact creature splashed to the ground—completely dismantled, now nothing more than a collection of spare parts.

Glissa sidestepped as the shiny bits of the leveler's insides spread out on the ground before her. Dodging an ill-timed strike by the other killing device, the elf twirled the Sword of Kaldra over her head. Grasping it in both hands as it came around, she brought the sharpened, magical edge of the blade down on the leveler's head. The legendary sword parted polished metal as easily as it parted rotting nim flesh. Gears strained, and springs groaned, but they couldn't overcome the might that Glissa had brought to bear.

With the unmistakable sound of metal crashing against metal, the leveler fell facedown onto the ground.

"What happened?" asked Glissa. "Why'd the nim stop attacking us?"

As if in answer, a trio of undead creatures lurched toward the two women.

"They didn't." Bruenna twirled her staff.

Glissa was faster. Bringing to mind the verdigris spires and thorny growths of the Tangle, the elf pulled in mana and funneled it into a spell. The ground shook and tiny motes of green light seeped from the cracks between the metal plates on the floor of the plain. The zombies before her, caught within the maelstrom of magic, withered and melted, dropping before they got close enough to strike with a blade.

"Why didn't you do that before?" asked Bruenna.

Glissa shrugged. "Magic is a delicate art form," she said, a smile blossoming on her face. "It takes a lot of concentration—"

"You mock me now, but—" Bruenna was interrupted by a clawing nim. She cut the shambling beast in half then continued. "We should have this conversation later—" she glanced around, indicating the battle raging around them— "perhaps when we're not in such immediate danger."

Straight ahead, Glissa spotted Bosh, his head rising high above the rest of the battle. Al-Hayat stood beside him, Slobad on his shoulders. They were surrounded by a ring of attackers, metal and putrid flesh alike.

Meanwhile, all around, nim battled with levelers.

"So they haven't stopped attacking us," said Glissa, "but they *have* started attacking the levelers as well."

"To their eyes, we all look like invaders," replied Bruenna. "The nim don't care much for who is chasing whom. As long as we're in their swamp, they'll fight to keep us all out."

Glissa bashed aside another shambling undead. "Then let's let the nim deal with the levelers."

* * * * *

Malil stood knee deep in rotten flesh. He had no conflict with these creatures. Why were they getting in his way? Didn't they know who he was? Didn't they know how badly he needed to get the elf girl?

The metal man raised a heavy sword in one hand and brought

it down on an advancing group of zombies. Gummy flesh parted, and the oncoming ghouls fell to the ground in a bloody mess.

"Flesh is weak," snarled Malil, cutting down another score of slogging creatures with a single flick of his wrist. "You will not stand in my way."

The rest of his levelers were having an equally easy time with thenim, but the sheer numbers were staggering. Where a scythe blade cut one down, two more stepped up to take its place. There was an unending supply for these undead creatures, and they swarmed in. To make matters worse, in order to stop them from coming, a leveler had to cut the beast to shreds. Simple wounds didn't stop their advance as they did with elves or humans—or sometimes other levelers.

"Damn," shouted Malil.

He didn't mind cutting down the beasts. He didn't care who he had to slay to get what he wanted, but all this fighting was inefficient. He didn't care if these creatures lived or died. He'd be glad to oblige them if what they wanted was a second death. Right now all he wanted was the elf girl.

But he couldn't reach her.

He'd waited in this miserable swamp, separated from his master and the serum he desired, now only to be stopped by piles and piles of weak, rotting flesh.

Across the battlefield, Malil could see the elf and her companions. They too fought the nim.

"They like no one," he said, taking the head from a desiccated figure that looked as if it once might have been an elf.

It appeared as if the elf was making her way toward the swamp. Caught between Malil and the nim, Glissa had chosen the undead, and now they were trying to once again get away from him. Driven by his desire, Malil pressed forward, urging his troops to cut their way to his prize. But the harder he fought the more his devices were mired in putrid flesh, and his levelers came to a lurching halt.

As Glissa disappeared over the edge of the slope, down toward the swamp, Malil felt his burning desire well up again in his belly.

"I must have her," he said to an undead humanlike creature. Malil stabbed his greatsword through the creature's belly and pulled it straight up, cutting the beast in half. "I must. I must."

* * * * *

Slipping over the lip of the slope, the only living flesh creatures in all of Mephidross fought their way toward the water. It was a hard fight, and Glissa's sword arm was nearly numb from smashing nim to bits.

Bruenna had lost many of her wizards in the battle, but she had managed to consolidate the remaining few, and the group followed the elf down toward the swamp. Al-Hayat and Slobad were next, and Bosh came last.

The big, mostly metal golem moved from the plain onto the downward slope. The ground was slick with vile things—rotten organs, broken shards of bone, melted flaps of rubbery flesh, black fluids, red gobs of meat, and yellow bits of putrescence. Bosh stepped on a pile of this slippery stuff, and his foot slid out from under him. His arms flailing, he tried to bring his other foot around, but it too sank into the filth. With a tremendous clank, the iron golem hit the ground on his back.

"Look out," shouted Slobad. The goblin pointed to the falling golem.

His arms waving and his legs kicked up in the air, Bosh slid down the steep slope, hydroplaning on a layer of filth.

Ruined zombies worked better than grease at lubricating metal, and the big guy picked up speed as he skidded toward the swamp.

Ten paces down Bosh crashed into a line of advancing undead. Even with eight legs, the creatures weren't nimble enough to get from the way of the sliding golem. With a crunch and a splat, Bosh ran over them, squashing the nim flat against the hill and adding more lubrication to his decent.

Glissa watched this out of control slide. Where he slid, he cut a swath, and in his wake, Bosh left a wide corridor in the middle of the marching, gas-belching nim.

"Come on," shouted the elf. Waving her hand over her shoulder to indicate the way, Glissa jumped into the air. Kicking her legs out in front of her, she landed on her rear and slid after the golem.

The filthy swamp smell was nothing compared to the odor coming off of the flattened nim. Glissa tried to hold her breath, but it was hard enough to stay upright. Using her sword as a rudder, she sat up, moving around the larger chunks as she slid toward the swamp. Down and down she went, picking up speed.

Ahead, Bosh tumbled over once, crushing more undead into paste. The slow moving swamp creatures couldn't get out of his way fast enough, and a mound of ruined bodies piled up before him as he approached the bottom. With a splash the giant golem slipped into the briny liquid at the edge of the swamp. A wave of black swill shot into the air. Tendrils of the stuff separated, reaching up over Bosh like a skeletal hand.

The splashed swamp water peaked. The top curled over, making the hand look like a gaping, hungry mouth. Then it fell back down to the earth with a tremendous clap. The black, viscous slime completely devoured Bosh, and he disappeared from view.

Glissa didn't have time to even blink after that. Scratching, clawing, and digging into the ground with her sword, she still couldn't slow her descent.

Here I go, she thought. Then her feet hit the slime, and all went black as her head slipped under.

CHAPTER 15

Memnarch stood at the window of his laboratory. A light breeze rattled the jagged bits of glass, reaching in through where the window had been to brush against his flesh. The cool air felt good against his hot skin, and he breathed it in, calming himself.

Out in the interior of Mirrodin, the mana core crackled and sparked. It was pregnant with energy, and soon it would release it. Already the blue-white sphere had begun to take on a greenish tinge. Time was getting short.

When the mana core did finally erupt, it would shake the foundations of the world, unleashing terrible force and temporarily unbalancing the perfection of Mirrodin.

The perfection of Mirrodin. Memnarch shook his head. The perfection of Mirrodin indeed. It was a myth. This world had never been perfect. Mirrodin had always had one fatal flaw—it wasn't a natural world. This plane, like so many others around the multiverse, was a creation of a planeswalker. But for all their magic and wisdom, the most powerful beings in all of Dominia had never been able to create stable worlds.

Many a day had Memnarch stood and pondered this conundrum.

His creator, his god Karn, had the power to forge whole worlds from nothing more than a thought. Unless he stayed on his world, though, maintaining it through his own force of will, it would collapse, imploding like an overripe star.

Karn had not been back to Mirrodin in a very long time.

The stuff of perfection was unstable. Could something that did not last truly be considered perfect? Was there such a thing as temporary perfection? Memnarch hoped so. But what really boggled his much-enhanced mind was the thought of natural worlds. If Karn could not create a stable world, then who could?

There were worlds beyond this one. Many, many worlds in fact. Memnarch had seen some of them. He had visited a few when the Creator had seen fit to take him along. These worlds did not collapse. They did not need a planeswalker to maintain their existence.

That meant Memnarch's creator had a creator. In fact, Karn had spoken of another planeswalker, a man named Urza, who had created him. But if Memnarch's Creator had a creator, then perhaps that Creator had a creator as well. And that Creator likely had a creator and he a creator too…. Could it really go on and on forever? There must be a starting point—one true Creator who created all other creators. If that were true, then how did that Creator come to be . . . created?

Memnarch's head hurt. He'd been down this line of reasoning so many times, and each time he reached this very same point, the point at which he no longer cared to think about it any longer.

That wasn't why his head hurt. It had been a long time since his last serum infusion. His mind ached for the lift, the joy, the mental strength that an infusion gave him.

He turned his enhanced gaze back out over the interior of the plane, trying to put that thought out of his mind. A giant blue-green spark arced through the air, hissing as it orbited the glowing orb. Then, with a popping sound, the energy dived back into the surface of the mana core.

The super-charged interior sun of Mirrodin had erupted exactly four times since its creation. Each time it created one of the four moons. There was one for each color: white, blue, black, red—but not green.

Green would be the next.

When the time came, another lacuna would be created. The mana core would shoot out a glowing ball of plasma with such force and with such heat that it would burn straight through the mile-thick, solid metal crust of the plane. The new moon would breach the surface and rocket off into the sky, joining the other four moons and falling into its natural orbit around the plane.

Once the moon punched through the crust and shot off into the atmosphere, it would find its place among the other moons. Each of them would push or pull on it, as if they were magnets. The moon would wobble back and forth, finally settling into its place among the others. Until that happened, the forces of nature would be terribly out of balance.

First, the blinkmoths would disappear. There was nothing about the plane of Mirrodin the Memnarch did not understand— except where the blinkmoths went during that first moon cycle. He couldn't explain it. After witnessing it the first two times, and being without serum for an entire moon cycle, he'd scoured the entire plane, inside and out. There was just no logical place for them to go. They simply left Mirrodin.

Memnarch was fully aware of the power of magic. He considered himself an accomplished spellcaster. But there were no spells to his knowledge that could move a creature from one plane to another. Only planeswalkers could do that.

He doubted very much that the blinkmoths were planeswalkers.

Wherever they went, it was a mystery to Memnarch.

The next noticeable change after the new lacuna would be the irregular moon orbits. As the green moon worked its way into it natural rotation, the others would be pushed and pulled in and out of their own orbits. Days and nights would blend together. At first there would be two short periods of light followed by two equally short periods of darkness. It would be a relief to the surface dwellers after having endured the long, hot days and the pitch-black nights of the Convergence. Still, the constant rising and setting of the moons would make sleep hard to come by, and it would put all of the wild animals in a frenzy. Their mating, hibernating, and hunting habits would be confused.

That all would pass.

Eventually, though, things would settle back into their normal rhythms. It always amused Memnarch to see how regular and predictable the organic creatures were. They loved their patterns and their rituals. Everything needed to be just the way it always had been for the past generations. Of course, it never really was exactly the same. Things changed, slowly—imperceptibly to the mortal folks. That was the beauty of evolution. Things improved, much like Memnarch had improved himself.

There was devolution as well.

Whatever had caused the mycosynth growths had also caused what Memnarch referred to as the "Spore." The Spore was a virus. It attacked metal, got into places it shouldn't be, and it broke things down. The Spore tarnished what little perfection Memnarch had to hold onto. It caused flesh to evolve into metal.

It caused metal to devolve into flesh.

Memnarch suspected that the Spore existed for a very long time, but he couldn't be sure. He assumed that it appeared after Master Karn had left Mirrodin. A planeswalker would have noticed such a virus in his own plane and eradicated it. He also knew that the Spore either originated in the mana core or was fed by the waves of energy it gave off. The mycosynth only grew on the interior of the plane, and each of the towering chrome spires reached toward the glowing blue-white orb, grabbing for it like greedy fingers.

As time passed, Memnarch had ever so slowly become more fleshy. He could only hope that when he ascended, found the spark and became a planeswalker, that he would be able to overcome the effects of the Spore and destroy them before they destroyed the plane.

That was where the elf girl came in.

She had the spark—that vital piece of a person's soul, the one in a million difference that made her capable of becoming a planeswalker. Given the right circumstances, she could ascend herself.

Master Karn had once spoken of ascending. He had told Memnarch of how it had happened during a terrible fight on another world. Before the Creator had become a god, he had been a metal golem—a creation just like Memnarch.

In the story, Master Karn spoke of an invasion of his home world by a sickness. He called it the Phyrexian Plague. Memnarch knew nothing more about it, but he imagined it was much like the mycosynth and resulting Spore here on Mirrodin.

This plague had taken hold of the world to such an extent that Karn and his master had been forced to build a last-ditch weapon—one that required them to sacrifice themselves in order to use it. Both creator and creation willing sacrificed themselves for the good of those left on the plane.

While the blast of the weapon vaporized the planeswalker creator, it did something different to the metal golem Karn. Maybe it was the trauma of being seared by a beam of holy light so powerful it could cleanse an entire planet of a virulent plague in one blast, or maybe it was the heroic action the metal golem had chosen. Whatever the cause, Master Karn ascended. His metal golem body was destroyed in the blast, but a new body was formed—one of quicksilver, one that with just a thought could walk among the stars.

Memnarch smiled at the thought. That was what he was planning to do, vaporize his own body and become a planeswalker. He did not have a super weapon, but he had something just as good—the mana core.

When the green moon was birthed from the surface of the interior sun, it would strike the shell of the plane and burn its way out. Using the information he'd collected from the other moons, Memnarch had pinpointed the exact location of where the eruption would occur.

He had built Panopticon precisely on top of this spot.

That eruption would provide the catastrophic power needed to destroy Memnarch's body. He'd have the elf girl with him when the blast hit his tower, and just like Master Karn, the planeswalker would perish—and the created metal man would ascend.

"A perfect plan," he said.

Turning away from the broken window, Memnarch made his way over to the Darksteel Eye, hoping to catch a glimpse of the elf girl.

* * * * *

Marek walked though the curved corridors of Lumengrid, on his way to finalize his preparations to leave with Pontifex. Taking a sharp corner, he nearly ran straight into councilor Orland.

"Whoa," said the councilor, losing his balance. "Marek, where are you off to in such a hurry."

"Excuse me, Councilor," he said. "Please forgive my haste." He bowed and stepped around Orland.

The councilor reached his arm out, blocking Marek's path. "Must you go so soon?"

Marek looked back over his shoulder, but the corridor was clear. "We should not been seen together," he said.

Orland smiled. "Relax, Marek. There is nothing odd about a member of the Synod talking to a guardsman."

Marek checked the hallway. "You know as well as I that Lord Pontifex did not get where he is by being careless and overly trusting." He gave Orland a cold stare. "Even my years of service do not lift me above his scrutiny." He looked the councilor over from head to toe. "You risk my life by detaining me."

Orland looked surprised. "It was quite by accident that I have run into you here, Marek." The councilor flashed a winning smile. "I was just on my way to see Councilor Sodador." He pointed behind Marek.

"Yes, I am aware of where Councilor Sodador resides, Orland. Don't treat me like a fool or waste my time. This meeting was no accident, so tell me what it is you want."

Orland nodded. "Yes, forgive me." Lowering his forehead, the councilor looked up, past the ridges of his creased brow. "I have it on good authority that you, my friend, would like to see the Synod dissolve and the vedalken people rule themselves."

"Where did you hear that?"

Orland smiled. "A little squid told me."

"Is that so?"

The councilor nodded. "It is, but I don't put much stock in rumors, so I came to find out for myself."

Marek straightened himself up, standing at attention. "You have the wrong vedalken, Councilor."

Now it was Orland's turn to look Marek over from head to toe. "I don't think I do." He shook his head. "No, I think a man who has spent his life protecting the vedalken empire's ruling class might have seen a thing or two. Someone like that might have his reasons to want to see a change in the way things get done."

Marek softened. "And?"

Orland smiled. "And I need to know: When the time comes, can I count on you, Marek?" The councilor leaned in closer to the warrior. "Are you willing to fight for yourself as hard as you've fought for Lord Pontifex?"

CHAPTER 16

Slobad looked down the slope at the black swamp that had just swallowed Glissa.

"What crazy elf do now? She think we follow her, huh?"

Al-Hayat nodded. "Yes." With his muzzle, the great forest beast gave the goblin a shove.

Slobad slipped down the slope. Flipping over on his stomach, he scrambled over broken bones, treading the ruined flesh as if it were water. Climbing back to the top of the slope, the goblin scowled at the wolf.

"Slobad not like so much, huh?"

Al-Hayat shook his head. Grabbing Slobad by the back of the neck, the wolf lifted him in the air and turned him toward the battle taking place behind them. Nim swarmed over levelers. Bruenna and the few remaining wizards had all left the field and were making their way through the remaining undead toward the swamp, following the elf into the filth.

"Behind, all that awaits us is death," explained Al-Hayat through closed teeth.

"Ahead only filth and rot, huh?" replied Slobad, dangling from the wolf's fangs.

Al-Hayat set the goblin back down on his own feet. "But in that filth lies potential," he explained. "We may yet live to see another day—or even a world free of Memnarch. Isn't that worth getting dirty for?"

Slobad looked back over the battlefield. The nim had the levelers bogged down, but it wouldn't take long for them to cut their way through. Turning around he looked down at the swamp. The swath Bosh had cut through the horde of undead was beginning to narrow as the shambling beasts closed ranks.

"Since you put it that way." The goblin threw up his hands and jumped into the air.

Landing on his rump, the rumpled, green creature slid down the slope. Beside him, Bruenna's wizards charged down the hill. One hovered as he descended, using magic to slow his descent. Two more took the same way as Slobad, using the sloughing pool of liquefied flesh as a quick route to the bottom.

The other three fought and died as they tangled with too many nim. Their bodies were slowly ripped to shreds, and their remains were devoured by the hungry undead.

Slobad swallowed hard, trying to keep the contents of his stomach from coming up. He'd seen many unsettling things in his life, but this was by far the worst.

Below him, the swamp came up fast. Looking over his shoulder, he caught a glimpse of Al-Hayat, slipping down the slope in the most awkward, uncontrolled fashion imaginable. Each of the wolf's four legs went in a different direction, and his whole body spun as he picked up speed. Scrambling with his front legs, he managed to keep his head above the layer of rotten flesh—but only for a moment. Then his feet hit a slick patch, and they parted, each going the opposite way of the other.

Al-Hayat's proud muzzle slapped to the ground, sending a wave of black filth into the air. His rear end slipped sideways, and the wolf careened backward down the hill toward Slobad.

The goblin laughed, seeing the majestic forest beast in such an undignified position. Then the cold, wet swamp hit his feet, and Slobad could see no more of the wolf, as he plunged under. His mouth filled with foul liquid, and his whole body seized up in disgust. Sinking quickly to the bottom, the goblin slid deeper into the swamp.

No longer able to control his gag reflex, Slobad puked, the vomit forcing the swamp water from his mouth.

Never before had the contents of his belly tasted so sweet on their way up.

* * * * *

In the Tangle, deep puddles of water collected under the biggest trees. All manner of creatures gathered there to drink or bath. When Glissa was young, she and Kane would climb up the tallest tree they could find and jump off into these puddles, scaring away all the other animals.

Once her head slipped under the surface of the swamp water, she tried to pretend she was back in the Tangle, jumping into a puddle. The image worked, for a time. Unlike those carefree days as a youth, now she was in real danger, and the water in the swamp was . . . like nothing else she'd ever encountered. Bits of debris touched her skin as she descended. At one point, it felt as though a fish were nibbling at the tiny hairs on her legs. Something told her that whatever it was, it wasn't a simple fish.

Her careening slide had been slowed upon impact with the swamp, and she had glided gently under the water. But where she thought she should reach a stop, she just kept going, sliding deeper and deeper with each passing second. Her breath began to run short, but she fought the urge to open her eyes.

The last time she had been in the Dross, she and Slobad had found Bosh. He had been buried in the filth that was now sucking her down. When they had run across him, she had wondered how such a creature could be devoured by a swampy liquid. Now she knew.

When she had hit the water, she felt her body twist. Stuck somewhere between the bottom and the surface, not sure of which way she was facing, she had no idea how deep she was nor which way was up. She'd hoped, like she had in the Tangle, that once she fell still, she'd start to float back to the surface. Without stopping, she wouldn't know which direction to swim. Why wasn't she stopping?

Realization came to her in a flash, and fear gripped her chest. A current! The swamp, like the Quicksilver Sea, had underwater currents, and this one was pulling her down.

Throwing her arms out wide, she reached in all directions, hoping to find the bottom or breach the surface—anything that could tell her which way was up. Her left hand struck something, but when she reached, it slipped away. All she could find was more of the viscous liquid that surrounded her and held her tight.

The deeper she slid the colder the water grew. The current picked up, and she felt her body pick up speed as she sank even deeper into the swamp. The air in her lungs burned, and the pressure of the water on her ears increased. She felt as if a giant were squeezing her head between his two mighty palms, and sharp pains blossomed in spots all over the inside of her skull.

The pain grew, and Glissa flailed. Panic filled her from head to toe.

* * * * *

Visions flashed in front of her eyes in rapid succession, and Glissa temporarily left this world as a flare consumed her.

She saw her mother standing in a tree in the Tangle. Then she saw Slobad, tinkering with a leveler, his hands and face covered in grease. Bruenna, Al-Hayat, and Chunth the troll appeared to her then just as quickly slipped away.

Bosh edged all the other images from her mind. He stood before her, his hands bleeding. He looked sad. Instead of his stoic and immovable expression, his mouth was actually in a frown, and his eyes seemed sunken. He looked right at her. Behind him Glissa could see the interior of Mirrodin. The bright mana core was high overhead, and the tower Bosh had called Panopticon was in the near distance.

In the vision, the half-flesh, half-iron golem's lips turned up, and he smiled at her, though his eyes remained sad. He turned and walked off, toward Panopticon.

* * * * *

Glissa felt the back of her head hit something, and she came out of the flare. She was moving at a tremendous clip now, and her fingers and toes were touching the edge of something. She was still under water, now surrounded on all sides by curved metal.

The rushing current carried her through a series of twists and turns. Each time the direction changed, her head hit the surrounding wall. The crashing impacts threatened to knock the air from her lungs, but she held tight, despite every urge to let go and just pass out.

She felt her feet skid along the bottom then slip free. Then she was falling through air. Her head broke from the swamp water, and reflexively she gasped in a breath. Flecks of the fetid swamp water sprinkled over her tongue, but she didn't care. The air exhilarated her, forcing the panic away, and now she could feel the wild beating of her heart.

Dragging her hand across her face, Glissa opened her eyes in time to see a huge lake of swamp water coming up fast below her. Gasping, she gathered in one more precious breath before splashing again into darkness.

Down and down she sank. From what she could tell, she'd fallen a long way. Bubbling, frothing air accompanied her as she plunged. Slowing, the bubbles peeled off, one at a time, rising again toward the surface, and Glissa could feel herself come to a stop—the way she'd hoped she would when she had started into the swamp in the first place.

The air in her lungs buoyed her, and she rose. Her legs felt week from the cold water and lack of air, but she kicked with all the energy she had left. It seemed an eternity, stuck in the syrupy swamp water, then her head breached the surface, and once again she drew in breath.

The edge of the lake wasn't far off, and Glissa swam to it, lifting herself gratefully from the water and resting her body on the firm metal ground. Lying there on her back, she breathed in huge gulps of air. There was water in her lungs, and as she sucked in, she could hear a thick rattling in her chest. She turned her head and coughed, trying to force out the liquid. Her hacking dislodged a big piece of flemmy gook, and she spit it out on the ground.

Rolling again to her back, she looked up to see how far she'd fallen.

High above, a series of intertwining grimy pipes covered the walls. They wound around each other, shooting off in all directions and crossing over to cover the ceiling, obscuring it from view. Black water and bits of refuse dripped from every pipe, but there was no doubt where Glissa had entered this room.

One of the pipes had a huge, gaping hole in the bottom. From it issued a heavy waterfall of putrid fluid. Beads of black liquid bursts apart, separating from the rest of the flood on the fall, finally coming down to splash into the underground lake that had caught Glissa on her plunge.

Pallid, yellow-green light filled the chamber. Glissa couldn't see where it was coming from, but the room was bright. Slipping over onto her belly, the elf lifted her head. The lake took up most of the chamber. Around it, a metal shelf ran around the outside of the room just wide enough for three elves to stand side by side. The pipes that ran all the way up the walls and across the ceiling jutted from the ground on the outside of this walkway.

To her left, behind a space between two of these pipes, was what looked like a tunnel leading out. Beside it sat Bosh. His partially rusted body blended flawlessly with the tubes, making him nearly disappear into the background.

"Bo—" Glissa's voice was raw, and there was swamp water in her throat. Burping and spitting out as much of the foul fluid as she could, the elf coughed out her words. "Bosh. Are you okay?"

"Yes," he said. He pointed to the waterfall above. "I fell."

"Me too," she said. Getting to her feet, she traversed the walkway over to the iron golem.

"I know," he said. "I watched you." He continued to sit on the floor as Glissa approached.

She looked him over, and he looked back, but he didn't move. "Are you sure you're okay?"

The golem nodded. "Yes, but I feel weak. I would like to rest for a moment."

Glissa nodded and sat down beside him. "What do you think this place is?"

Bosh shook his head. "I don't know. I've never been here before."

"Well, wherever it is, it's deep under the swamp." She breathed. Her lungs still rattled a bit, but she was improving. "It's a good thing there was a hole in that pipe. Who knows where it leads, and I don't think I could have made it much longer without any air."

"There was not a hole there," said Bosh. "I got stuck going around a corner and smashed it open."

"Then you saved both of our lives."

Bosh looked down at her then back up at the waterfall. "Yes."

Just then a large piece of debris plummeted from the ceiling. Glissa watched it fall, tracking its course toward the underground lake. It was round and wrinkly, and it toppled end over end. It sprouted arms and began to flail.

Glissa jumped to her feet. "Slobad!"

The goblin didn't hear her. His eyes were so wide that Glissa could see his pupils from where she was standing.

The elf turned toward the golem. "We should do something."

Bosh began to get to his feet. "What?"

Glissa shrugged and turned back in time to watch the goblin hit the lake with a loud slap. "Fish him out. He'll drown!" She circled around the narrow walkway closer to where he landed.

Round waves moved out from where Slobad had impacted the underground lake. The swamp water moved slowly, dampening the splash because it was so thick and dense. Glissa watched the center of the waves, waiting for Slobad's head to pop up, reassure her that he didn't get crushed when he landed, or drowned shortly there after.

"Where is he?" she said, nervously scanning the water.

Bosh clomped up behind her. "I do not see him."

A chunk of something surfaced near the impact point.

"There," pointed Glissa. "Is that him? We've got to get him out."

Bosh leaned over, trying to get a closer look. "I do not think so. It's too small."

"Too small? He's a goblin."

Bosh shrugged. "If that is him, it is only his head."

Glissa scowled at the golem, but he paid her no mind.

Near the center of the lake, bubbles started to rise and breach the surface. They were small at first, but they grew in size and frequency. Pretty soon the lake seemed as if it were going to boil, starting with the very middle and moving out slowly to the edges.

Glissa took a step back from the lake. "I don't think that's Slobad."

"Nor I," replied Bosh.

Both the elf and the golem flattened themselves against the wall. Then Glissa spotted something at the far end.

"Look," she shouted.

"That is him," confirmed Bosh.

The two took off at a run.

Slobad had surfaced on the other side of the rising storm of bubbles and was swimming toward the farthest edge of the lake, on the opposite side. His little arms didn't carry him very fast, and the burbling dome threatened to overtake him in only a few strokes.

Glissa bunched her fists as she ran. Whipping around the end of the lake, she and Bosh closed in on their friend. Slobad reached the edge, and grabbed hold of the walkway. Behind him, the bubbles peaked then stopped altogether as swamp water shot into the air.

A column of tarnished metal rose from the lake. Putrid, black water streamed from its sides, clinging to every crease and seam, uselessly trying to pull back into the depths something that could not be contained.

The metal monstrosity climbed into the air, nearly four times the height of Bosh. It looked like the trunk of a tree or the mycosynth on the interior of Mirrodin—only this thing was pitch black, and completely cylindrical. Then it opened up in front, seeming to uncross hundreds of folded arms—each one a razor-sharp blade.

"A giant centipede." Glissa whispered out the words, fearing that saying them any louder would make the creature more menacingly real than it already was.

As it unfolded, the creature's face and head came into view. On top, long, thick antennae sprouted, twitching this way and that. Under those, two beady, pulsing red eyes scanned the room. It had no nose or mouth to speak of, at least not on its face.

With the grinding sound of metal on metal, the centipede scissored its arms closed then back open, like a zipper. Undulating from the top to the bottom, a wave raced down the creature's body. With each passing curve, hundreds of blades slid closed then open again, ready to cut to shreds anything that came close.

The creature swung its head around, two beady little eyes scanning the chamber. When they crossed over Slobad, Bosh, and Glissa, the centipede reeled back. Then it came flying forward, its scissor arms moving at double speed.

"Grab Slobad," shouted Glissa, bolting for the goblin.

Bosh beat her to him. At a full run, the golem reached his huge hand down into the muck. Scooping a handful of water from the lake, he ran on at top speed. Black swamp muck drained from his palm, leaving Slobad in a heap against the golem's closed fingers.

Seeing that Bosh had the goblin, Glissa skidded to a halt. The centipede's head was high in the air, but it came down on the trio in a blink. Backpedaling, the elf fell away, letting Bosh and Slobad go off in one direction while she turned and ran in the other.

The centipede's head whipped down, slamming into the edge of the lake—right where Slobad had been only moments before. The impact shook the chamber, and Glissa was thrown to the ground. Looking back, she could see the centipede's head buried deep in the dented walkway. On the other side were Bosh and Slobad. They had escaped, but they were separated from her by the monstrous bug.

That would be a fitting way to die for a goblin, thought Glissa as she scrambled to get away from the centipede.

Once again on her feet, she shouted over her shoulder. "Run to the passage. I'll meet you there."

If there was a reply, she didn't hear it, because the centipede pulled its head out, bending the complaining metal of the walkway as it did. The motion filled the entire chamber with a wretched squealing that vibrated down Glissa's spine and rattled the metal on her legs and forearms.

Freed from the dented walkway, the centipede reeled back again, shaking its head side to side. It looked at Glissa then at Bosh and finally turned its attentions back on the elf.

Glissa's lungs were starting to hurt again. She could feel the water she'd inhaled on the way down the tube. With every breath it felt as if someone were stabbing a sharp fingernail into her chest. Worse, she could feel a bit of liquid floating around in there, bubbling away with each inhale.

With a quick flick of its long body, part of which was still concealed under the black water, the centipede closed in on Glissa. Tilting its head, it coiled the top of its chest, like a snake about to strike.

Glissa watched it do this, and her heart skipped a beat. It was so big. She didn't see how it could miss her.

Watching the monster instead of the walkway, Glissa tripped and went sprawling onto her face. The room got darker as the monster's shadow grew around her. Rolling over onto her back, the elf looked up at the scissoring blades as they came crashing down on top of her.

CHAPTER 17

The centipede was huge and so very fast. The creature's razor sharp arms opened wide, and Glissa closed her eyes, not wanting to watch them as they tore into her flesh. Metal screeched. A whoosh of air rushed through the elf's hair, followed by a shower of foul smelling swamp water that stung her face.

Glissa opened her eyes. She was still alive. The centipede's opened arms had crashed into the walkway, burying themselves up to the elbow. The floor had kept the blades from scissoring closed around her, but now the bulk of the creature's body was on top of her, squeezing her life away.

The centipede's great bulk threatened to pop Glissa like a grape. Her chest was restricted, and her arms were pinned to the ground. She couldn't breathe, except in quick short breaths, and she could feel all the blood in her body being pressed into her head.

The giant bug twisted and pulled, shaking the platform as it did. Metal complained, and its arms lifted a few centimeters. Relief flooded through the elf's body. She took in a deeper breath, and the pressure in her head subsided. Then that relief gave way to the reality of her situation. The centipede was struggling. It was only a matter of time before the blades were free, and then they would close—catching her in between.

Taking stock, she looked for a way out. To her left, a hundred killing blades waited for her, barring her escape. To her right, more of the same. She tried to lift her sword, but it was too long, and she couldn't get it into a useful position, and even if she could, what good would it do against such a creature?

The floor heaved again, and the centipede lifted another six inches, releasing her enough to pull her arms to her chest. Still, she was trapped. One more good heave by the centipede and its scissoring arms would be free of the platform, ready to cut her into little bite-sized chunks.

A rhythmic tinkling sound, like a set of wind chimes, rang through the confined space between the centipede's chest and the floor. Shards of metal cascaded over Glissa, and a huge hand reached in and grabbed her by the shoulder.

"Time to go," said Bosh.

Though part of him was becoming fleshy, his feet were still metal, and he'd kicked through two dozen of the centipede's razor-sharp arms.

"I couldn't agree more," replied Glissa. With Bosh's help she pushed the ground, sliding out from under the big bug.

Free of her prison, Glissa got to her feet and ran, Bosh right beside her. Behind them, Glissa could hear the walkway complain as the centipede heaved again. Metal shrieked, and the creature let out a high-pitched squeal. The elf didn't know what it meant, but she was pretty sure it wasn't good.

Up ahead, Slobad was waiting in the opening between the pipes, but he was distracted by something. His eyes were glued to the ceiling, and he was wringing his hands. Glissa followed his gaze.

"Oh, no."

There, seemingly stuck in the hole Bosh had punched through the pipe on the ceiling, hung Al-Hayat. His back legs were tangled up. His front paws flailed, and his whole body swung. With each swing, the wolf lifted his head to bite at something near his tangled back feet. Back and forth he went, and Glissa watched, unable to do anything for her friend.

Al-Hayat caught whatever it was that he'd been trying to reach, and the wolf slipped free, plunging toward the underground lake.

"Bosh!" shouted Glissa over her shoulder. "We've got to keep the centipede busy long enough for Al-Hayat to get out of the lake."

"How?"

She stopped running and turned to face the golem. "We keep its attention focused on us."

Over Bosh's shoulder, Glissa could see that the centipede had retreated a bit. It followed her and the golem with its beady eyes, but it hadn't given immediate chase. Perhaps Bosh's attack had been more damaging than it appeared. Glissa could clearly see the blank spot on the creature's left side where it was now missing several of its limbs. Still, in the grand scheme, the damaged blades were only a tiny fraction of the centipede's legs. It still had hundreds, if not thousands more.

Its attention wholly on the elf and the golem, the big bug clearly hadn't seen the falling wolf, and this gave Glissa a small amount of confidence.

"Hey, bug face," she shouted, waving her hands over her head. "We're over here. A tasty meal, just the way you like it."

Bosh stopped beside her and turned. "Do you really think it is a good idea to taunt such a creature?"

"It's not chasing us."

The centipede stared at her, unmoving—no, it was moving. Now that she looked at it again, Glissa realized that the creature was rising higher from the water. Its head rose farther into the air, and its body just kept coming and coming—no end in sight.

"No wonder its not chasing us. It doesn't have to," she said, gripping the hilt of her sword tight in her hand. "It can reach us from anywhere."

As if the centipede heard the elf's words, it reared its head back and flung itself at the pair.

"Jump," shouted the elf.

Both she and the golem leaped into the lake. Glissa's head dropped below the surface, and she could feel the dull thud of the centipede's head impacting the walkway.

Blindly she swam back toward the edge of the lake, staying underwater the whole way. The trick was going to be surfacing without coming up underneath the bug's scissoring arms. There was very little more she could do other than guess. When her hand reached the edge, she slid two full arm lengths to her right then poked the tip of her sword from the water. It hit nothing, and she lifted her head.

She had guessed right.

The creature had impacted the walkway just to her left. Its giant head lay in the indentation its smashing attack had made, and it struggled again to free itself.

Tossing her sword up onto the shore, Glissa took the opportunity to pull herself from the water. It was a struggle. She was tired now, and even breathing seemed like a tremendous effort. Finally, she got out and onto her feet. Picking up her sword, she scooted along the wall, keeping her back to the pipes. The centipede, so busy pulling its head out, didn't immediately notice her, and she rested against the wall, scanning the water for Al-Hayat.

The last time she looked, he'd been falling. She hadn't seen him land, but she knew it would be near where she saw Slobad hit. And sure enough, she spotted the wolf in the middle of the lake dog paddling toward her.

At least he was headed in the right direction she thought, as she turned her attention back to the centipede. The creature had lifted its head again and was scanning the walkway. It hadn't spotted her yet, but it would. Both she and Bosh needed to be— where was Bosh?

Glissa scanned the walkway and the edge of the lake. He was nowhere. She'd lost him when they jumped into the lake. She was pretty sure he'd made it out from under the centipede. His flattened body wasn't smashed to the bottom of the indentation the big bug had left with its last slam. Where could he be?

Just then bodies began to rain from the sky. Falling from the hole in the pipes, four human-shaped creatures flailed. Each of them was covered in the same oily sludge that Glissa was. They plummeted toward the lake, right in front of the centipede.

This time the big bug saw the falling creatures, and it turned to watch them fall. As it spun its head, Glissa caught a glimpse of something shiny on its back.

Her jaw dropped. "Bosh."

The iron golem hadn't jumped into the water. He had jumped onto the centipede's back, and now he was climbing toward the creature's head.

Slobad was suddenly at her side. "Crazy golem gonna get killed, huh?"

"Let's hope not."

Halfway to the lake, the falling figures slowed their decent and began to float in midair.

"It's Bruenna," shouted Slobad, jumping up and down and pointing.

Glissa looked up at where the goblin was pointing. Sure

enough, though her face was covered in slime, it was clearly Bruenna. Even from here, the elf could see that the human wizard was chanting something, and she hoped it was a spell that would destroy or immobilize the centipede.

The bug watched the flying humans, its scissoring arms opening and closing in anticipation. It reared back and lunged.

Glissa cringed, and Slobad squeezed her leg.

The flying wizards all darted away, avoiding the creature's bladed arms. But the rush of air from the centipede's attack knocked the whole group of them sideways in twisting gulf-streams. To Glissa they looked like a swarm of flies being swatted by a giant.

The swamp creature, its head bent, its body curled over like a question mark, tried to steady itself. Bosh held onto its back for dear life, pressing his face against the centipede's metallic hide and squeezing with all of his might.

The bug straightened itself and scanned the room. Bosh took advantage of the momentary lull, climbing higher up to reach the back of its head. Grabbing hold of the centipede's wavering antennae with both hands, the iron golem pushed away from the bug's body with his powerful legs. He swung out then back, gaining momentum as he came, and kicked the creature with his right foot.

A loud clang rocketed through the chamber, echoing off the walls and ringing off the pipes. The centipede whipped its head side to side, and Bosh flailed around, still holding tight to the creature's antennae.

Next to the flailing beast, the huge iron golem looked like a child's toy. Hanging on for dear life, his body was flung this way and that. His limbs flapped wildly, and the only evidence that he wasn't already dead from the thrashing was the fact that he still clung to the centipede. Each time the bug twisted in a different direction, Bosh's body struck its hide, clanging like a tolling bell.

The swamp beast continued to flop, showing no sign of slowing, and the rest of its body got into the act. The length still under the dark waters thrashed, turning the thick underground lake into a frothing mess. Swamp water flooded up onto the walkway, washing against the walls and splashing up on the already wet companions.

Bruenna and her wizards steered as far away from the angered beast as they could, coming down on the pathway beside Glissa and Slobad, not far from the tunnel leading from this room.

"We must flee," said the human wizard as she came into earshot of Glissa.

Glissa nodded. "Not without Bosh."

Bruenna put her hand on the elf's shoulder. "What he does, he does as a gift. Don't let his bravery be lost." She guided Glissa toward the tunnel.

The human wizards filed into the passage. One scouted down a ways, disappearing from view. Glissa reluctantly let herself be pulled toward the opening, glancing up at Bosh with every step.

The golem remained stubbornly attached to the thrashing centipede.

Glissa glanced down. Slobad clung to her thigh. With every step she took, he took two, and now the goblin looked up into her eyes. They were sad, scared. He looked like she felt. Reaching down, she grabbed hold of the goblin's hand. She expected him to say something, but all she got was a tight squeeze. He knew what was going through her mind. It was going through his as well. There was no need to say the words.

The elf and goblin crossed into the tunnel. As the lip of the ceiling came over them, they ducked down, not wanting to look away from their friend.

"We must go," said Bruenna. "The sooner we get what you have come for, the sooner we can face Memnarch."

Glissa didn't budge.

"Bosh would want you to go," said the wizard.

The elf looked down at the goblin. He shook his head.

"No," she said. "No, he wouldn't." Squeezing Slobad's hand she broke away from Bruenna's grasp.

"Come on," she said. "Let's go save Bosh."

Glissa bolted back from the tunnel and into the chamber. Slobad ran right beside her. High above, their friend clung to the thrashing centipede.

"How we get him off, huh?" asked the goblin.

Glissa shook her head. Looking around the room, she searched for something, anything that she could use to help her. Half way up the wall, near the side of the lake closest to Bosh and the centipede, she found what she was searching for.

Grabbing Slobad's shoulder, she pointed. "You see that?"

Slobad narrowed his eyes. "What?"

"The joint. The big round thing with the seam in it." She shook her hand as she pointed.

"No," replied the goblin.

"There, half way up. The silvery bend. Can't you see it?" She got down on her knees so that she was closer to his level and pointed with both hand.

Realization blossomed on Slobad's face. "Yes. Slobad see now."

Glissa smiled. "If I can get you up there, can you take it apart?"

Now it was the goblin's turn to smile. "Slobad can take anything apart, huh?"

She grabbed him by the cheek and kissed his little face. "That's why I love you." Then she stood up, lifting Slobad under her arm.

"Hey," he said. "Goblins not toys, huh? Ride up here." He climbed under her armpit and onto her back, wrapping his arms around her shoulders.

Glissa nodded and began reciting the words to a spell. Relaxing the muscles along her spine, she opened herself up to the powers of green mana. Here, deep under the Dross, there was little of the arcane energies that she sought. But the spell she was about to cast needed very little, and she could improvise with what was abundant here in the stronghold of darkness.

Gathering to her the powers she needed, Glissa began to form the framework of her spell. It was an incantation many of the forest elves were taught when they were very young, useful in many different situations, this one being no exception.

When the words were spoken and all the pieces in place, Glissa focused her attention on the pipes on the ceiling near the coupling and let the spell loose.

Long, stringy white strands of sticky silk shot from her fingertips, reaching high into the air. As they flew, they spread out, expanding like fingers reaching to grasp hold of the ceiling. Squeezing hold of the silk, Glissa and Slobad were lifted from the ground, propelled toward the wall by the web the elf had spun.

The first moment was the most exhilarating. Having been jerked from the floor, the pair accelerated, and everything became a blur. As they continued upward, the chamber again came into focus, and Glissa turned to check on Bosh.

In the time it had taken the elf to cast her spell, the centipede had slowed its thrashing, and the iron golem had come to rest against the great creature's back.

"Uh oh. It see us, huh?" said Slobad from her back.

Glissa shivered. It was true. The centipede was watching her and the goblin as they sped toward the wall.

With lightning speed, the bug lunged, snapping its razor arms together, trying to catch the soaring elf.

Glissa twisted in midair. There was nothing she could do to control her flight. All she could do was cling tightly to the strand of webby silk. The creature moved in on them, rustling the air and pushing before it the foul stench of the underground lake. Glissa's hair whipped around, and the unnatural breeze whistled as it whipped through the metal on her shins.

The centipede's closing arms reached out, grasping for the elf and the goblin. Metal closed down on metal, missing flesh but slicing right through the magical web and sending the pair spinning off toward the wall.

The room whirled, and Slobad's grip tightened around Glissa's shoulders. Closing her eyes, the elf quickly ran through the words to another spell. It was all she had, and she wasn't even sure it would work, but she forced as much power into it as she could.

The final word spoken, Glissa let loose. Strands of wire that looked like leafy green vines sprouted from her hands and feet.

Slobad gasped then giggled. "Hey," he said, letting go with one hand. "Stop. Tickles, huh?"

Glissa ignored him. As they spun, falling back toward the floor, she grabbed hold of the wires with both hands. Whipping them around like a lasso, the elf flung them toward the wall with all of her might. It was her only chance, and she took it.

The wires clanked as they collided with the tubes, slapping around and spanking off the slippery, slime-covered metal.

"Damn!" shouted the elf.

The vines trailed down the wall as the pair fell, slapping and flapping the whole way. Then one of them got stuck in between two of the pipes—and it jammed. The other end of the cable—attached to Glissa's foot—pulled tight. The goblin and the elf were flipped over, upside down, and flung sideways as their descent was stopped cold by the wire.

The pair swung out over the lake, suspended upside down by Glissa's magical vine. All the blood in her body ran down into her head, and she struggled to recover from the sudden stop.

"You okay?" she asked Slobad.

"Yeah," replied the goblin, though his words seemed labored.

Reaching the end of their swing, the vine brought the two back toward the wall. Glissa squeezed her gut and leaned into the vine, trying to accentuate the swinging.

The centipede loomed up large behind her, getting ready to strike again.

"Slobad," she shouted. "Can you grab hold of my hand?" Reaching back up over her upended shoulders, she spread her palms out for the goblin.

Without a word, the goblin grabbed hold. Immediately his body flipped over, righting itself. The force of the shifting bodies changed the course of their swinging, and the vine gave way.

Glissa gasped as they fell again. A loud creak filled the chamber, and their descent was stopped once again. Only a few inches below where they had been, the vine caught again.

Suspended there, arms outstretched, looking up into the eyes of the upside down elf, the goblin said, "Now what, crazy elf?"

"Now I'm going to toss you onto that pipe coupling."

Slobad's eyebrows lifted. "What?"

"We're going to swing as hard as we can, then I'm going to toss you up toward the coupling."

"Why?"

"So you can take it apart."

"What 'bout you, huh?"

Glissa smiled at him, her head still filling with blood. "I'm just going to hang out."

The pair swung away, reaching the apex of their arc, slowing, then coming back down and gaining speed. They were headed back toward the coupling.

"This is our best chance," said Glissa. "It's now or never."

Slobad looked up and only nodded.

From the corner of her eye, Glissa could see the centipede ready to strike again, its head curled back, its eyes pointed at her and Slobad.

"Here we go," she shouted, and she swung her arms with everything she had. At the top of their arc, as close as they would come to coupling, Glissa let go of the goblin. As soon as she did, the vine complained once again, then it snapped, and she fell, head first, toward the ground.

As she dropped she watched Slobad soar through the air. He looked as if he were hanging on an invisible hook, weightless and unconcerned about being ten times his height from the floor.

The centipede's head filled her vision. It came down, and the rest of the world rushed up to greet her. She could hear the scissoring sound of the bug's arms closing and opening again. She hit something hard, and everything went black.

* * * * *

At the other end of the lake, a new predator emerged. Unseen but all seeing, it stalked from between the pipes. Scanning the room with its hawklike eyes, set deep above a birdlike beak, the four-legged creature stayed concealed within the shadows. It would watch and wait.

The myr had all the time in the world.

* * * * *

Slobad was weightless. One minute he was swinging from a vine like a monkey, the next he was being hurled through the air. The falling part he didn't so much like, but the moment just before he fell—the point at which he wasn't travelling up or down but was just stuck in midair—that he kind of liked.

Now he was falling again. Glissa had done her best to throw him toward the coupling. He hadn't made it, and he was starting back down. Slobad felt his stomach rise as he began to pick up speed. He definitely didn't like this part, and he reached out, reactions taking over for reason.

His fingers closed around nothing but air, and the goblin continued to fall. Then something solid hit his leg, and he lunged for it. Nimble hands caught the edge of a broken, magical vine, and Slobad crashed into the pipes.

His heart raced, and terror flooded through his veins. Looking down, he saw Glissa falling then saw the centipede dive after her—Bosh clinging to his back.

Glissa hit the water, and the swamp creature plunged its head under, leaving the room eerily quiet. Slobad clung to the wall, listening to himself breathe, trying to piece together what had just happened to him.

The sound of bubbling water interrupted his thoughts. The surface of the underground lake exploded upward, and the centipede's head shot into the sky. This time, though, Bosh wasn't attached.

Great, thought the goblin. Bosh and Glissa are gone, and Slobad is the one stuck up here with angry centipede, huh?

Before the creature could get its bearings, Slobad decided to climb. Grabbing hold of the smallest pipe he could find, hugging it as if it were Glissa's back, the goblin shimmed up toward the coupling.

The going was tough, but Slobad was a good climber, and he managed to make progress. The coupling, however, was on a different pipe, and eventually he'd have to find a way to cross from where he was over to where he was going.

Now that he thought about it, he didn't know why he was going there. Glissa had wanted him to take it apart, but that was when Bosh was still on the creature's back. But, even when the golem had still been attached to the bug, Slobad didn't know what good taking apart the connective coupling was going to do.

He'd almost reached the connection when he heard a loud chittering sound. Turning around, he looked into the beady little eyes of the giant centipede.

Slobad swallowed. "Nice bug, huh?"

The swamp monster reared and lunged at the goblin.

Slobad barely had time to scamper onto the neighboring pipe before the creature's head impacted the coupling.

A dull gong, followed by a high-pitched hissing sound, rolled through the chamber. A flood of filth shot out, blinding the centipede and forcing it back. The creature's attack had punctured the coupling, and all the swamp fluid stored within the pipe was released in one large shot.

"Oh," said Slobad. "Now Slobad understand crazy elf."

Below he could see that Glissa and Bosh had surfaced and were getting out of the lake. Bruenna stood below him, waving her hands.

"What?" he yelled.

Bruenna cupped her hands to her mouth. "Jump."

"Oh." Slobad shrugged and leaped into the air.

CHAPTER 18

Memnarch's body hummed in anticipation. Every cell, every molecule of metal and flesh combined wanted more serum. No, they needed more serum.

Drinking in giant quaffs from a large mug, the guardian of Mirrodin leaned over the controls of his Darksteel Eye. When he had built the Eye, he asssumed he would always have his infusion device. Consequently, the viewing chamber was too small for him to fit inside while wearing his serum tanks.

It had been a miscalculation.

Images buzzed around him. Each of the eight different screens showed him the view through the eyes of his myr. Right now, he was unconcerned with all of it—except for the unfolding events in the Mephidross.

Capturing the elf girl was his priority. The rest of the plane could wait just as he had waited.

Through the eyes of his spy, he watched the elf girl and her friends evade the centipede and scurry into the tunnel. Memnarch had watched that interaction barely taking a breath. There would be no end to the torture he would unleash on the denizens of the Dross if she were killed in the swamp.

Damn this frustration. If only he could lay his hands on her. If only he were in his original body, his created, perfect body, then he would be able to chase her himself. But alas, he was not. He was cursed to have this sagging, fleshy monstrosity that served no other purpose except as a vessel for his greatness. With it, there was only one thing he could do in the search for the elf—watch and wait.

Each time his servants had her cornered, the elf girl had managed to escape. That would not be the case this time.

Now as his myr stalked behind its quarry, Memnarch was much relieved. She only needed to step through the end of the passage, and he would have her in his grasp.

* * * * *

Glissa and Bosh fished Slobad from the underground lake. His body was mostly limp, but he was coughing up swamp water, so the elf figured he was still alive. Looking up one last time at the disoriented centipede, Glissa dodged into the passage with the rest of the group, the goblin in tow.

The eerie yellow glow from the large chamber behind them didn't seep too far into the tunnel. About a hundred yards in, everything was dark.

"Anybody have a dry torch?" said Glissa.

Suddenly the passage lit up with a cool blue glow. In front of the elf, Bruenna and two of her wizards held their arms in the air. In their outstretched palms, each held a small glowing ball of light, about the size of a baby squirrel. It wasn't much, but it did the trick.

"That's better."

Glissa scanned the tunnel. It was large enough to accommodate the iron golem, though his head occasionally touched the roof, depending on how much sludge had collected on the floor. The walls were covered in a shiny film that reminded her of the sludge she'd swum through to get to the bottom of the swamp. Looking down at her hands, the same shiny slime had attached itself to every crevice. The lines on her hands were set in a deep black, and her skin looked like it belonged to someone twice her age.

"I don't think I can remember the last time I was clean."

The group continued on, following a series of twists and turns. Al-Hayat had a hard time keeping his balance. His paws kept slipping in the slime, and his claws made a screeching noise when they ground across the metal pipe beneath.

Finally the passage straightened out, and a clear white light filled the tunnel from the other end. It wasn't bright or harsh, but it was certainly more powerful than the dull blue glow from Bruenna's spell. Seeing the new light reminded Glissa of exiting the blue lacuna. That time she had stepped from the tunnel to find a whole new world, one that she had thought was the stuff of legends but was in fact real.

Now she wondered what new thing she was going to find when she stepped out into the light. She didn't know if it was possible for her entire world to be turned upside down again, but even the thought made her stopped where she stood.

"What is wrong?" asked Bosh. The deep resonant base of his voice woke the sleeping Slobad. The goblin rubbed his eyes and leaped down, standing beside the elf.

Glissa shrugged. "Last time we stepped from a tunnel like this I discovered a hollow world. What will I find this time?"

Al-Hayat had turned and come back to join the conversation. "Is finding out something new such a bad thing?"

"No," replied Glissa, "not always." She smiled. "But I didn't find you at the end of a tube."

The wolf laughed. "So everything at the end of a tube is bad?"

Glissa shrugged. "I don't know. This is only my second tube."

Al-Hayat stuck his muzzle against her back and urged her forward. "Maybe this one won't be so bad."

Bruenna appeared, her glowing blue ball now extinguished. "Don't be so sure."

Glissa looked up at each of her friends in turn. She'd come this far. No reason to stop now. Steeling herself, she stepped forward and out of the tunnel.

She was greeted by the back of a tall, bright metal throne sitting on a multitiered dais. The walls of the chamber were of a dark, etched metal that looked as if it had been eaten away at by acid—or something worse. Stepping out from behind the throne, Glissa spotted a pair of exceptionally tall double doors. They were closed at the moment, and they glowed around the edges with a magical red light.

"I've been here before," she said.

The others filed from the tunnel. Slobad stepped up beside the elf, sticking close.

Glissa walked up the dais to touch the cushion on the seat of the throne. "We're in the Vault of Whispers. This is Geth's chamber."

The double doors swung open. A rush of fog flooded in, spreading out over the floor like a wave, filling up the room from corner to corner.

Behind the fog, a pale, human-looking man stepped into the room. His bald head shone under the warm lights. A strip of metal ran over his forehead and down the back of his neck, disappearing into the folds of his gray robe.

"So nice to see you again, young Glissa," said the man as he entered. "You really shouldn't drop in so unexpectedly."

Glissa pulled her sword from its sheath. "Hello, Geth. I hope that our visit this time won't be as unpleasant for you as our last."

"Don't be so hard on yourself," replied Geth, moving around the wall, getting deeper into the chamber without getting any closer to Glissa. "I quite enjoyed our last visit."

Glissa watched the strange, gaunt man as he circled in the room. "Yeah, I'll bet," she said. "So tell me, how's your vampire?"

Geth visibly bristled. "Fine. Fine."

Bruenna and her wizards had entered the room. They stood against the wall opposite Geth.

"And Yert?"

Geth frowned. "I'm afraid Yert is no longer with us."

Glissa stepped down from the dais. "What did you do to him?"

Geth continued around the wall but stopped when he saw Al-Hayat come out from behind the throne. The leader of the Vault held up his hands. "Nothing. I swear."

"Then where is he?"

Geth eyed Al-Hayat one more time, then Bosh stepped out beside the wolf. He glanced from the pair back to the human wizards then panned over to Glissa. "He met with a tragic accident."

"Accident?"

Geth nodded. "Turns out he wasn't much of a handler after all." He held his hands out wide and shrugged. "I gave him a new reaper as you requested, but the poor man got caught within its grasp only a few hours after you left here."

Glissa felt the bile inside her rise to the surface. "If you—" She took a menacing step forward, but Geth held out his finger, waving it side to side.

"You didn't come here to check on Yert, young Glissa. So why don't you tell me what it is you require, and perhaps we can speed your visit here."

Glissa stopped, but she gripped the hilt of her sword tightly in both hands. Taking a deep breath, she calmed herself. "All right, Geth." She held up her hand, showing him the ring the troll had given her. "I need the last piece to the Kaldra Guardian."

Geth took a step back. "My, my. That's no small request."

Glissa narrowed her eyes. "What is it you're angling for, Geth?"

The pale man smiled. "Angling for? There is nothing that you have that I desire. Besides, I do believe I owe you for sparing the life of my vampire."

The elf cocked her head to one side. Geth seemed entirely too happy to see her and even more happy to be helpful. "This isn't right," she said. "What is it that's amusing you so much?"

"Amusing me?" Geth's smile widened. "I'm just enjoying the irony of this. The last time you were here, you stormed in, cut the arm from my vampire, demanded that I tell you who was ransoming your life, then absconded with my vial of serum." He held his hand up to his face, trying to hide the smile behind, but it was no use. He began to laugh. "Now you need my help. Isn't that grand?"

"Yes, grand, Geth." Glissa was growing impatient. "So tell me where the last piece is, or this time it won't be your vampire who loses a limb."

Geth tried to swallow his laughter, but he couldn't. He held his finger in the air and began taking deep breaths in an effort to calm himself.

"Don't you see the beauty in all of this? It's like the cycle of life. First you are nothing. Then you're born. You live your life, and then you die." Geth rubbed his hands together. "If you're lucky, you end up here in the Dross, continuing to be productive in the unlife. If you're not, then that's it. You're nothing again."

A chill ran down Glissa's spine. This was not right. Looking back, she could tell Bruenna and her wizards were feeling the same thing. On the other side of the throne, Al-Hayat too was uncomfortable, shifting his gaze side to side, keeping himself hunched and ready to pounce.

Beside her, Slobad crouched near the ground. He looked tired, almost distracted. The plunge into the lake must have taken more out of him this time.

Only Bosh seemed unfazed by the strange situation. Then again, Bosh's expression was always stoic, neither happy nor sad.

"All right, Geth," said Glissa, raising her sword again and taking two large steps toward the pale man. "You can laugh about this all you want when we're gone."

Geth pressed himself tight up against the wall, his eyes bulging.

Glissa moved in closer, letting the tip of her blade hover just below his throat. "Tell me where the last piece is."

"What makes you think I'll just hand it over?"

"Only this." Glissa whipped the tip of her blade across the gaunt man's cheek, drawing a thick line of red blood.

Geth squealed and pulled his hands up, covering the fresh wound. The look of horror and betrayal on his face was plain.

"I spared your life once, but at the moment I'm not in such a generous mood." She looked down at herself, covered in muck. "I've been through too much, haven't slept or eaten, and I don't trust you." On this last word she shoved the tip of her blade again at Geth, punctuating her point.

"Okay. Okay." Geth held up his hands in surrender. "I'll show you."

The ruler of the Vault placed his fingers to his lips and let out a high-pitched whistle. The acid-etched walls of his chamber tipped forward, as if an invisible giant had been holding them up and now had let go.

Glissa grabbed Geth by the collar of his robe and pulled him back, out from under the falling wall. As she pulled back the lord of the Vault slipped from her grasp and disappeared in the swirling fog.

As the walls collapsed in, everyone else charged toward the center of the room, pilling onto the dais. There was barely enough space, and Bosh was forced to climb on top of the throne.

With everyone collected safely from the way in the center of the room, the walls fell with a tremendous clang, pushing before them a gust of wind. The fog that had blown in with Geth was pushed back into the air, and the companions were surrounded by a dense ring of opaque whiteness.

"What have you done, Geth?" she shouted out into the gloom.

The leader of the vault cackled, his voice coming from farther away than Glissa had expected. "Only completed the circle."

Everyone stood on guard, straining to see. The fog began to settle again, slowly drooping to the floor. As it descended, objects began to take shape. Tall and narrow, they looked at first like human-sized statues. The fog clung to them as it fell, making the figures seem to rise up from the floor.

Then one of them moved.

"Hello, elf," said a voice that sounded muted and far away, as if it were underwater.

Bruenna raised her hands. Magical energies playing between them. "Vedalken."

* * * * *

Pontifex watched the walls to Geth's chamber fall. A thick fog lifted into the air, obscuring his view.

"Marek, are your troops in place?"

"Yes, my lord," replied the head of the guard. He held a glowing halberd in the crook of one arm, and in his other hands he gripped an old-fashioned trident.

"Excellent." He rubbed two of his four hands together. "Now we wait and see if our friend Geth has come through."

As the walls settled fully to the ground with a loud clap, an island rose from the fog in the center of what used to be Geth's private chamber. Clinging to that island like a pile of rats atop a sinking ship were the elf and her companions.

"Hello, elf," said Lord Pontifex. He took a step forward.

Atop the island, a pair of hands cloaked in magical energies rose into the air. Pontifex heard someone say, "Vedalken," then a jagged bolt of blue lightning shot out and enveloped a warrior standing next to him.

He turned to give Marek the order to charge, but his bodyguard and commander of the vedalken guards had already moved in.

Though most of the fog had cleared, it still clung to the floor, obscuring from view the bottom half of the onrushing warriors. They held their charged lances high above them as they ran. The glowing heads lit up the shifting white cloud below, washing out every color in the spectrum and replacing it with a pale blue.

In the next second, Pontifex's warriors tore into the huddling mass in the middle of the room. Metal clashed against metal. The sounds of flesh tearing and bones breaking drifted over the fog like a lilting horn. The flash of blue-headed halberds cast exotic shadows on the white cloud, and Pontifex came one step closer to acquiring his prize.

*   *   *   *   *

"It's a trap," shouted Glissa, steeling herself for the charge.

Bruenna had already reacted, sending a jagged shot of power out into the foggy distance.

What had appeared to be statues were vedalken warriors. The fog obscured most of their bodies, but Glissa could clearly see the glowing heads of their magically tipped halberds. They seemed to float on the cloud, casting a pale blue glow as they came. It was a strangely calming color.

The warriors were upon them, and Glissa had no more time to ponder the beauty of the killing blades.

Magic arced out from the dais, crashing into the oncoming warriors. Several fell, but the rest came on, and Glissa launched herself forward, her blade biting into vedalken flesh.

The fog on the floor swirled up and around the combatants. Blades clashed, and sparks flew. Spells were cast, and warriors were frozen in place. Nowhere on the dais was safe from the assault, and in seconds the entire group was surrounded.

Glissa's blade sang as it cut the thick, dank air. With one swing she cut cleanly through the shaft of a vedalken halberd. With the next she cut down the warrior holding the two halves.

Standing where she was, she couldn't see the rest of her friends. Occasionally she would catch a glimpse of blue magic flying toward the vedalken warriors, or hear Al-Hayat growl. Even if she had time to turn and check on Slobad or Bosh, she doubted she'd be able to see them through all the fog.

Kicking aside the dying warrior before her, the elf turned to the next vague figure looming in the wispy white cloud.

The head of his charged halberd came into view, and Glissa sped up her swing, barely able to block the attack before it smashed into her shoulder. Spinning away, she came around onto the balls of her feet.

The head of the halberd came at her again, but this time she was prepared, and she batted it away with ease—but a sharp pain blossomed on her thigh. The halberd blade had been a feint. Looking down, Glissa saw the head of a trident pull back into the obscurity of the fog.

Drawing air through her clenched teeth, Glissa took a step back, the stinging burn of her fresh wound causing her to limp. The trident had punched three deep holes in her leg, and they wept blood. The entire left side of her body was beginning to ache. She couldn't fight like this. She needed to heal herself.

Glancing over her shoulder, she looked for some help—there was none in sight, only a swirling cloud of white and jags of blue magic. Her only chance was to try to duck back into the fog, hide herself long enough to heal her leg.

Just as this thought flashed through her head, the warrior she'd been fighting stepped out of the fog—the vedalken Bruenna had called Marek. He held a glowing halberd in one hand and a short, sharp trident in the other. The tips of the trident were shiny, and though the blue glow of the vedalken's lance was washing out the color, Glissa knew it was her blood tipping the tines.

Marek wasted no time, bringing his halberd down in a chopping blow. Glissa batted it away, but her injured leg slowed her. Pain flared again in her thigh, and she watched the vedalken pull his trident, for the second time, from her wounded leg.

Dropping to the ground, she pressed her back against the floor. The thick fog swirled up, concealing her from view. Pressing her sword tightly against her body, Glissa rolled to her right, hoping to mask her whereabouts.

The sounds of battle filled the air above her, and a heavy boot pounded the floor right beside her head. He's found me, she thought. A chill ran up her spine, and panic flooded her veins. She had failed.

Then the warrior who belonged to the boot moved on, and Glissa breathed a quick sigh of relief. Dropping her sword, the elf placed both of her hand on her injured left thigh. Even placing light pressure on the skin made the wound throb more, and Glissa winced. Taking a deep breath, she clamed her thoughts and drew in mana. Like the spell she had cast beside the underground lake, this one only needed a small amount of the energies of the Tangle. The rest she could improvise.

Feeling the spell fully powered, Glissa pushed the arcane magic from her finger tips, flooding the healing warmth into her thigh. The pain subsided immediately, and Glissa closed her eyes, lost in the brief moment of painless bliss.

Cold, sharpened steel pressed tightly against her throat.

"I suggest you surrender," said a far-away, watery voice.

Glissa opened her eyes and looked up at an image of herself reflected in the shiny surface of Marek's facemask.

CHAPTER 19

Marek lifted Glissa from the ground and held the elf's hands behind her back with two of his own. With the other two he pointed the tip of his halberd at Bruenna. The vedalken warriors had captured or killed everyone on the dais.

Behind Marek, a dozen of his guardsmen held their weapons against the giant wolf, pressing the points into his hide. Another two dozen held the big golem who still stood atop the throne. The goblin and the sole remaining wizard had been disarmed and were under guard as well.

Pontifex strode up to the dais, Geth in tow, and looked down on the defiant elf girl. "We meet again."

"Pontifex. What a surprise. You're not still angry about that little incident in your pool?" said Glissa. She squirmed against her captor, but it was clear that Marek had a good grip.

The vedalken lord brushed aside the comment. "No, of course not." He stepped up much closer, putting his nose right in her face. "I have a much better reason to come find you."

Geth licked his lips and rubbed his hands together. Though he didn't say a word, he was clearly enjoying this.

"Oh really," replied the elf. "What would that be?"

"There are creatures on this plane—forces that you still don't understand. You, my young elf friend, have attracted their attention."

"And you've come to do their bidding?" asked Glissa. "The ruler of the vedalken has become a petty thug?"

Pontifex smiled. "No, Glissa. On the contrary, I'm here to make sure those forces never succeed." He lifted his sword, testing the edge with the tip of his thumb. "I'm here to kill you."

Geth giggled.

Marek turned his attention from the elf girl and the human wizard to stare at his lord. He meant to kill the elf. He'd been trying to do just that for some time. The real question was what would happen after?

A huge crash and hum interrupted Marek's reverie.

"Let her go, Pontifex," boomed a voice.

From the fog rolled a squad of levelers.

Lord Pontifex turned away from the elf girl. "Go away, Malil. This doesn't concern you."

Malil rode up astride his leveler, his greatsword already out of its scabbard.

Something looked different about the metal man. Marek had only seen him a couple of times before, but this time he seemed more . . . human, tired even, as if he suffered from the same ailments that inflicted the organic creatures of Mirrodin.

Malil rode up to the foot of the dais, only a few feet from Pontifex. The other levelers formed up behind him—two rows deep.

"Yes," said the metal man. "Yes, it does. Now let the elf go, and turn her over to me."

Pontifex shook his head. "After all I've done to track her down, do you think I'm going to let you take her back and get all the credit?"

"Memnarch wants her alive, Pontifex."

From the corner of his eye, Marek spotted a four-legged

creature dart through the shadows. He didn't so much see the creature clearly, only its movement and its outline as it crept from one spot of darkness to another.

Pontifex zigzagged the head of his halberd through the air, making a whipping sound. "You'll have to come take her from me."

Malil didn't even blink. "If that's what it takes."

The levelers lurched forward, cutting into the vedalken guards standing on the first step of the dais.

*   *   *   *   *

Her hands held tight behind her back by Marek, Glissa fished around on the floor with her foot. She'd dropped her sword when she'd cast her last spell, and since she'd been taken captive, she'd been searching for it.

She shifted her feet and stepped on something hard. It skidded a bit, making a grinding metallic sound, dampened by the dense fog.

I found it, she thought. The notion filled her with a brief glimmer of hope. Then the levelers attacked, and Marek's grip on her hands loosened.

Glissa lurched away from her captor, diving to the ground. Her hand closed around the hilt of her sword, and she climbed back to her feet.

More than half of the vedalken had turned to take on the levelers. Marek was nowhere to be seen, and already Al-Hayat had a four-armed warrior pinned to the ground with each paw and another nearly eviscerated between his teeth.

Bosh reached down to grab a couple of vedalken, but when he shifted his weight, the throne he stood upon tipped backward, and he lost his balance. The iron golem disappeared as the chair toppled. Fog and dust shot into the air, and Glissa bounded over the top of the dais trying to get to her fallen friend.

A few of the remaining vedalken guards tried to bar her way, but they were overwhelmed by an icy magical blast from Bruenna, and the elf managed to skirt past. With her next step the floor seemed to disappear, and she fell.

She shouted as she dropped, caught off guard. Her rump landed on something hard, and she rolled sideways, throwing her hands out to catch herself and stop her fall. The floor she landed on seemed lumpy and uneven. It moved under her and gave off a jingling sound.

Glissa tumbled once then came to rest on her feet. The room around her was dark, illuminated only by a beam of light coming through the hole she had just fallen through. She could see that the ceiling was only three or four times her height, not far in comparison to the fall she had taken into the underground lake. The hole she had fallen through was perfectly round, as if it had been put there intentionally or made by magic. Above it, Glissa could make out the toppled legs of the throne Bosh had been standing on.

"The hole was under the throne," she said. That thought made her feel a little bit better. It seemed as if in the past day she had managed to fall into nearly everything that an elf could fall into on Mirrodin.

At least there was a reason I didn't see it when I walked in, she thought.

Climbing to the point closest to the hole, Glissa tried jumping. She thought if she could catch the edge of the hole, she could pull herself out, but her leap wasn't nearly high enough to reach, and each time she tried, the ground shifted below her, making the same jingling sound it had when she had landed.

Above she could hear the sounds of battle.

Giving up on the idea of getting out by herself, Glissa spun in a circle, squinting to help her eyes adjust. She could just make out the shadows marking the corners and walls of the room. It was small, nothing fancy, and it appeared as if she was the only one there.

She chuckled. "That's what I thought about the lake."

Bending down, she grabbed hold of a handful of the shifting, jingling ground and lifted it into the light. It sparkled.

In her hand she held several dozen gold disks. Looking down she could see that the floor was covered with stacks them. She was standing on the largest pile, right under the hole in the ceiling.

Walking down to the floor, she examined the other piles. It looked as if larger objects had been buried under the smaller ones. Letting the metal disks in her hand fall back to the floor, she bent down again to examine some of the other objects.

Pushing aside large handfuls of the jingling metal, Glissa uncovered a large, intricately designed metal plate. Made from a dark gray metal, the protective piece just seemed to go on and on. It wasn't just big, it was huge. She could just make out the edge of a symbol that appeared to cover most of the front half of the shield. Clearing away the metal disks as fast as she could, Glissa uncovered the rest of the marking.

It was the same circular sigil as on the ring the trolls gave her.

"The Kaldra Shield."

Suddenly, something fell from the ceiling, landing on the big pile of disks with a shriek. Glissa took a step back, picking up her sword and getting ready to fight.

The falling creature rolled and came to a stop right at her feet.

"Slobad." Glissa lowered her blade.

The goblin rubbed the side of his head with his hands. "Slobad tired of falling, huh?"

Glissa helped the goblin to his feet. "How did you find me?"

"Crazy elf run toward Bosh then disappear, huh? When you not stand up, Slobad look. Goblin fall through hole." He looked up, pointing at the ceiling, and stuck his tongue out. "No goblin make this room, huh? No goblin cut hole in floor where people fall through. Who make such a place, huh?"

"One who's trying to hide this." Glissa grabbed Slobad's arm and turned him toward the shield she had found.

The goblin's eyes grew as big as his head. "Is that . . . ?" Slobad walked over to the rune-inscribed artifact, touching it lightly with his fingers.

"The last piece of the Kaldra Champion," finished Glissa.

Slobad licked his lips then looked over his shoulder at the elf. "You still have helm, huh?"

Glissa nodded. Fishing around inside her pack, she pulled out the helm. Slobad reached out both of his hands, taking it from her.

"You'll need this as well." The elf lifted her sword, admiring the sharpened edge. Turning it around, she offered the hilt of the Kaldra Sword to Slobad.

The goblin took it but scowled. "If Slobad take your blade, what crazy elf fight with, huh?"

Glissa bent down and picked up a dark-bladed sword stuck in the piles of metal disks. "I'll find something."

The goblin nodded then turned and began digging out the rest of the Kaldra Shield.

* * * * *

Damn that stupid metal man. Pontifex turned aside the attacks of a leveler then laid his palm on the creature's hide. With a thought, he released a flood of blue mana into the artifact beast, freezing its joints.

Stepping around the now-inoperative killing device, Pontifex closed in on Malil.

The vedalken lord brandished his halberd with a practiced flare. "I've been waiting for this for a very long time."

Malil stood motionless, his greatsword in his hand by his side. "You fail to see the bigger picture, Pontifex."

"No, Malil, it is you who fail to see." Pontifex took a fighting stance one long step away from his opponent. "Do you really think Memnarch will recognize the sacrifices you made to bring him the elf girl? Do you think you will be rewarded for your hard work?"

Malil stared back at the vedalken, unmoved. "Memnarch wants her alive. I am not here to quibble with you over who brings her to him. I do not care about your childish jealousies." He lifted his sword. "I have my instructions, and I will abide by them."

His hand flew from his side. His blade flashed in the pale light of the Vault, but Pontifex was fast and caught the tip of the metal man's sword with the shaft of his polearm.

"As I said before—" a smile grew on Pontifex's face—"I have waited a long time for this."

Tossing Malil's blade back at him, Pontifex wove the head of his halberd in a lightning-fast pattern before the metal man's eyes.

Malil studied the moving blades. Pontifex watched his eyes follow the pattern.

Lunging forward, Malil tried to take advantage of an opening. This was what the vedalken lord had been waiting for. As the blade came forward, Pontifex changed the pattern, catching Malil off guard.

The metal man's strike slipped past Pontifex's halberd. The vedalken dodged, getting inside his opponent's reach and driving the point of his weapon into the crease between Malil's shoulder and arm.

Malil pulled back, Pontifex's polearm still stuck in his joint. His left arm had been immobilized by the strike.

Pontifex released his halberd and retrieved a short sword from inside his robe. "You have only four limbs," he said, showing off his own six-limbed body. "I have three more blades."

* * * * *

Bruenna was in the fight of her life. Levelers swirled all around. She fought off a vedalken with each hand. Over the course of the past day, these odds had been common. Though she used every trick and skill at her disposal, the assault was overpowering, and all she could do was keep herself alive, never having the opportunity to counterattack. Without the chance to strike back, all would be lost. It was only a matter of time.

The only other remaining wizard fared the same. He fought only to keep himself alive.

She traded blows with the two warriors, wielding a sword in each hand, moving back and forth as if she and her opponents were involved in an intricate dance. Her foot caught on something on the fog-covered ground, and she nearly tripped. Checking the floor, she took a step sideways, trying to avoid whatever it was that she'd stepped on.

When she lifted her eyes, the two vedalken were gone.

Fighters all around her continued to clash, but she was now without an opponent. Scanning the battle, she saw why. A new challenger had arrived.

"Well, well, well. Bruenna," said a far-away, watery voice.

The human prepared herself for a fight. "Marek." The head

of the vedalken elite guard had also been in charge of the human enslavement process inside Lumengrid. The sprawling vedalken fortress that resided below the waves of the Quicksilver Sea had been built on the backs of forced labor.

Bruenna and her tribe had been enslaved by this monster. It had been Marek who had overseen the beatings and punishments meted out to those who did not work hard enough.

"I should have known I'd meet you here," she said, "in the bowels of Mirrodin."

The vedalken took a step toward the wizard. "What is that supposed to mean?"

Bruenna began gathering mana. "Only that a creature like you deserves to die in a place like this."

"And what exactly is a 'creature like me'?"

Bruenna narrowed her eyes. "One who doesn't understand the value of human life." Lunging forward, she jabbed at the vedalken's midsection.

Marek dodged away, easily turning aside her attack with the haft of his halberd. This was what the wizard was hoping for, and she reached up, touching the warrior's facemask with her open palm and casting her spell.

Icicles formed on the metal frame of Marek's helmet, and the serum inside turned bitter cold then froze solid. As the liquid turned to ice, the glass plates, which enabled Marek to see out, shattered.

Marek thrashed about, dropping his halberd and grabbing hold of his head, now trapped inside a block of frozen serum. Bruenna took advantage of the blinded, frantic slaver and drove the tip of her sword deep into his body.

Marek fell back and disappeared into the fog.

* * * * *

Malil pulled the head of Pontifex's halberd from his arm. The vedalken's petty jealousies were getting in the way. For the love of Memnarch, all he wanted was another dose of serum, another burst of enlightenment. Surely that was not too much to ask for.

Malil's life on this plane had been relatively short in comparison to Pontifex's. He'd had the opportunity to see many strange and interesting things. He'd also had the occasion to fight. Most of the time it was in doing Memnarch's bidding, and never had it been against a skilled opponent. So he'd never really had the opportunity to fully test his own capabilities as a warrior.

Until now.

Tossing Pontifex's blade to the ground, Malil took three quick steps. His metal body had been made to react to emergency situations by making him thrice as strong and thrice as fast—but only for a short distance. This had been Memnarch's way of making Malil capable of getting himself out of trouble, should the situation arise.

Malil had never needed this function before, but it seemed as good a time as any to try it out.

His body moved in a blur. In three steps, the metal man managed to get around and behind Pontifex.

The vedalken lord tried to spin, but he wasn't nearly fast enough. Malil punched the four-armed lord squarely in the back, sending Pontifex to his knees. Raising his greatsword into the air, the metal man looked down on the back of the vedalken's bent neck. He could cut right through it and be rid of this childish fool.

The Vault of Whispers rumbled, and dust cascaded from the ceiling.

"Stop this fighting, and bring me the elf girl." The words filled the cavernous chamber, seeming to come from everywhere at once.

Malil lowered his sword. "Yes, my lord."

Pontifex too seemed unnerved by the command. He stood up, his eyes darting this way and that. Then he looked at Malil, and the metal man looked back.

Both men stared into the other's eyes for a long, tense moment.

Pontifex broke the silence. "We will finish this later."

Malil nodded. "After the elf girl is captured and returned to Memnarch." He squeezed the hilt of his sword.

The vedalken looked away. "Agreed."

CHAPTER 20

Bosh stood up.

One minute everyone was fighting everyone else, then a booming voice filled the chamber—a voice Bosh recognized as Memnarch's. Now it seemed everyone had turned to fight the metal golem.

Levelers and vedalken swarmed over him. They poked his fleshy parts and pounded his iron ones. He fought back. With each wave of his hand, he bashed back the advance of a half-dozen attackers. Still more came on.

They climbed up his arms, swung at his head, made him bleed. Again he crashed to the floor.

* * * * *

Blue blood dripped from Al-Hayat's muzzle.

Tossing his latest victim aside, he lashed out, trying to catch another. His teeth closed around the scythe blades of a leveler beast, and the razor-sharp edge cut right through his lip. Yowling in pain, his own red blood mixing with that of his foes, the wolf retreated a step.

The leveler charged in, and it wasn't alone. Six other levelers were right beside it, and a dozen vedalken added their halberds as well. Their blades cut into him, tearing off fur and reaching straight down into flesh.

He swatted at them, growling and barring his teeth, but something made these combined foes more aggressive, less afraid. And in moments they swarmed him.

Al-Hayat backed off the dais. His rump bumped into the back wall of the chamber. Looking around, all he could see were four-armed warriors and scythe-bladed levelers. Not a single one of his friends was in sight.

Cornered, trapped like a common animal at the end of a hunt, the great forest beast crouched down and bared his fangs.

If he was going to die here, then so were they.

* * * * *

Bruenna turned away from Marek. He might live, but she didn't have time to finish him off just now, not while the other wizard who had accompanied her into this hellhole was fighting for his life right behind her.

She stepped behind a vedalken warrior. With all of her strength, she jammed the tip of her blade into the small of his back. The four-armed guard squirmed like a bug on a pin and dropped his sword.

Something hit Bruenna in the back of the head, and she fell forward. The force of the fall pushed her blade deeper into the vedalken's back, and he let out a gurgling cry.

She was hit again and let go of her sword, her arms flying out in front of her to stop her fall. Turning over onto her back she looked up just as a leveler's scythe blade descended through the fog and bit into her shoulder.

* * * * *

"Do you have those damn things working together yet?" screamed Glissa.

Slobad, kneeling on the ground near the big pile of disks, waved his hand at her, not bothering to turn.

The sounds of battle were getting louder. Glissa's nerves were shot. Who knew how many of her friends were dead or dying up there right now. She felt powerless, trapped down here, waiting for Slobad to summon a creature she wasn't even sure would help her.

"If you don't hurry, they're all going to be dead," she said, pacing around one of the smaller piles.

The goblin stood up and brushed himself off. "Finished."

The heavy shield Glissa had uncovered lifted itself up. The pile of metal disks that had been covering it cascaded away. Jingling as they hit the others, there were so many of them landing all at the same time, they sounded like a heavy downpour—only all the raindrops were made of metal.

When Glissa had landed in this room, she had thought the floor was not so far below her feet, simply covered in a thin layer of these strange metal disks. She had been wrong. This chamber ran deep.

The elf and the goblin stepped away, pressing their backs against the wall. Gold disks continued to roll from the avatar's shoulders as it rose and rose.

The disks fell back, filling the empty space in the piled gold. The floor became like quicksand, dissolving underneath their feet, grabbing at their ankles and threatening to pull them down into the crushing pit of gold. Glissa and Slobad struggled to stay on top, almost running in place as the floor sucked them down.

Slobad tripped. Landing flat on his chest, the little goblin slid backward, caught in a roiling current of metal disks.

"Help!" screamed the goblin, trying to swim through the gold.

Glissa dropped to her knees and reached out. "Grab on." The moment she stopped running, she too got stuck in the wave of gold, and the two of them slipped toward the edge of the empty pit.

Try as they might, they couldn't stop their descent. The closer they got to the hole the faster they went. Glissa grabbed Slobad's hand and squeezed it as they slipped off the edge and fell into darkness. The jingling noise grew louder the farther they fell, and gold disks pelted them from all sides, falling into the pit and bouncing off their skulls.

"We're going to be buried alive," shouted the elf.

"Not if we die from fall, huh?" Slobad shouted back.

A pale blue-white glow filled the pit. Glissa could see the sides of the hole as the disks sloughed off and fell. Then the glow coalesced into an enormous five-fingered hand and wrapped itself around the falling pair. The gold stopped pelting them, and they stopped falling.

"What the—?" Glissa's question was cut short when she was tossed against the side of the hand as it lifted her and Slobad back up to the top of the pit.

Up and up they went, then just as suddenly as their fall had been stopped, so did their ascent. The hand opened up, and Glissa looked out over a ghostly white palm.

"Oh." Slobad's jaw dropped.

The Kaldra Champion floated before them. Its head, arms, and hands were formed from a glowing, pale blue-white plasma. At first, Glissa thought it was magical energy, but sitting in the middle of its palm, she could feel its substance. It was rubbery and soft, almost like flesh.

Its arms were strong and inscribed with hundreds of tattoos. Some formed rudimentary pictures of animals and monsters. Others appeared to be simple runes—letters or words in an alphabet Glissa did not understand.

Under the great helm its face looked human—only much, much larger, and blue. It had a strong, angular chin that jutted out past the rest of its face, and its eyes were empty white orbs, like those of an old blind man. In its right hand it clutched the sword, whose power Glissa already missed.

"So you're the Kaldra Champion," said Glissa looking up into the towering creature's white orbs.

It nodded.

"Help us save our friends, huh?" asked the goblin.

The Kaldra Champion smiled then nodded.

"Hurry." Glissa pointed to the hole in the ceiling.

The Kaldra Champion closed his fist around the goblin and the elf and looked up. Glissa could just see between the creature's fingers as he launched toward the light. The ceiling came up in a blink, and Glissa covered her head.

* * * * *

The floor exploded.

Bits of blackened metal scattered across the room, ricocheting off the levelers and pinning several vedalken to the walls.

A pale blue-white giant shot up and hovered above the broken ground. With a wave of his hand the fog covering the floor completely disappeared, revealing the wounded and dying creatures who had been concealed.

"What in the nine hells is that?" shouted Pontifex.

Malil stood beside him, shaking his head.

The creature opened his palm, and two figures stood up.

Pontifex grabbed the metal man by the arm. "It has the elf girl."

"I can see that."

Pontifex turned to find Marek. The leader of his elite guard was squirming on the floor about twenty feet away. He appeared to be in no condition to give orders.

Pontifex shouted at the top of his lungs, "Get the elf girl!"

The vedalken warriors who hadn't been knocked down by the flying debris immediately disengaged and charged the floating blue creature holding the elf.

"Do you think that's wise?" asked Malil turning to Pontifex. "I'm not entirely certain we shouldn't be very afraid of this creature."

* * * * *

Levelers covered Bosh from head to toe. Vedalken poked at him with their halberds. One group of attackers he could handle, but two . . . He smashed at them, crushing them between his mighty palms, but there were too many of them.

He was going to die.

Something exploded, and Bosh felt the floor rumble under him. The fog lifted, and he heard someone yell, "Get the elf girl!"

The vedalken turned and ran. The odds had improved.

Rolling over to one side, the half-iron, half-flesh golem pushed himself up onto his elbow. Levelers cascaded from his chest, bouncing as they hit the hard metal floor. Unlatching the compartment on his chest, Bosh flung it open. The big door swung down, creaking on its hinges, and slammed into the ground. Reaching over, the big golem closed the hatch and admired the two smashed leveler carcasses on the floor before him.

Pushing himself onto his feet, Bosh looked down at the little metal constructs before him. With no fog, he could see them all clearly.

"Time to smash." His deep voice rumbled, and he brought his fist down atop the nearest foe. Bits of broken metal spun off into all directions.

* * * * *

A leveler pinned Bruenna's shoulder to the ground. The metal burned inside her skin, and she couldn't move. Worse, she couldn't even see where the thing was. Lying on the ground, the fog blocked her view of everything except the first few inches of the scythe blade that jutted from her shoulder.

The artifact creature pulled back, yanking the blade from her flesh and disappearing into the fog. A wave of relief rolled over her only to be replaced by a dull throb and panic. It's preparing to hit me again, she thought. If only she could see it.

The fog swept away from the floor, revealing the entire room—and the leveler about to strike. The killing device's blade came whistling through the air, but Bruenna kicked and rolled, throwing herself just barely out of harm's way. The blade crashed into the ground, sticking into the metal floor, and the human wizard placed her hand on the leveler's hide.

Bruenna flooded the device with a combination of blue and black mana. Gears ground to a stop, and the beast shook. Smoke seeped from its seams, and the light in its eye sockets grew blindingly bright.

"This is for my shoulder," she said, and she placed her other hand on the creature as well.

Another spell flooded into the leveler. Metal plates collapsed, crushing the creature's insides. The artifact shook more violently, shuttered once, then came to rest as the light inside it went out.

* * * * *

The great forest wolf looked out at more than two dozen levelers and vedalken combined. They closed in, fearless but cautious all the same.

Al-Hayat waited, growling at them, watching each inch closer. A vedalken was the first to step too close. In a flash, Al-Hayat bounded forward, closed his powerful jaws around the blue-skinned warrior's head, then stepped back against the wall.

The vedalken's body stood upright for a moment longer. Its hands still gripped tightly around its halberd. From the stump of its neck, blue blood rushed over its shoulders, flooding to the ground in pulsing bursts.

The wolf spat out his mouthful. His bite had been so big that he didn't even break the seal on the vedalken's helmet—taking the head clean off the neck in a single piece.

The warrior's body toppled to the floor, and everyone else charged.

Al-Hayat slapped the first leveler away with the flat of his paw. His claws made a grinding sound as they scratched across the creature's metallic hide, and the artifact creature went flying.

The rest piled on top of the wolf. Levelers and vedalken alike slashed and stabbed the forest beast. Flailing and growling, Al-Hayat tried to beat them back, but it was no use. They were on him, and they cut his flesh from his bones.

With each slash, he howled. With each stab he growled. Finally, covered in his own blood, Al-Hayat's legs gave out, and he collapsed to the floor. Lying on his side, he snapped at all he could reach with his sharp fangs. Many died, but many more were out of his reach.

Something exploded from the floor. A creature, the likes of which he'd never seen, rose toward the ceiling as if it were the blue moon coming over the plane. Al-Hayat had lived many long years on Mirrodin. He had seen the birth of the blue moon and the black and red ones after that. One day he had hoped to see the green moon shoot from the Tangle and make its place in the heavens, as the others had. The time for that was nearing.

He felt the tip of something sharp pierce his gut, and his whole body shuddered. His energy waned, and his vision narrowed. Looking up at the rising blue column, he saw Glissa standing on the creature's palm. She looked down on him, caught his eye, and he tried to smile.

"You have done well, Glissa," he whispered knowing she could not hear him.

He felt more blades enter his flesh, but oddly they did not hurt.

It is my time, he thought and closed his eyes.

* * * * *

Glissa turned, standing on the Kaldra Champion's palm. There, behind where the throne had been, lay Al-Hayat. He was surrounded by vedalken and levelers. His lip curled, exposing his great fangs, covered in blue blood.

A leveler jabbed its scythe blade into the wolf's gut.

"*No,*" shouted the elf.

Al-Hayat lurched once, looked up at her, then closed his eyes and laid his head on the ground.

Glissa pulled her new sword from its scabbard and leaped into the air. The ground was a long way down, but she tucked into a roll as she landed, breaking her fall.

The levelers and vedalken turned away from the fallen beast, converging on the elf.

"You want some?" she shouted at them as they came on. "Come and get it!"

Behind them Al-Hayat jerked once, and a puddle of blood began to form under his limp mouth. Rage bubbled up inside the elf, mixed with grief. From now on, the wolf would be only a memory.

She let the rage fill her. Every cell in her body tingled with hatred, and her eyes were half blind with tears. Finally, she could hold it in no more, and she screamed at the top of her lungs.

The sound echoed off the walls, filling the cavernous space and rocking the ground. Those levelers who were charging toward her exploded. Bits of silver housing and sinew flew in all directions. What had once been a dozen killing devices was reduced to a pile of spare parts in the blink of an eye.

It wasn't just the levelers. The vedalken's halberds disintegrated as well. Blades glowing with magical power fell to dust, leaving the four-armed warriors with nothing. They stopped in their tracks, their eyes wide with terror.

Sword in front of her, Glissa sneered. "Who's next?"

A huge pale blue hand came crashing to the ground on top of the stunned vedalken. Not one had the time nor the speed to move out of the way, and a half-dozen of them were smashed to pulp.

The remaining warriors gathered their wits and ran.

Glissa looked up at the Kaldra Champion. "After them," she shouted.

The Champion nodded. Setting Slobad to the floor with his other hand, he turned toward the retreating troops and gave chase.

* * * * *

Marek's whole body throbbed. The icy serum in his helmet was freezing his head. Fortunately, the glass of his facemask was less resilient than his flesh, and it burst out, releasing some of the pressure and sparing him from having his skull crushed like a melon.

Still, the cold stung his skin, and it sent an icy burning down his spine all the way through his hips and into his legs. That wasn't the most immediate problem. With a block of ice surrounding his head, he couldn't see or breathe.

Groping around, he tried to find something he could chip away at the ice with. He found nothing and in desperation smashed his head against the floor.

Each time he made contact, the impact raced through the solid ice and vibrated through his skull. At first it hurt, but his head became numb from the cold, and after a few attempts, he couldn't feel it any more.

His lungs began to burn, and his oxygen-starved body grew weary. Panic raced through his veins, and he smashed his face harder against the ground. Blackness filled his head, and he became dizzy.

Lifting himself to his feet, Marek jumped into the air and kicked his legs up over his head. The commander of the vedalken elite guard threw all he had into this last attempt to free himself, and the top of his head crashed down, the rest of his body behind it. The impact of the blow was enough to put a crack down the middle of the ice, and the block began to give way.

Wheeling back, he felt himself drifting off into unconsciousness as he smashed his head one more time against the ground. The ice broke away, clearing his face, and the dank air of the Dross filled his lungs.

The cloudy blackness in his head receded, and the rest of the world came back to him. The skin on his face felt burnt, and his legs were still numb from the cold running down his spine, but he could breathe, and at the moment that was all he cared about.

He lay facedown on the floor for a long while, only vaguely aware of the goings on around him. Finally, someone rolled him over, and he looked up into the face of Lord Pontifex.

"Marek. You're alive."

Marek could only blink and grunt.

Malil came into his view. He tapped Pontifex on the shoulder.

"We should go," he said.

The vedalken lord looked up at something Marek couldn't see then nodded.

"Damn. All right."

Bending down, Pontifex wrapped his arm under Marek's shoulders and lifted the stunned warrior to his feet.

The chamber spun, and Marek flopped his arm over Lord Pontifex's shoulder. Looking up, he saw now what had forced the retreat. A huge ghostly blue-white creature was pounding vedalken warriors and levelers alike to pulp.

Marek rolled his head toward Pontifex. "How will we . . ." His voice was scratchy and hollow, and it hurt to speak. He cleared his throat. "Find her . . . again."

Without looking at Marek, Malil answered his question. "Memnarch will know where she is."

Pontifex shouldered most of Marek's weight, and the two of them hobbled from the Vault of Whispers. Malil was close behind.

CHAPTER 21

Glissa knelt next to Al-Hayat.

The great forest beast was dying.

"Can you heal yourself?" asked Glissa.

The wolf smiled then winced in pain. "I have no more magic."

"What can I do?"

"You can finish what we have started," replied Al-Hayat. "You can free the rest of Mirrodin." The wolf lay still. "Rejoice with the coming of the green moon."

Al-Hayat closed his eyes, and his breath slipped away.

Glissa lay her hand on his fur. Large chunks of it had been cut and torn away during the fight, but she stroked it all the same.

Slobad came up behind her and put his hand on her shoulder. She looked back and him.

"I could have saved him if I hadn't fallen into that hole."

Slobad shook his head. "Crazy elf not fall into hole, we not find giant, huh? We all be dead."

Glissa took one last look at Al-Hayat then got to her feet. The inner sanctum of Mephidross lay silent. The Kaldra Champion had smashed his way through the ranks of levelers and vedalken and sent them running. It was true, he had saved their lives—most of them anyway. They had won this battle, but it felt more like a defeat than anything else.

Bruenna came over to the pair. "Where to now?"

Without hesitation, Glissa replied, "We have all the pieces. It's time to meet Memnarch."

"How do you intend to get there?" asked the wizard.

The elf shrugged. "I don't . . . The only way in I know of is through the blue lacuna. Marching back out through the swamp and then into the vedalken fortress again doesn't sound like such a good idea. I don't think we're in much shape to fight another battle just yet. Anybody have any other ideas?" She looked at both Bruenna and Slobad.

"I do," said Bosh in his rumbling voice. His hands had been bandaged by the last of Bruenna's wizards, and he stood now looking down on the other three.

"Well," said Glissa, "let's hear it."

"The black lacuna is somewhere inside Mephidross. It leads into the interior as well."

"Golem know where it is, huh?" asked the goblin.

"No," replied the golem, "but he does." Bosh pointed toward the far end of the room.

There, pinned under a smashed, smoking leveler, was Geth.

"Grab him," shouted Glissa.

The pale man squealed and struggled harder to free himself, but the Kaldra Champion lifted him from under the broken construct and off the ground by the back of his robes.

"Where is the entrance to the black lacuna?" demanded the elf. With the walls to Geth's personal chamber gone and the fog blown away, her voice echoed in the large chamber.

Geth hung silently, dangling from the fingertips of the Kaldra Champion.

Glissa walked over to stand just beneath him. She crossed her arms over her chest and looked up at the gaunt ruler of the Vault. "You can tell us, or I'll have my friend here squeeze your head until it pops." She shrugged. "The choice is yours."

The Kaldra Champion grabbed the sides of Geth's head with two fingers.

Geth batted at the Champion's fingers with his balled up fists. "All right. All right," he shouted. The leader of the Vault began sobbing. "I'll tell you anything, just put me down and leave me my head." Geth whimpered. "I'm fond of my head."

* * * * *

Unseen by any inside the Vault of Whispers, Memnarch's myr waited patiently in the shadows. In Panopticon, deep inside the plane, the Guardian stood inside the Eye. One of his six scrying mirrors tuned to the eyes of the myr.

"Yes, Glissa Sunseeker," he said as he watched. "Come find Memnarch, you and your Champion." He laughed. "Come find Memnarch."

* * * * *

The journey down the black lacuna was much like the journey down the blue one, only this time there wasn't an army on Glissa's tail. Like the blue lacuna, it followed the slight curvature of the plane on its way from the surface to the interior. The first few thousand feet of their decent, the walls of the tunnel looked like burned steel. Bits of shiny silver metal shone through a patina of black charring. Down farther, the surface was covered in the same, glowing mossy substance, which lit the way toward the end of the tube.

Down and down they went, resting for a time along the way. As they got closer to the end, Glissa could feel her power growing. Mana became easier to tap the closer they came to the interior, and her healing spells became more potent. She hoped her battle magic would be more powerful as well.

The lacuna ended, and Glissa stepped into the interior of Mirrodin. It was only the second time she had been here, but now it didn't seem so mysterious. It was familiar to her now, and somehow, it almost felt like home.

Above, the mana core cast blinding blue-white light on everything. Nothing was shaded, nothing was safe from the penetrating gaze of the hovering internal sun. But though it had been only a full moon cycle since she'd been here, the mana core looked different.

Glissa hadn't really taken the opportunity to examine it the last time she was here. There hadn't been time for that. Now she could see arcs of green energy leaping off the mana core's surface. They appeared as if from nowhere, circled the core once, then dived back into its surface as if they were fish in the Quicksilver Sea. She didn't remember seeing any such thing last time, and even as distracted as she was, she felt certain she would have remembered a jagged bolt of green mana circling the sphere.

The rest of the interior looked different too. There were the same spindly towers that Bosh had called mycosynth, and the same mossy substance on the ground, but the landscape was more jagged, less open, and the tower in the distance was nowhere to be seen.

Everyone else piled out of the tunnel behind Glissa, shielding their eyes from the bright light.

Slobad put his hand up on his forehead and peered around as if he were a sea captain. "Where are we, huh? Look different."

"It's a different lacuna," reasoned Glissa. "We're in a different place." She turned to Bosh. "Where do we find Memnarch?"

Bosh raised his still-bandaged hand and pointed through the

mycosynth forest of chrome structures. "Through there. A long walk from here."

Glissa started walking toward the microsyth. "Then we'd better get moving."

* * * * *

Marek rested on the plains outside the swamps of the Dross. Fewer than half the warriors who had come on this mission had survived, and most of those who had were badly wounded.

Malil's force of levelers fared just as poorly. The head of the vedalken elite guards had heard the metal man say he had left the interior with over a hundred of the killing devices. Now there were barely more than two dozen.

Despite the fact that Malil had lost more soldiers, he had a decided advantage over the beaten vedalken. The devices didn't feel the emotional impact of defeat. The remaining levelers stood ready, prepared to fight to the death, even in the face of such tremendous losses.

Marek's troops, however, were dispirited and broken. They had lost, and now they were tired, frustrated, and ready to go home. Sitting here on the plain, Marek hoped that they didn't spot the elf girl and her retinue leaving the swamp. He and his men couldn't take another battle right now.

* * * * *

Pontifex paced beside a field of razor grass, watching the edge of the swamp for any sign of Glissa.

Whatever that thing was that had come from the floor and wiped out half of his elite guard was going to pose a problem.

For that matter, Malil too was going to be a handful, but the metal man would be easy enough to manipulate.

Pontifex chuckled. That was the best part about constructs. They didn't understand the subtleties of a simple lie. Somehow, while they could perform multiple complex tasks, often times more efficiently and effectively than an organic creature, they still maintained a childlike innocence. Malil would believe anything Pontifex told him. It was in his nature to do so, and the vedalken lord intended to use that to his advantage.

He'd keep the fool thinking that they were trying to capture the elf girl. Once he had his opportunity, he'd simply slip his dagger into her gut, and that would be the end of his problem.

Malil stepped up beside him, interrupting his reverie.

"She's not coming out," said the metal man.

"No? How do you know this?"

Malil tapped the side of his skull. "Memnarch has seen them enter the black lacuna."

"The black lacuna? She's going to the interior?"

The metal man nodded.

Why would she go that way? Pontifex wondered. Certainly the swamp and his own force weren't a factor, after seeing what their protector did. Had he overestimated the power of that swirling blue monstrosity? Was it just a temporary spell?

Pontifex shook his head. "Well, if she's going through the center of the plane to try to escape, she's taken the long way out."

Malil nodded his agreement.

Pontifex turned away from the razor grass field. "The question is where she's headed."

"It does not matter," said Malil. "If we chase her down the black lacuna we will be perpetually in pursuit. We must travel North to the Knowledge Pool. We can move much faster on the surface than she can on the interior, and we'll cut her off."

Pontifex nodded. "Yes, but what if she heads South to the red lacuna? We'll lose her in the mountains of the Oxidda Chain."

Malil once again tapped his head. "If she does, Memnarch will tell me so, and we will be waiting for her when she surfaces."

Pontifex smiled. "Then we're off to Lumengrid."

* * * * *

Orland stood on the floor of the People's Grand Assembly Chamber. He looked up at the expectant faces of over a hundred representatives of the soon-to-be Republic of Vedalken.

"My fellow vedalken," he said just above a whisper. His words were lifted up to even the highest perched citizen in the hall. "Until today, the name of this chamber has been a farce." He paced the room, exhilarated by each and every set of eyes that silently followed his movements. "The People's Assembly Chamber, indeed. With notably few exceptions, only the members of the elite—the lifetime appointed councilors who sat on the Synod—were allowed to debate within its walls." Orland stopped and spun on his heels. "It wasn't always like this. There was a time in our republic's history when decisions were made by the people. When we were not ruled but ruled ourselves." The vedalken councilor nodded, smiling. "A pleasant notion, don't you think?"

The assembled representatives nodded silently.

"It is time that we took back that which rightfully belongs to us." His voice rose. "It is time that we once again ruled ourselves." Now he was nearly shouting. "It is time that we decide once and for all that no vedalken has the right to go on making poor decisions in the public's interest, while the elected representatives sit powerlessly on the sidelines—" he paused, quieting himself—"no avenue of recourse available to them."

There was a rustle of robes as the representatives nodded their approval.

Sodador and Tyrell sat on a bench on the floor of the chamber. They nodded their approval as well, even lightly clapping—a gesture which had all but been outlawed in the People's Assembly Hall.

Orland continued. "My friends, those days are soon to be over." He pulled a rolled up red scroll from a pocket in his robe, lifting it high in the air for all to see. "The measure before us today, good representatives, will create a free society for all vedalken residing in the fortress of Lumengrid. I trust you have all received a copy of this document."

The rustling of robes again filled the chamber as each of the vedalken in attendance pulled from his or her garments a scroll, the exact shape, size, and color of the one Orland held.

Councilor Orland smiled. "Excellent." He looked to the other two representatives who urged him on with a wave of their hands. "As you may know, age old vedalken bylaws require that in order to change the voting structure of our government, a unanimous vote by all the members of the Synod is required. In the absence of Lord Pontifex, you have been summoned here to vote in his stead—" he turned slowly around the room, taking in each and every face—"much as you voted to accept me into the Synod only a moon cycle ago." He stopped and looked down at the parchment in his hand. "This time, there is no tie that needs to be broken. It matters not the weight of each vote, for any vote against this measure will be the end of it."

Orland took a deep breath. This was the moment he had been waiting for since the day he had become a councilor. "So, I ask you now, good representatives—" he looked at Sodador and Tyrell—"and councilors, how do you vote? Up or down?"

Orland held two of his four arms out before him, his thumbs pointing toward the ceiling.

Sodador and Tyrell stood up from their bench. They too held their hands out, their thumbs stretched to the sky.

Orland smiled. His insides jittered in anticipation. Scanning his eyes up the long spiral, he took note of each representative's vote.

Every thumb in the chamber pointed up.

"Congratulations, my friends," he said, lifting all four of his arms in the air in celebration. "Welcome to the new Free Republic of Vedalken."

* * * * *

The trip to the Quicksilver Sea had taken no time at all. Pontifex and his soldiers had climbed aboard Malil's levelers. The vedalken's four hands made it easy for them to hold onto the killing devices' steering tails and hides. The remains of the elite guard had ridden the whole way atop the swift metallic beasts.

Crossing over the rippling ocean with the aid of Pontifex's magic, they entered Lumengrid. Inside, the halls were quiet, save for a handful of low-level functionaries carrying on mundane business. When the vedalken citizens saw Pontifex and his retinue, they disappeared into doors or around corners.

"What's going on here?" demanded Pontifex.

"The people are afraid of the levelers," replied Marek.

Pontifex was irritated. "I am their lord. They should not cower from me."

Just then another vedalken stepped out of an alley, his attention focused on a memo in his hands. When he looked up and saw the group, his eyes opened wide, and he tried to dart away, but Pontifex grabbed him by the front of his robes.

"Why do you run, citizen?"

"I . . . I . . ."

"Where has everyone gone?" shouted the vedalken lord.

The vedalken swallowed hard. "They're in the People's Assembly Hall."

Pontifex released him, and the vedalken citizen stumbled backward, dashing away as fast as he could.

"The Assembly Hall," said Pontifex. A cold chill ran over his skin. "Orland." He took off, dashing down the corridors, running straight for the inverted cone-shaped hall near his own chambers. There could be only one reason—

Turning the corner, Pontifex burst through the doors of the People's Assembly Hall.

"Pontifex? What a surprise." Orland stood on the floor at the bottom of the chamber. Sodador and Tyrell near him, a look of contentment on their faces.

"Don't you mean 'Lord Pontifex,' Councilor Orland?"

Around the outside of the room, arrayed on the viewing platform, all of the vedalken elected representatives were in attendance. They stared at him, their expressions ranging from shock to amused silence.

"No, Pontifex," said Orland. "There are no more lords among the vedalken."

"What are you talking about, Councilor?"

"We have taken a vote." Orland waved his hands in the air, indicating all the vedalken in the room. "The Vedalken Empire is no more."

Pontifex laughed. "That's preposterous. If there is no more empire, then why are you all still here? The people and the empire are one and the same."

Orland nodded. "How right you are, Pontifex. Only, we prefer to call it a republic."

"Oh, please," spat the former vedalken lord. "Who will lead the people? Who will make the laws and instill order in the masses? Surely you don't think the representatives can rule?"

A loud rustling sound filled the chamber as the assembled citizens shifted and scowled, reacting to Pontifex's words.

"Actually," replied Orland, "that's exactly what *we* think."

Pontifex beat his hands against the railing. "This cannot happen. I will not allow it. I am still the leader of the Synod. Nothing happens in Lumengrid without my approval!"

"No, Pontifex," said Sodador, "the Synod no longer exists. We've formed a parliament. The elected representatives now have all the power." He took a step, leaning heavily on his cane and limping. "In fact, you're the only one here without a vote."

Pontifex looked around the room. How could they do this to him? After all he had done for the empire, this was how he was rewarded. He had dedicated his life to the service of all vedalken, and now he was cast out.

Tyrell stood up from the bench where he sat on the floor of the chamber. "Now, for the next piece of business," he said. "I bring before you a resolution of imprisonment." The older statesman held out a piece of metal parchment, holding it at arm's length and leaning his head back to view what was written on its surface. "Wherein: The Free Republic of Vedalken has found citizen Pontifex to be within the jurisdiction of this governing body and its limits of prosecution and retributive justice. And Wherein: This parliament has found the former lord of the empire to have committed numerous crimes against the people. Let it be resolved that free citizen Pontifex be immediately apprehended and imprisoned, to await trial and punishment for his repeat offenses against the republic and its denizens."

"You're imprisoning *me?*" shouted Pontifex.

Orland nodded. "Yes."

The door behind him opened, and a pair of armed guards burst in. One leveled his halberd at him. The other produced a set of four manacles.

Pontifex narrowed his eyes, glaring down on the three former councilors standing on the floor. "You will not get away with this," he said. "Mark my words, I will make you all pay for this treachery."

Turning around, he lowered his eyes to the ground and stuck his arms out straight, presenting his wrists for shackles. As the guard moved to take him custody, Pontifex lifted his head. He finished mouthing the last word of a spell, and a jet of brilliant blue energy shot from each of his hands.

His spell struck both guards. Pontifex lifted his arms over his head, and the guards shot into the air, their arms flailing, their legs moving as if to run, but both were held fast by powerful magics.

A gasp escaped the lips of the collected representatives, filling the Assembly Hall with the booming noise of a million whispers.

Spinning around, Pontifex lifted the two suspended guards over his head and looked back down at Orland. Their eyes met. The former vedalken lord hurled his fists toward the floor. Both guards shrieked. Magnified by the chamber, it bounced off the walls, overtopping the collective gasp. Both vedalken fell.

Orland jumped away, but the older Tyrell and the lame Sodador were not so quick. The falling guards landed atop the two councilors, and the crunching sound of bones breaking replaced all other noise in the hall—amplified a hundred fold.

Pontifex smiled as he looked over the rail. Only Orland remained moving. The other four lay on the ground in a broken pile, their blue blood mixing as it seeped out onto the floor in a large puddle.

Pontifex pointed at Orland. "You're next, councilor," he said. "If it's the last thing I do, you will be next." He turned and darted from the People's Assembly Hall.

* * * * *

Glissa and the others marched through a forest of mycosynth. The going was slow, as the mossy ground grabbed at their feet. The tall spires made travel difficult as well. It was like navigating through the dense Tangle, only here the growths were less predictable. Several times the entire group marched through the mazelike mycosynth, only to find a dead-end and be forced to retrace their steps.

Pushing deeper into the forest, Glissa nearly lost her balance as she tried to avoid stepping on a squirming critter beneath her feet.

"What the . . . ?" Glissa slipped back, but Bosh managed to catch her in his meaty palm. She looked over her shoulder at the golem. "Thanks."

Bosh nodded, and the corners of his mouth turned up in a grin.

"Bosh," she shouted, spinning around and grabbing hold of one of his fingers. "You smiled."

"I did?"

"Uh huh. Here, kneel down."

Glissa reached up, and the golem bent down. Her hand touched his face. It was soft and squishy. Though it retained its metallic look, there was no doubt, the golem's face had turned to flesh.

"When did this happen?"

Bosh shrugged. "Just now."

Glissa ran her hand along his cheek. "Your face is almost all flesh."

The golem sighed. "Yes."

"Well," said the elf, "at least now you won't always look so dour and serious."

"Is that good?"

The elf smiled at him. "Yes. Very."

At this the corners of Bosh's mouth bent up again.

Another of the creatures that had tripped Glissa brushed against her leg. The animal was rectangular with very angular edges—no curves or organic irregularities at all. It had two skinny arms with three opposable digits attached to each, and its movements were smooth and swift, as if it traveled on wheels.

The creature moved back and forth between diamond-shaped objects embedded in (or perhaps overgrown by) the glowing mossy ground cover. Each time it reached one of this things, it fondled it with its fingers, then moved on to another, as if it were adjusting something or tending a plant.

Glissa reached down and grabbed the beast off the ground. It was the same metallic color as Bosh, but it too was soft and pliable. On its underside, as Glissa had guessed, there were three little wheels, and they spun now, trying to get free of the elf's grip. Its arms too reached back and began pinching at her skin.

"Ow." Glissa put the creature down. "What is that thing?"

"It is a grendle," replied Bosh.

"A grendle?"

The golem nodded.

"What do they do?"

Bosh shook his head. "I do not know. I have only vague memories of them." He looked down on the little creature. "They were made by Memnarch."

From all around, more grendles came out from behind the towering mycosynth monoliths. They moved in a pack, touching and prodding the diamond-shaped boxes on the ground then moving on. They didn't seem to mind Glissa or the others, simply moving around the obstructions where they stood.

"If Memnarch made them," asked Glissa, "how did they become fleshy? Can he create organic creatures?"

Bosh shook his head. "No. They began as metal constructs." He pushed a finger into his own skin. "They are like me, made from metal turned to flesh."

Slobad knelt down to get a closer look. He poked at one, pulling his finger out of the way when it snapped its little hands at him. "These all flesh, huh? You only part flesh."

Glissa scratched her head, then she looked up at the mana core. "Maybe something here in the interior causes metal to turn to flesh." She scanned the mycosynth. "If this is the source, then it would make sense that these creatures would transform faster." She shrugged. "Maybe they've been like this for a long time."

"Look at this." Bruenna was several steps away, standing at the base of a monolith. She poked at something on the ground with her toe.

Glissa walked over. Bruenna was looking at a grendle. Only this one was unmoving, and it looked pale and stiff.

"It's dead," said the wizard.

"From what?"

Bruenna looked up into Glissa's eyes, then glanced up at Bosh. "Old age, presumably."

Glissa understood immediately. "We need to go." She grabbed Bosh by the hand. "We need to get you out of here as fast as we can—before you end up like them."

CHAPTER 22

Malil had never experienced desire such as he felt just now. Every pore of his body hated him and rebelled. His vision blurred. His arms were weak. His thoughts were scattered and incoherent, punctuated periodically by lucid moments of understanding and hatred.

This was one of those moments.

Leaping down from his leveler, he crossed the threshold and entered Panopticon. He had not waited even a moment for Pontifex. Who knew what that fool was after. Right now, Malil didn't care. All he could focus on was getting to the top of the tower and acquiring some serum. Once inside the staging area at the base of Panopticon, the metal man hurried up the stairs and into the lift.

He had failed in his task, but he could go no further. Certainly Memnarch would understand this. Certainly he would give Malil another dose, something to aid him in his quest to capture the elf girl.

The lift rose.

If he'd only had more serum in Mephidross, reasoned Malil, he would have her by now. He tapped his fingers on his leg in anticipation.

He'd tell Memnarch about his newfound understanding.

Explain to him that in order to accomplish his goals, he'd need more serum. He'd relate the tales of his long days and nights on the plain, waiting for the elf, no serum to be had—the tremors and shakes, the delusions and aching. He'd tell Memnarch of his suffering, and surely the creator would give him what he wanted.

He rose through the floor of the observation deck and climbed the spiraling walkway to the laboratory.

If that didn't work, he thought, gripping the hilt of his sword in his weary, aching hand, he'd do whatever would be necessary.

The door to the laboratory slide open, and Malil stepped inside. The place was ruined. Shards of glass covered the floor—inches deep. Bits of broken metal lay in bent heaps. The windows were broken out. The tables were turned over, and all of the experiments were smashed on the floor, their liquids mixing with each others, their results lost.

Memnarch lay on the floor near his ruined serum-infusion device. His body heaved and shook, and he did not look up at the sound of the door opening then closing again.

Scanning the room, Malil looked for serum. The opalescent liquid was impossible to mistake. There was nothing else like it on the entire planet. The whole lab had been full of it. Big tanks and tubes were constantly pumping the stuff from one place to another—or into Memnarch. Certainly there would be some left.

Malil dropped to his knees. He pushed the shards of glass away, uncovering what lay beneath. The more he looked, the less he found. Getting back to his feet, he began kicking aside the debris on the floor, shuffling through the piles faster and faster.

"Where is it? Enlightenment! I must have it!" he shouted. Metal bent and a still-whole beaker, apparently saved from whatever had hit this room, spun across the floor.

Malil's eyes lit up. The bottle came to a stop, rotating in place. Its sides were painted with the opalescent color of serum. The viscous liquid clung to the edges, slowly falling back to the bottom of the beaker—but only reluctantly.

The metal man lifted the vial to his lips. The sticky liquid rolled over his tongue and down his throat.

It was as if his eyes had been covered over with grease. His vision cleared, and he could see the world for how it really was. Suddenly, everything was right in Mirrodin. It did not matter that he hadn't caught the elf. He had time, and now he had an increased mental and physical capacity.

"She's mine," he said.

Standing up, Malil wiped the last of the serum from his lips with the back of his hand. But when he pulled it away, he didn't see the pure shimmering color of blinkmoth serum. His hand was covered in a thin red liquid—like elf blood. He touched his lip again, and more of the substance came away. The flask as well had traces of the stuff on its broken edge.

Now that he thought about it, the strange sensation he had felt while searching the floor was still bothering him. Turning over his hand, he examined his palm.

It too was covered in this red liquid. A piece of glass protruded from just under his index finger, and the liquid seemed to be pumping from a scratch in his hide.

Malil dropped the beaker and grabbed hold of the shard of glass. Pulling it out, he touched his palm. A small patch of it had become soft. Where the glass had been, there was an incision, and it wept fluid.

The metal man touched his lip. It too felt soft, and a small wound just like the one on his hand was leaking.

He was bleeding.

Memnarch stirred.

"Master." Malil shook the prone frame. "Master, are you all right?"

Memnarch stared at him with unseeing eyes. "Serum. We must have serum. We must . . . *know.*"

"Yes, Master," replied Malil. "Where do I find it?"

Memnarch pointed to the ruined infusion device.

Malil nodded. "It's broken."

Memnarch shook his head, pointing emphatically to something beside him. There, lying on the ground, was a large hose. On one end was a sharp-tipped needle.

* * * * *

Glissa stepped out around an unusually wide monolith, and suddenly she was outside of the mycosynth forest. Directly before her, a short hill dropped softly down into a valley, and beyond that, a wide, rolling expanse opened up underneath the humming mana core. In the far distance, just below the point where the ground curved up, disappearing from view, she could just make out the base of Panopticon.

"It's still a long way," said Bruenna, stepping up behind her.

Glissa nodded. "Perhaps we should rest here. Something tells me the opportunities will grow fewer the closer we get to the tower."

Bruenna nodded. "A wise decision," she said. "What about the golem? The longer we linger, the more he turns to flesh."

Glissa looked up at Bosh. He still appeared much the same as he had when she first met him. Now, though, he was far more expressive. His stoic, unmoving jaw smiled or frowned, depending on his mood—and his mood, Glissa found, changed quickly.

Right now, he was happy. The edges of his lips curled up, and his eyes seemed more open. Maybe all the things she had been telling him about being flesh were true. Perhaps it wasn't so bad after all to become like her, live a life that was more frail but more enjoyable because of that vulnerability.

"You're right," replied Glissa finally. "We should keep moving."

The elf headed down the hill, moving slowly closer to the far distant Panopticon. The others followed close behind. When they reached the bottom of the valley and headed back up, Glissa heard a strange noise.

"What's that?"

Bruenna turned her head to listen. "I do not know."

Slobad recognized the sound. "Threshers."

As if the goblin's words summoned a pack of hungry beasts, a line of buzzing threshers rolled over the hill and descended on them. Similar in design to levelers, threshers were smaller, faster, hunched-backed killing devices. In place of the scissoring scythe blades, these creatures had a rotating cylinder of interlocking, curved cutting devices.

Glissa had seen them before on the plains, roaming around when the razor grass fields had grown too long to see over. They dug deep, mazelike pathways into the growing blades.

What purpose their ritual served, Glissa was uncertain. She'd seen the leonin use the cut grass to built weapons, but they were not responsible for these killing devices. Memnarch was.

The threshers rolled down the hill, their spinning blades chewing up the mossy ground covering. Glissa drew her sword. The wizards had already drawn mana, and their spells flew. The long blue tracers of their arcane magics lit up the sky. Glissa flashed back to the many fights she'd faced with these human spellcasters. They were fast. Their spells always struck first, taking a heavy toll on whatever was coming at them.

The wizards' spells splashed against the advancing line of threshers, and for a moment a few of their number were lost in a cloud of mystical energy. Bruenna let out a whoop, but she fell silent when those same devices rolled out of the cloud, unharmed.

"What happened?" asked Glissa.

Bruenna shook her head. "They are either immune to magic or—" she turned to look Glissa in the eye—"they are no longer made of metal."

That was all the conversation they had time for, as the rolling devices crashed into them.

Bosh was the first to encounter the foe. Kicking out, he smashed the first in line in the side, expertly avoiding the spinning blades, aiming for a spot right beside the creature's eye. A well-placed blow here could incapacitate it, shaking loose the constructs that made it run, leaving it an empty shell that could be ignored on the battlefield.

The golem's foot landed squarely where he aimed, but instead of the pounding boom of hollow metal, Bosh's foot sank deep into soft, pliable skin. The creature let out a squeal and skittered back, as if it had felt pain. It shuddered and jolted from side to side. Bosh's blow hadn't incapacitated it, but it seemed to have confused the creature. He didn't have time to worry about it, as the next thresher fell on him, its blades spinning.

Glissa too was engaged in a fierce fight. She cut down, sending her blade into the spinning teeth of her opponent. She had yet to really test her new weapon. The Sword of Kaldra would have cut through anything, bone, metal, flesh, it didn't matter. She had grown accustomed to its power, and she fought now as if she still wielded it.

The steel blade slashed across the leveler's mowing cylinder, and it cut deep, but it wasn't metal it bit into; it was flesh. Blood spurt from a tremendous gash, washing over Glissa and covering her in the sticky red fluid. The wounded thresher shied back, and two more took its place.

Glissa fought off the two devices. Though they had become flesh, their blades were still sharp. They left long gashes in the metallic floor of the interior, and the elf knew enough to keep herself away.

Fighting these part-flesh, part-metal artifacts was like fighting a forest beast in the Tangle. That thought reminded her of something her father had told her as a young elf going out on her first hunting party. "Some bits are metal, other bits flesh, but you always want to stay away from the teeth."

Glissa pulled her blade back, coming across with both hands and swiping at a thresher in a flat slice. The tip of her sword cut into the creature's eyes, and she took a step back. Her swift attack bought her enough time to spare a glance over her shoulder. What she saw didn't make her happy.

The Kaldra Champion floated over a pack of threshers. The smaller creations were fast and more agile than their leveler counterparts. The Champion smashed his fist to the ground, but the devices darted away unscathed. Against bigger, slower targets, he was a superb fighter. Against these little creatures, the Kaldra Champion was nearly useless.

Turning her attention back to the thresher, Glissa barely managed to fend off its blow, as the quick device darted in. Her sword hit the creature's sharp teeth. Lodging it into the spinning cylinder, she put all of her weight on the blade and shoved off.

Lifting from the ground, the elf's body lurched. The forward movement of the thresher forced her back, and she balanced her lithe frame against the hilt of her sword. The creature began spurting blood, and it stopped its charge, letting Glissa fall back to the ground. It moved back, trying to pull the elf's weapon from its belly. Its own bladed cylinder clamped down on the sword, and it jerked, pulling the handle free of Glissa's grasp.

A cold chill ran down the elf's spine as she watched the agile device dart back up the hill, her blade stuck inside. All around, the valley was flooded with these threshers, and the others fought for their lives. Slobad rode on top of a device, holding on for dear life. It looked as if he was trying to pry the thing open, but judging from the bloodstains on his chest, he was more a butcher than a mechanic. Bosh had his hands full, fighting off a half-dozen of the monsters.

Glissa wouldn't be much help if she didn't have her sword. Sidestepping a charging thresher, she went after the wounded device that had stolen her blade. As she turned, she clearly saw Bruenna battling with a pair of devices. Her shins bled. She was isolated—and she was losing. The other wizard from her tribe had fallen into hand to hand combat with the threshers as well. He was tied up, unable to get to her.

Parrying the attacks of one device, Bruenna turned too late to catch the attack of the other, and the creature gave her a nasty slash across the back. The human wizard fell to the ground, clutching at her wound.

Glissa jolted at the sight, forgetting her sword in the flurry of battle. She ran toward her downed friend as fast as she could. A thresher jumped out in front of her, its spinning blades turned to tear her apart.

Pushing the ground with her back leg, the elf leaped into the air, her front leg outstretched. The thresher reared back, but it was too slow, Glissa had already cleared its teeth, and she landed on top of its head. Its top was soft, and it caved in under her weight. She slipped, and her knee gave way. Tilting to the side, Glissa pushed off again.

Her off-center jump sent her flying to the ground. She tucked into a ball, curling her shoulder under as she hit. The world spun once, and Glissa popped back to her feet.

Before her, the threshers closed in on Bruenna. One of them seemed to open, lifting its head and cutting blades up off the ground. Behind those spinning teeth, the creature revealed a hollow chamber. Bruenna looked up, her eyes wide, and she lifted her hands in the air, hopelessly trying to hold off the advancing creature.

Darting forward, it scooped up the injured mage and closed down, swallowing her whole.

Glissa couldn't believe her eyes. Bruenna was gone. Threshers weren't supposed to be able to do that.

Anger and grief welled up inside her, the same feelings that had driven her powerful spell in the past. She thought of Al-Hayat, the trolls, and all the wizards who had died on this quest. Then she thought of Bruenna, trapped inside the gut of that thresher, and her blood began to boil. She could feel power course through her, as it had many times before. Her control was getting greater, and she focused her rage on the threshers, willing them to disintegrate into tiny piles of dust.

Nothing happened.

Glissa felt the same release she had each time before when the spell had worked. For some reason the creatures she had focused on were unaffected.

It hit her. "They're no longer metal."

Each time before, when she had used this mysterious power, she had only been able to destroy levelers or weapons—never flesh. Standing there, empty handed, watching the thresher with Bruenna inside dart away, Glissa felt numb. Her head buzzed, and her limbs felt heavy. She hadn't realized before how draining that experience had been.

A thresher hit her from behind, knocking the elf face first on the ground. She had time to turn over and see the creature open wide, before she too was swallowed whole.

CHAPTER 23

Memnarch opened the door to the Eye and waved Malil over. "Come. Memnarch wishes to see the elf girl."

Malil crossed the laboratory and climbed into the Eye with Memnarch. The guardian touched the appropriate controls, and all of the screens lit up. Each of them showed a different scene, each giving a different view of Mirrodin. The plains, swamp, mountains, oceans, and forest of the metal planet were all represented.

Memnarch turned another knob, and five of the six screens changed to a picture of the interior. They were all the same, but each from a different angle. In the center of all five screens, a lone thresher rolled across the open ground.

On the sixth screen was a view of the inside of the Eye—the view from Malil's point of view. The metal man looked into that screen, and it reproduced what he saw a billion times—like two mirrors facing each other. Malil looked at what Memnarch saw when Memnarch looked through his eyes, and that image layered itself upon itself into infinity, making an endless hallway, surrounded by the interior of the Eye.

An unexpected discovery, thought the Guardian, something he'd have to explore later, when the elf girl was firmly within his grasp.

Malil turned his attention to one of the other five screens, and the view through his eyes too showed the lone device on the interior of Mirrodin.

"Why are we looking at a thresher, master?"

"Because, Malil, the elf girl is inside."

Memnarch squinted, spotting something heading toward his prize. One of the screens shifted its view, narrowing in on another lone creature, speeding toward the thresher atop a hoverer.

"What is *he* doing here?"

* * * * *

The inside of the thresher's body was very dark. It reminded Glissa of the time Bosh had placed her in his chest cavity. Only this time, the world wasn't spinning. Considering the circumstances, it was a comfortable ride. The chamber was spacious enough for her to sit cross-legged and not have to duck her head, and the sides of the creature were soft.

After having hit the thresher with her fists—and even kicking until she became winded—Glissa concluded that it didn't feel any pain, at least not from the inside. So she sat waiting.

What a predicament. Swallowed whole by a thresher after having lost her sword. It was a wonder she'd made it this far at all. She laughed at that thought. Slobad had been so worried about what she would use for a weapon once they'd put the Kaldra Champion together. Evidently, it didn't matter.

She thought about what awaited her at the end of this ride. Was Bruenna being taken to the same place? Would she finally meet Memnarch? This wasn't exactly the way she had envisioned it.

Glissa felt the thresher slow down. Her heart raced, and she prepared to draw mana. The creature came to an abrupt stop. It jerked backward, then the sharp tip of a short blade cut through the creature's exterior, nearly punching straight into Glissa's forehead.

The blade slid sideways, and the thresher shook. Blood poured into the hollow cavity, and light seeped in through the wound. Glissa could only make out the hand and forearm attached to the blade—blue skin.

Another blade struck the beast and punched through. Glissa pushed herself back in the chamber, staying as far from the weapons as possible, then she drew as much mana as she could.

The arcane energies flowed to her, and she cast a spell, growing to nearly twice her size in the blink of an eye. Her body quickly filled the confined space, and her arms were pinned to her sides by the thresher's flesh. She had known this would happen and avoided just this situation earlier in the ride. Kicking with all of her might, her engorged legs connected with the front of the thresher—right beneath where the blade had cut into its hide.

Flesh tore, and light flooded in. Glissa was free.

Getting to her feet, the giant elf pulled the remaining bits of the thresher's corpse from her head and looked down on a vedalken.

"Pontifex."

The four-armed lord glared back at her. "You have taken from me my god. You have taken from me my kingdom." He lifted a bloody sword in each hand. "Now I am going to take your life."

The vedalken lunged at the elf, cutting two long gashes in her thigh before she could react. The wounds would have been much worse had Glissa not been so big, but they were still painful, and the elf gave ground.

Lifting off into the air on his hoverer, the vedalken brandished a pair of matched short swords. Pontifex shot forward, swooping around the giant elf, charging right at her head.

Glissa ducked, shuffling forward and putting her hand to the ground to keep from falling. The hoverer just missed her, tussling her hair as it shot past. Catching her balance, Glissa stood up and turned, keeping the vedalken where she could see him.

Pontifex stopped dead and with a thought twisted the hoverer in mid-air. Its nose pointed at Glissa, he rode at her again. This time Glissa sidestepped to her right, swatting at the vedalken as if he were a buzzing fly. Pontifex anticipated her move and swung the hoverer to his left, bringing the sharp edge of his blade across her shoulder.

The elf hissed at the wound and jerked away from the attack, bringing her other hand up in defense. Pontifex's mind urged his vehicle away, but he was too close. The elf's hand swung by him, swirling the air around his hoverer.

Pontifex bounced through the windstream, then the hoverer flipped over and spun, tossing the rider from his mount. The vedalken dropped to the ground.

Glissa lifted her foot in the air, prepared to step on her foe. "I'm going to squash you like a bug." She lowered her foot, casting a great shadow.

Pontifex got to his knees. One of his left arms had been wounded in the fall, and he held it tight against his body. "I have nothing left to live for," he said. He shouted a one-syllable spell, extending his two good arms out at the big elf.

A whirlwind of swirling blue energies enwrapped Glissa, whipping her hair about her head and draining from her the magics that had enlarged her to giant size. The elf shrank. The world around her grew larger, and the powers that had made her bigger and stronger were sucked away.

When she reached normal size, the whipping wind released her. The swirling storm glided over the ground, pushing the mossy covering this way and that, headed straight for the wounded vedalken.

Once again the storm enclosed its victim. Pontifex disappeared from view, surrounded entirely in the swirling energy. Then, just as quickly as it had started, the wind died, and the storm stopped, dropping away to reveal the vedalken beneath. Pontifex was fully healed, and he began to grow. His arms stretched and his legs lifted him high in the air. His head, already big for a vedalken, became larger than a troll's.

The blue-skinned vedalken grew to titanic proportions, towering over the elf.

Glissa put her foot down. "Can we talk about this?"

Pontifex took a giant step forward, and Glissa had to jump to one side to avoid being squashed.

The elf darted away. Spotting a cluster of four or five small mycosynth monoliths, she made for the cover they provided. When she reached the growths, she fell in behind them, putting her back up against a monolith, trying to catch her breath. At least they were sharp, so Pontifex would have to think twice about trying to step on her.

"You cannot hide forever," shouted the giant vedalken.

"Don't count on it," said Glissa under her breath.

Pontifex began pacing around the cluster. "Come out and face me."

Glissa slid behind a different monolith, staying hidden and quiet.

The vedalken got down on his hands and knees, and peered into the middle of the mycosynth. Pontifex's huge eye glared down on Glissa. Though she tried to scoot down, hiding between two of the metal formations, she couldn't escape his gaze.

Reaching in with his enlarged finger, Pontifex poked around inside the cluster. He sneered, keeping his eye on her as he dug around for his prize, but the formation was too tightly packed, and he was too big. The sharp edges of the mycosynth cut his skin, and frustrated his attempts to get Glissa.

Finally Pontifex stood up. "Fine. We shall do this the hard way." Waving his arms in the air, a wisp of blue mana flared from each of his four hands. The vedalken disappeared from sight.

Glissa stood up. She peered around the edge of the monolith. No Pontifex. Craning her neck, she looked the other way. No Pontifex.

Grabbing a handful of the mossy ground cover, she tapped into the flowing mana here in the interior and forced some into her hands. The sticky substance bent to her will, elongating and weaving itself into a long thin fiber. Folding over one end to make a thicker handle, Glissa gave her makeshift whip a quick flick. The end shot out and snapped with a loud pop. She nodded. It would do. She took a deep breath and burst into the open, guessing at where Pontifex must be.

Coming out from behind the cluster of monoliths, the elf lifted her whip for a quick, surprise strike—only there was no Pontifex. Spinning around, she scanned the area—still no Pontifex.

"Looking for me?" came a voice.

Glissa's head darted. She looked up, down, side to side, but she couldn't see anything. Dropping into a crouch, the elf spun a slow circle, trying to be prepared for anything.

Behind her, she heard the mossy ground shuffle, and she turned—too late. Something hard hit the back of her head, and the world spun. Glissa dropped her whip and fell.

*　*　*　*　*

Pontifex stood over the incapacitated elf. She rolled around on the ground, holding the back of her head, finally turning over on her back and looking up at him.

"That wasn't nearly as hard as I thought it would be."

Glissa's eyes were nearly crossed from the pain. He'd hit her hard. It was a wonder the blow hadn't killed her outright.

But he was glad it hadn't. He wanted this to last a while. He wanted to torture her as much as she had tortured him.

Dropping to his knees, he straddled the elf's chest, pulling her arms down and pinning them under his legs. Then he grabbed her chin in one of his hands and examined her face, holding his matched short swords near her throat with two others.

"What is it that Memnarch sees in you?" Pontifex roughly shoved her head from side to side. "What is it you have that I do not?"

Glissa remained silent, her eyes mostly closed, her lips curled in a grimace of pain.

Pontifex shook his head. "How is it that such an insignificant creature could take my place at his side? Look at you. Your body has yet to evolve past having only two arms. What use is a creature such as this?"

Glissa's eyes were beginning to clear. Though she was hardly lucid, it was evident that the pain in her head was beginning to subside.

"It's no matter, really. Once I've killed you, Memnarch will have no choice but to take me back. He'll see that I was the only choice and understand the folly of his thinking." The vedalken nodded, decidedly convinced of his own words. "The only question now is how swiftly will your death come."

The glowing blue blade of a vedalken halberd slipped up under his chin. "It will not come at all," said a voice.

A cold chill ran down his spine, and Pontifex lifted his chin as far as it would go, touching the top of his head to his back. Another vedalken came into view.

"Marek," he said, relief replacing the fear. "You startled me." He reached up and put his fingers on the halberd blade, pushing it away.

Marek pressed back, and the blade sliced into Pontifex's fingers.

"What is this?"

"I won't let you kill her, Pontifex," said Marek, his eyes narrow.

Pontifex tried to lean forward. Marek held his halberd tight against Pontifex's throat, unmoving.

"After all I did for you . . ." said Pontifex. "To do this to me now . . ."

"Yes," said Marek, "I owe you my life."

"Then why are you doing this?"

"Because I have a duty to the Vedalken Republic."

"Vedalken Republic? Don't tell me you buy into all that nonsense Orland is spouting about representation for the people."

Marek nodded. "Yes, Pontifex. That's exactly what I'm telling you."

"Please, Marek, we were friends, partners." Pontifex swallowed. "You helped me hunt this very elf. You, as much as anyone, wanted to see her head on top of that pike, and now you can have it. All that work. All that time we spent chasing this prize, and now she is within reach." He looked back into Marek's eyes, the back of his head still touching his shoulder blades. "Please. Release this blade and let us talk about this . . . as friends."

Marek's eyes focused on the distance, his mind somewhere else. Pontifex watched, hoping that his words had gotten through. His neck hurt from craning back so far, and the skin on his throat was tight against his Adam's apple, making it hard to breathe. If he got out of this, he would kill the elf, and then he would kill Marek for this betrayal.

Marek's glassy gaze came back to Pontifex, and he shook his head. "I owe you much, but if I let you go through with this, let you betray Memnarch in the name of the Vedalken Empire, you will doom us all. Your actions will cast a shadow on all that we have accomplished. Your greed and petty jealousies could be the downfall of the greatest revolution in vedalken history." Marek's eyes grew soft, sad. "I'm not about to let you do that."

Pontifex rolled backward, away from Marek's halberd, bringing his twin swords up and thrusting at his attacker as he tumbled. Each blade bit deep, puncturing skin, bone, and lung.

Completing his somersault, the one-time vedalken lord came up to his feet, the front of his robes drenched in blue blood.

Marek stood for a moment longer then dropped to his knees. The lengths of Pontifex's matched blades were buried to the hilt in his chest.

"Mar—" Pontifex tried to speak, but his voice wouldn't work, and a sharp pain ran down his spine as he tried. Touching his throat, he felt a long gash where Marek's halberd had been. Looking down at himself, he realized that the blood on his robes was not Marek's. It was his own.

His head felt light, and the mana core seemed to grow brighter, nearly washing out all color, turning everything to a hazy white. Marek toppled forward. Pontifex could see the ends of his blades protruding from his back.

The head of the vedalken elite guard shuddered once then fell still.

Pontifex slumped down beside his one-time friend, his vision narrowing, his thoughts drifting away before he could finish them. A warm, soft buzz filled his whole body. It seemed to brush aside the pain in his throat and the anguish in his heart.

What have I done?

Slowly, the last leader of the vedalken Synod lowered his head to rest on his friend's shoulder and closed his eyes.

CHAPTER 24

Glissa awoke to someone poking at her head. The elf sprang to her feet, spinning on her attacker, mana already drawn.

"Whoa, crazy elf!" shouted Slobad. "Take it easy, huh?" He waved his hand in front of her face. "Slobad." The goblin flashed her a toothy grin.

Glissa relaxed, funneling the mana into a rejuvenating spell that immediately found the throbbing pain in the back of her head.

On the ground beside her lay Pontifex and Marek. Their blood mixed and pooled together below them.

"What happened? How did Marek get here?"

"We were hoping you could tell us," said Bosh. "They were both dead when we arrived."

Glissa shrugged, feeling the back of her head. Her spell had significantly reduced the bump, but it hurt when she pressed on it. "I had a fight with Pontifex. The last thing I remember was getting hit on the head."

"Maybe Marek saved you?" said Slobad.

Glissa smiled. "Not likely." She looked around. The Kaldra Champion stood behind them, towering over the other three. "Where's the other wizard?"

"He went after Bruenna."

In the chaos, Glissa had forgotten. Immediately she felt the urge to give chase, go find her friend and rescue her from whatever fate awaited her when the thresher stopped and let her free. But Bruenna's image arose in her mind. Glissa could see her shaking her head, saying, "Finish what you have started—for the good of all."

Bosh handed Glissa her new blade. "You might need this."

She took it, gratefully. "Thank you."

Grabbing hold of Pontifex's hoverer, she hopped on. "It's time we paid Memnarch a visit."

* * * * *

In the distance, a four-legged, bird-headed creature stalked the elf and her companions. It crouched low behind a mycosynth monolith. From its hiding place, the myr could see where they headed, but it did not pursue—not yet.

Also in its field of view were several other artifact creations just like itself. They were a pack. Five in all, they hunted the elf.

Back in Panopticon, Memnarch watched her through the Eye as she headed to his palace.

* * * * *

As they approached the glistening tower, Glissa couldn't help but be amazed. Though she knew it was made of steel, aluminum, and titanium, parts of Panopticon looked like sparkling crystals.

Memnarch's fortress climbed high into the air, higher than any other structure on the interior. Where each of its five walls joined the next, the line was so sharp and straight, it looked as if it would cut through flesh like a razor. The top rose to a needlelike point, perched atop a room made entirely of glass, opened to the world for all to see in—and for those inside to see out.

From a distance, the tower looked like just one more perfectly formed mycosynth monolith. Up close, it looked more like the scepter of a giant king. Its base was thick and heavy. Its top was adorned with a hefty jewel. Its sides were intricately designed to give off a regal air of power and grace.

A pair of wide doors on the ground floor opened up, and Glissa stopped. She looked up at the Kaldra Champion, then she looked at Bosh and Slobad.

"You ready?"

All three nodded.

The doors lay open, the light of the mana core reflecting off the edges, not penetrating into its depths. Then the darkness beyond began to move. Shadows coalesced into nightmares, and an army burst forth, their shiny hides reflecting back the interior sun's blinding rays.

"Levelers," said Glissa and Slobad in unison.

Glissa stepped off the hover hoverer and drew her sword. In a flash the metal beasts were on them. Scythe blades rang out, and the elf parried blow after blow. Catching the tip of her darksteel sword in a joint, she pried free a bolt. After so many fights with these beasts, she knew where to hit them to do the most damage.

Her strike was clean, and one side of her foe sloughed to the ground. Its left half now unarmored, Glissa reversed her stroke and cut deep into the device. That was all it took, two strokes, and the leveler was dead.

Across the way, Slobad loosed his crowbar. Hopping into the air, he jumped over the razor blades of the attacking horde to land atop a leveler. With a practiced flare, the goblin tore into the killing device, taking apart its metal hide in a blink and disabling it with a twist of his hand. Then he was off, leaving the lifeless hulk to rust on the battlefield.

Behind them, Bosh beat the metal devices into the ground. He kicked holes in their hides and tore their insides out. He smashed their vision crystals, blinding them before he dented in their heads, and he ripped their steering sails off. Without them, the levelers could only turn right, and they spun in place, looking like ballerinas dancing a deadly ballet on the battlefield.

Towering above them all was the Kaldra Champion. With each of his great magical fists he smashed a leveler flat. With each of his feet he stomped them into foil.

It was a massacre of titanic proportions. For each victim these killing devices had claimed on the surface of Mirrodin, the elf, goblin, golem, and champion visited five blows upon their heads. The battlefield rang with the screeching of metal, and the ground was piled with debris.

The fighting stopped. The levelers, usually fearless and unrelenting, retreated. Behind them, the gates to Panopticon lay open, and a pair of figures emerged. One was bipedal. His skin shone brilliantly under the glare of the mana core.

The other walked on all fours, not like a wolf or a lion, but more like a spider with only four legs. Unlike his counterpart, this one did not sparkle or reflect the blinding light. Instead he looked a pale blue, as if he were made of flesh instead of metal.

As the pair marched toward them, Glissa recognized the shorter, two-legged creature. "Malil."

The other bore a striking resemblance to the metal man. Not in his body or even his face—for this creature had six eyes, each covered with a deep blue lens—but in his mannerisms. They were like a father and his son. Each looked different, but both came from the same lineage, carrying the same build, the same set of ancestors—and the same scars.

The levelers parted, and the two creatures stopped a handful of steps from Glissa and her companions.

"I have watched you for so very long, Glissa," said the spindly legged creature. "At times I have wondered if we would ever meet face to face. Now here you are."

Glissa gripped her sword. "Everyone seems to know me, but who are you?"

The creature lowered his head and front legs in an elaborate bow. "I am the Guardian of Mirrodin, keeper of all you see." He stood up. "You may call me Memnarch."

Something inside Glissa snapped, and she leaped forward, covering the distance between her and Memnarch in two great bounds. With a howl, she hurled her blade at the crablike creature, driven by more than strength or speed, but by the hatred she had harbored for this man since her parents' death.

Her steel blade whistled, and Malil lunged forward, trying to get between her and Memnarch, but he was too late. The elf's fury was swift, and the sword connected with one of the Guardian's legs.

With a great creak and a loud pop, Glissa's weapon clove through the joint, and the six-eyed creature listed to his left.

Time stopped. A cathartic release rushed through Glissa's whole body, grabbing her by the spine and shaking every part of her, from top to bottom. This was the moment she'd been living for. This was her revenge, and she'd struck the first blow. Happiness and grief warred with each other, and tears formed in her eyes. Justice was near.

There was a spine-tingling screech, and Memnarch pulled back, waving his hands in the air.

Glissa was lifted from the ground by an invisible force and

thrown back. The world blurred. Wind rushed in her ears, and the elf crashed into the ground a hundred paces away from where she had been standing.

Memnarch lifted himself up, rising to the full height of his long, spindly legs. "How *dare* you?" he shouted. Raising his hand again, he lifted Glissa from the ground with an invisible, magical force, letting her dangle in midair. "I am your *god*. You should *worship* me."

"There is no god in Mirrodin." Glissa kicked and struggled, but it was no use, she was held fast.

"Facts are fact, no matter if you believe them or not." Sidling over on his three good limbs, Memnarch looked her straight in the eyes. "That is inconsequential. You have something I want."

Glissa glared at him. "You took everything I had when you killed my family."

Memnarch titled his head. "Not everything." He grabbed the floating elf's chin, examining her face. "I do not know where the planeswalker spark resides, but it is enough that I have you." Turning around he found Malil. "Take her to the containment cell." He looked back at the goblin and the golem. "Kill the others."

Slobad started jumping up and down. "Smash him!" he shouted.

In a flash the Kaldra Champion swooped in. Malil jumped in front of Memnarch, putting himself between the Guardian and the Champion.

Raising his greatsword, Malil charged the construct. His blade connected then bounced away, having done no damage to the magical avatar.

With a swipe of its hand, the Kaldra Champion knocked Malil back against the wall of Panopticon. His body made a clang as it impacted, then he slid to the ground, disappearing from view behind a pile of ruined levelers.

The avatar moved in on Memnarch, raising his fists, ready to smash the Guardian.

Memnarch placed his hands to his forehead. A beam of brilliant blue mana shot from his eyes. The magical energy swirled around and around the towering Champion. With each revolution, the light spread out, like thread unwinding from a spool, and it surrounded the Champion in a giant sapphire egg.

The mana solidified, and the Kaldra Champion disappeared, swallowed whole by a throbbing blue sphere.

Glissa dropped slowly to the ground, her hopes of bringing justice to her parents' killer fading.

The giant egg cracked, and the hardened shell dropped away, cascading to the ground in a shower of tiny blue bits. Inside, the Kaldra Champion still stood, seemingly unharmed.

"You claim there is no god here, Glissa," said Memnarch. "Perhaps this will change your mind." He looked up at the immobile Champion. "Seize her."

The Kaldra Champion turned on Glissa. With its magical palms outstretched, it lurched forward, grasping at the elf. Its hand slapped the ground just as Glissa leaped away, just barely missing being smashed.

"Careful," shouted Memnarch. "We need her alive."

Glissa scampered behind a broken leveler. The Champion knocked it aside—sending it spinning through the air and floated forward, looming over the elf.

Glissa looked up at the magical construct she had placed so much hope in. It floated there, ready to snatch her up. Nothing in this world turned out as it should. Nothing she had been told since her childhood had been true. She had placed her trust in something that had been untested, and now she was paying the price.

There was nothing that could be counted on, nothing worth

trusting. If she lived through this, she promised herself, she would trust no one but herself—ever again.

The Kaldra Champion reached again for the elf. Glissa backpedaled, but her heel caught on something. It was Pontifex's hoverer, and she tripped over it. The Champion's hand closed down around her. Closing her eyes, she prepared to be squashed—or worse.

A long second passed. Nothing happened.

Opening her eyes, Glissa saw the Kaldra Champion being dragged backward away from her. Standing at the base of the Champion's lower body, straining with all of his might, Bosh had both of his arms wrapped around the magical creature, and he pulled it away from her.

Though Bosh was only a third of the Kaldra Champion's size, he still had the strength to be a formidable opponent. The golem yanked hard, twisting the Champion's body and hurling it toward Panopticon. The magical construct flew through the air, landing on the ground several meters shy of the tower's wall.

Bosh turned to Glissa. "Run," he shouted.

Glissa stood stunned for a moment. She couldn't leave him.

"Run," he yelled again, his eyes growing big in his head, his face creased with concern.

Slobad shot up beside her on Pontifex's hoverer. "Come on."

The Kaldra Champion righted itself and grabbed Bosh in one of its huge hands. The iron golem was lifted high into the air. He seemed resigned to his fate, not looking at the Champion but keeping his eyes focused on Glissa.

"Go," he said, his lips forming the words, but no sound emerging. Then he smiled.

The Kaldra Champion squeezed Bosh, and the golem's face wrinkled with pain. The sound of metal cracking filled her ears, and Glissa turned away. She couldn't watch.

Stepping on behind Slobad, she whispered, "Go."

At full speed, Glissa and Slobad flew away from Panopticon.

* * * * *

"After them," shouted Memnarch.

The Kaldra Champion opened its fist and let its contents fall to the ground.

"I want the elf alive," ordered the Guardian. "Alive!"

Silently, the Champion floated off in pursuit of the elf and the goblin.

Memnarch turned and headed back to Panopticon. Near the open doors he found Malil climbing to his feet behind a pile of broken levelers.

"Come, Malil," said Memnarch. "We will watch from the Eye."

* * * * *

When they had covered several hundred yards, Glissa looked back over her shoulder. As she did, the Kaldra Champion dropped Bosh's smashed body to the ground.

"I was wrong," said Glissa.

"'Bout what?"

The elf shook her head, fighting back her tears. "I had thought there was nothing worth trusting in this world." She turned away from the pursuing Champion to put her hands on Slobad's shoulders. "But there was . . . there is."

"He good golem, huh?" said Slobad. "Slobad miss him."

"Me too," said the elf. "Me too." Wiping her eyes she added, "Just do me a favor."

The goblin nodded. "What you want, crazy elf?"

"Don't get killed."

Slobad nodded. "Slobad try, huh?" He glanced at the Champion behind them. "Not so easy."

Glissa turned her attention back to their pursuer. Slobad was right, the Kaldra Champion was coming on fast.

"How far to the blue lacuna?"

"Close, huh?" replied Slobad.

CHAPTER 25

Glissa and Slobad sped on, the Kaldra Champion right behind them. In the far distance they could see the entrance to the blue lacuna. To their left, another mycosynth forest loomed up under the mana core.

"Never make it," said the goblin.

"We might be able to gain some ground if we went through the monoliths," she shouted against the wind into Slobad's ear.

"How? Slow us, huh?"

"But they'll slow him even more," she said, hitching her thumb over her shoulder.

Slobad shrugged. "Okay, crazy elf." Leaning to his left, the goblin steered their hoverer toward the mycosynth. They sped off, the Champion gaining ground fast.

The strange crystalline growth rose up before them, and the Kaldra Champion loomed behind. Mere seconds from the edge of the forest, something came out from between two monoliths, blocking their path.

"Thresher," shouted Slobad, and he leaned hard right.

Glissa wasn't ready for the abrupt turn, and she slipped, falling off the hoverer and rolling to a stop.

The Champion ignored Slobad, zeroing in on the fallen elf.

The thresher too had its sights set on Glissa, and the two pursuers sandwiched her between.

The thresher reached her first. It leaned back, opening up like the other she had faced near the black lacuna, ready to swallow her whole and carry her off. There was nothing Glissa could do but put her hands up to protect her head.

The Kaldra Champion bent down, ready to pluck her from the ground.

The leveler stopped dead in its tracks, its deep central cavern only inches from the elf's head. A figure stepped out from inside, her hands held high.

"Bruenna!"

The wizard shouted a single power word, the rest of her spell already spoken. Screaming lines of blue power shot from the woman's outstretched arms like a cannon. The blast hit the Kaldra Champion in the chest and froze him in place, bent over like a question mark, only a few feet from the two women.

Glissa got to her feet. "But how—?"

Bruenna interrupted her. "We must go. This spell won't hold him for long."

With that, the human cast another spell.

Glissa and Bruenna lifted from the ground, gifted with the ability to fly. Slobad had circled back, but seeing the two women soar into the air, he headed for the entrance to the lacuna.

The women followed the goblin, racing as fast as they could. As they entered the blue tunnel, they heard the Kaldra Champion let out a tremendous roar.

*　*　*　*　*

At the top of the Pool of Knowledge, Bruenna turned to the other two. "You must get to the Tangle," she said. "You will have a better chance of beating this foe on your own ground."

"You come with us, huh?" The goblin looked up at the wizard from the hoverer.

Bruenna shook her head. "I must go help defend my tribe."

"We help you," said the elf.

Bruenna once again shook her head. "You have problems of your own." She smiled. "We will meet again, I think. For now our destinies lie on different paths."

* * * * *

Glissa and Slobad shot from Lumengrid, headed for the elf's home. They had abandoned Pontifex's hoverer for Bruenna's magic, and they flew now, out over the Quicksilver Sea and onto the plain. Not far behind, the Kaldra Champion pursued, though he could not fly. Having to follow on the ground slowed his progress considerably, and the pair managed to stay ahead of their tormentor.

"Do you ever think we'll stop being chased?" asked the goblin.

"No," replied Glissa. "I think it's our lot in this life. Frankly, I was bored with it long ago." She shrugged. "But what choice do we have?"

The pair approached the Tangle.

"What's that?" Slobad pointed at the ground.

Glissa squinted. "Trolls," she said. "The trolls have come to our aid."

There, arrayed before the metal forest were about twenty-five burly, wrinkled trolls, each holding what looked like the trunk of a stout tree between his hands.

Coming down to the ground, Glissa was greeted by Drooge, leaning heavily on his staff.

"You are being followed." The old troll pointed to the Kaldra Champion, growing larger in the near distance.

"And you have come to fight," replied Glissa, "as you said you would."

Drooge took a deep breath and nodded sadly. "This fight has only just begun." He laid his thick palm on her shoulder, and he smiled. "Go," he said. "We will keep him busy until you have reached the cover of the deep Tangle."

Looking up into his eyes, the elf said, "Come with us. If we run deep enough, he won't be able to get us. He's too big."

Drooge shook his head. "The trolls' time has come," he said, "but you, young Glissa, have a long life ahead. You are Mirrodin's last and only hope." He pushed her toward the interior of the forest. "Seek out the Radix, in the deepest part of the Tangle. It is there that you will find the most power. Go now and prepare yourself. Your fight yet awaits you."

Glissa stumbled forward, the troll's hand on her back. "But—"

"Please," said Drooge. "You will do your part." He turned back to the plain where the Kaldra Champion was nearly upon them. "Now we must do ours."

Slobad grabbed Glissa by the hand and pulled her toward the deeper woods. "Come on, huh?"

Glissa took one look back, then she turned and headed into the Tangle, Slobad at her side. They ran as fast as they could, leaping over fallen trees and skirting razor-sharp vines. Soon the reflected light from the plain disappeared from view behind, replaced by the darkness of the deep forest.

A thumping boom reverberated, and the ground shook. The sounds of battle drifted in through the jungle canopy. Images of trolls fighting the Kaldra Champion ran through Glissa's head. She wanted to turn, make her stand with the brave forest creatures, but that was not her fate.

It seemed they had run forever, the landscape changing with each step, before they reached the great clearing in the deepest part of the forest. Here the trees just simply stopped growing. Their roots reached deep into the ground until they touched the circle. This was the Radix, marked from one end to the other with strange runes and symbols.

Glissa had come across it many times. It wasn't a place she liked to visit. It was here that the elves went for their memory cleansing rituals. The place seemed haunted with the thoughts and minds of generations past, and all those ghosts kind of creeped her out.

Already she could hear the sound of the Kaldra Champion smashing his way into the Tangle. She knew that meant the trolls were gone, and that now only Slobad and she remained.

"What do you think we do now, huh?" asked the goblin.

Glissa pulled her sword from her belt. "We fight."

The crashing grew louder, and Glissa could see the tops of the trees falling in the canopy.

Closing her eyes, Glissa tried to relax as she drew in mana for a spell. She could feel the magical energies of the Tangle flowing to her easily—as quick and as smooth as they had in the interior of the plane. Then she cast her spell, reaching out to all the trees and metal plants surrounding the Radix.

Green lightnings flashed over the surface of the forest clearing. Jolts of power surged over the ground, arcing between trees and plants, playing over Glissa's fingertips, and reaching into the sky.

The metal forest came alive, shaping itself into a wall around Mirrodin's savior. Boughs bent and stretched, weaving together. Bushes sprouted up, filling the gaps between. The thick branches formed a barrier around the circle. The leaves, vines, and thorns pushed their sharpened edges and points to the outside, becoming an imposing wall to any who neared.

Slobad padded over the newly formed hedge and climbed to the top. "I see him," he shouted. The goblin pointed across the circle. "There."

Glissa turned. Over the top of her barricade, she could just make out the great helm of the Kaldra Champion.

The magical construct beat his fists against it, shaking the trees and scaring a flock of birds out into the sky. Then the interior of the tangled wall began to glow blue. The vines and branches shrank, separating from each other and falling away.

A pair of glowing blue fists punched through the slowly growing hole. Fingers wrapped around branches, followed by the squealing sound of distressed metal. The Champion tore through the hole. His hands moved at a blinding speed, tearing away the Tangle, throwing bits of the woven barricade into the distance.

With another tremendous roar, the Kaldra Champion stepped through into the center of the Radix.

Glissa backed up reflexively. Glancing around, she realized the folly of creating her magical wall. Instead of keeping the Champion out, it now kept her in.

Raising her hands, she drew mana. The floor of the Radix sparked and crackled with green energies. Glissa's feet stuck fast to the surface as mana flowed through her and out into a spell. The same trees and brush that had formed the ringing wall now reached out to entangle the Kaldra Champion. Vines wrapped themselves around him. Trees battered him from all sides, and the brush clawed the magical construct to the ground.

The creature struggled, able to tear away large bits of the forest by the handful, but it wasn't enough. The mana continued to flow through the elf, and the Tangle rallied to her call. The Kaldra Champion was pulled to the ground and covered completely with writhing metallic brush.

Glissa shut down the flow of power, and the forest stopped moving. Every pore in her body tingled. Her head buzzed, and the sound reminded her of the humming mana core.

Before her, where the Kaldra Champion had been, a huge mound now obscured him from view. Glissa walked over to examine it. The vines were wrapped tight. The trees were firm. The brush would not let go of its captive. Nothing moved.

Looking back over her shoulder, she saw Slobad standing on top of a tree. The wall was no more, having been disassembled by Glissa's spell. The goblin clung to a stout branch, trying not to fall off.

"I think you can climb down now." She looked back over her shoulder, checking once again that the Champion was buried by the foliage. "He's not going anywhere."

A terrible tearing sound erupted. The ground shook, and Glissa lost her balance. Dropping to her knees she steadied herself. Slobad was yelling something, but she couldn't hear it over the ripping of vines and bashing sounds of metal being pounded.

Behind her, the Kaldra Champion tore himself free of his jungle cage.

Glissa prepared to cast another spell, but she was immediately lifted from the ground. The Champion had her in his crushing grasp. Her arms were pinned to her sides, and her legs were held tight. She felt several bones in her chest give way with a pop, and a blinding pain shot through her whole body.

Then they were moving, heading into the jungle. Glissa couldn't hardly breath, only able to take short, quick breaths without causing herself tremendous pain. Her vision began to dim, and she struggled against her captor with what strength remained. He was just too huge, too powerful, and nothing she did could make him budge.

She looked up at the avatar, his face calm, void of any triumph or emotion. He would simply carry her back to Memnarch, following the orders of his current master until he was given another. He had no concerns about the fate of Mirrodin. He couldn't be swayed by sympathy or rhetoric. He knew only brute force and blind loyalty, and he would do whatever it took to return her to his current master. It was over. The fight had been lost.

A green flash came from nowhere, landing on the Champion's shoulder.

Slobad!

The goblin had leaped from his treetop perch. Flopping to his belly, crowbar in hand the brave little green man began prying the Sword of Kaldra from the Champion.

Glissa's hope swelled. If Slobad could unsummon the Champion...

The goblin attracted the Champion's attention. The magical being swatted at Slobad. The goblin ducked, but the Champion swung again, and he was forced to scamper back, his work unfinished.

Turning his head to look down on the pest, the Champion flung a single finger at the meddling goblin, flicking Slobad off his shoulder like an elf shooing a housefly.

Glissa watched in horror as her friend flew backward into the dense Tangle. Branches broke, brush rustled, and the sound of the goblin's body falling was followed by a small thud.

Glissa felt empty inside. She had seen so many of her friends die, why did she want to live anymore? What was left here on Mirrodin for her except pain and more death?

But then that emptiness began to fill up. Her skin tingled, and her insides burned. She glared at the Kaldra Champion with a new hatred that overtopped anything she had ever felt. This creature, this construct that she had work so hard to revive had repaid her for her gift of life by killing her two best friends—killing the only two trustworthy creatures Glissa had met on this godless ball of metal.

A wave of warm, embracing rage flooded up her spine, erasing the pain in her ribs and filling her with a new strength. She wanted to torture the Kaldra Champion, make it feel the same betrayal that she had felt, make it suffer as she had, make it pay for the deaths of Bosh and Slobad.

The Radix lit up with green fire. The inscribed runes and symbols glowed with a preternatural light, and jags of power leaped from the ground to the trees and up against the Kaldra Champion.

In that moment, Glissa felt the mana of the Tangle flow to her without her willing it. The power of the forest, the entire forest, was at her command, and she funneled it into her rage, shaping it with her anguish, focusing it with her pain into the Kaldra Champion.

Suddenly, the Radix exploded. A ball of green mana, as large as the moons of Mirrodin, burst through the ground. In a blink the plate was evaporated, and the trees for miles in each direction fell to the ground, laid low by the force of the blast.

The green lacuna had come. The new green moon shot from the ground and smashed into the Kaldra Champion. The shield, sword, and helm were all consumed in a flash of green energy. His magical fists and head dropped away, and with them Glissa too dropped to the ground into the tangled burning wreckage.

Glissa awoke jammed between two downed, partially melted trees. Her head hurt. Her ribs hurt. Even her teeth hurt.

How long she'd been out, she did not know.

She sat up and looked around. Where the Radix had been, there was now a huge hole, much like the other lacunae. All around, the Tangle had been melted or bent. The trees lay in straight rows like neatly combed hair, and everything was burnished or molten.

Nothing moved.

Glissa laid her head back and closed her eyes. She thought of Slobad. She tried to imagine what the last few moments of his life had been like, falling through the trees... She had to stop herself. It was too painful.

Something poked her in the head. "Crazy elf going to lie there all day, huh?"

Glissa's eye's popped open. "Slobad?"

The goblin's face was covered in soot. He smiled, his dingy yellow teeth showing brightly through his blackened visage.

She grabbed him by the elbow, unable to get up for an embrace. "I thought you were dead."

Slobad shook his head. "Naw." He rubbed the back of his head. "Slobad just bounced, huh?"

* * * * *

Memnarch stood on top of the ruined wall of his laboratory. His skin was scorched, the wound on his leg was cauterized and sterile, and two of his eyes had been ruptured. He limped as he walked, barely able to keep himself up.

Panopticon had toppled to the ground, blown to bits by the green lacuna. Its insides were burnt and ruined. The windows in the observation level had all been blown out, their glass vaporized by the tremendous blast.

He looked up at the new hole in the floor of the interior. The green lacuna had finally come to pass. The world would be out of balance for some time to come.

In the wreckage of his tower fortress, Memnarch found Malil, lying on his side, still inside the darksteel Eye. The impervious metal frame of the scrying device had saved them both from being vaporized in the blast.

The Guardian of Mirrodin bent down and touched the metal man's chest.

Malil's eyes shot open.

Memnarch smiled. "Come, Malil," he said. "We have much work to do, much work to do indeed."

Tales of Dominaria

LEGIONS
Onslaught Cycle, Book II
J. Robert King

In the blood and sand of the arena,
two foes clash in a titanic battle.

EMPEROR'S FIST
Magic Legends Cycle Two, Book II
Scott McGough

War looms above the Edemi Islands, casting the deep
and dread shadow of the Emperor's Fist.

SCOURGE
Onslaught Cycle, Book III
J. Robert King

From the fiery battles of the Cabal, a new god has arisen,
one whose presence drives her worshipers to madness.

THE MONSTERS OF MAGIC
An anthology edited by J. Robert King

From Dominaria to Phyrexia, monsters fill the multiverse,
and tales of the most popular ones fill these pages.

CHAMPION'S TRIAL
Magic Legends Cycle Two, Book III
Scott McGough

To restore his honor, the onetime champion of Madara must
battle his own corrupt empire and the monster on the throne.

November 2003

Legend of the Five Rings

The Four Winds Saga

Only one can claim the Throne of Rokugan.

WIND OF JUSTICE
Third Scroll
Rich Wulf

Naseru, the most cold-hearted and scheming of the royal heirs, will stop at nothing to sit upon the Throne of Rokugan. But when dark forces in the City of Night threaten his beloved Empire, Naseru must learn to wield the most unlikely weapon of all — justice.

WIND OF TRUTH
Fourth Scroll
Ree Soesbee

Sezaru, one of the most powerful wielders of magic in all Rokugan, has never desired his father's throne, but destiny calls to the son of Toturi. Here, in the final volume of the Four Winds Saga, all will be decided.

December 2003

Now available:

THE STEEL THRONE
Prelude
Edward Bolme

WIND OF HONOR
First Scroll
Ree Soesbee

WIND OF WAR
Second Scroll
Jess Lebow

R.A. Salvatore's
War of the Spider Queen

Chaos has come to the Underdark like never before.

New York Times best-seller!

CONDEMNATION, *Book III*
Richard Baker

The search for answers to Lolth's silence uncovers only more complex questions. Doubt and frustration test the boundaries of already tenuous relationships as members of the drow expedition begin to turn on each other. Sensing the holes in the armor of Menzoberranzan, a new, dangerous threat steps in to test the resolve of the Jewel of the Underdark, and finds it lacking.

Now in paperback!

DISSOLUTION, *Book I*
Richard Lee Byers

When the Queen of the Demonweb Pits stops answering the prayers of her faithful, the delicate balance of power that sustains drow civilization crumbles. As the great Houses scramble for answers, Menzoberranzan herself begins to burn.

INSURRECTION, *Book II*
Thomas M. Reid

The effects of Lolth's silence ripple through the Underdark and shake the drow city of Ched Nasad to its very foundations. Trapped in a city on the edge of oblivion, a small group of drow finds unlikely allies and a thousand new enemies.

FORGOTTEN REALMS

The Hunter's Blades Trilogy

New York Times best-selling author
R.A. SALVATORE
takes fans behind enemy lines in this
new trilogy about one of the most popular
fantasy characters ever created.

THE LONE DROW
Book II

Chaos reigns in the Spine of the World. The city of Mirabar
braces for invasion from without and civil war within. An orc king
tests the limits of his power. And *The Lone Drow* fights
for his life as this epic trilogy continues.

Now available in paperback!

THE THOUSAND ORCS
Book I

A horde of savage orcs, led by a mysterious cabal of power-hungry
warlords, floods across the North. When Drizzt Do'Urden and
his companions are caught in the bloody tide, the dark elf ranger
finds himself standing alone against *The Thousand Orcs*.

The original Chronicles

From *New York Times* best-selling authors Margaret Weis & Tracy Hickman

These classics of modern fantasy literature – the three titles that started it all – are available for the very first time in individual hardcover volumes. All three titles feature stunning cover art from award-winning artist Matt Stawicki.

DRAGONS OF AUTUMN TWILIGHT
Volume I
Friends meet amid a growing shadow of fear and rumors of war.
Out of their story, an epic saga is born.

DRAGONS OF WINTER NIGHT
Volume II
Dragons return to Krynn as the Queen of Darkness launches her assault.
Against her stands a small band of heroes bearing a new weapon:
the DRAGONLANCE.

DRAGONS OF SPRING DAWNING
Volume III
As the War of the Lance reaches its height, old friends clash amid
gallantry and betrayal. Yet their greatest battles lie within each of them.

The Minotaur Wars

From *New York Times* best-selling author Richard A. Knaak comes a powerful new chapter in the DRAGONLANCE® saga.

The continent of Ansalon, reeling from the destruction of the War of Souls, slowly crawls from beneath the rubble to rebuild – but the fires of war, once stirred, are difficult to quench. Another war comes to Ansalon, one that will change the balance of power throughout Krynn.

NIGHT OF BLOOD
Volume I

Change comes violently to the land of the minotaurs. Usurpers overthrow the emperor, murder all rivals, and dishonor minotaur tradition. The new emperor's wife presides over a cult of the dead, while the new government makes a secret pact with a deadly enemy. But betrayal is never easy, and rebellion lurks in the shadows.

The Minotaur Wars have begun.